PAUL TEMPLE AND THE MARGO MYSTERY

Francis Durbridge

WILLIAMS & WHITING

This edition published in 2023 by Williams & Whiting

Cover design by Timo Schroeder

9781915887207

Williams & Whiting (Publishers)

15 Chestnut Grove, Hurstpierpoint,

West Sussex, BN6 9SS

Titles by Francis Durbridge published by Williams & Whiting

1 The Scarf – tv serial
2 Paul Temple and the Curzon Case – radio serial
3 La Boutique – radio serial
4 The Broken Horseshoe – tv serial
5 Three Plays for Radio Volume 1
6 Send for Paul Temple – radio serial
7 A Time of Day – tv serial
8 Death Comes to The Hibiscus – stage play
The Essential Heart – radio play
(writing as Nicholas Vane)
9 Send for Paul Temple – stage play
10 The Teckman Biography – tv serial
11 Paul Temple and Steve – radio serial
12 Twenty Minutes From Rome – a teleplay
13 Portrait of Alison – tv serial
14 Paul Temple: Two Plays for Radio Volume 1
15 Three Plays for Radio Volume 2
16 The Other Man – tv serial
17 Paul Temple and the Spencer Affair – radio serial
18 Step In The Dark – film script
19 My Friend Charles – tv serial
20 A Case For Paul Temple – radio serial
21 Murder In The Media – more rediscovered serials and stories
22 The Desperate People – tv serial
23 Paul Temple: Two Plays for Television
24 And Anthony Sherwood Laughed – radio series
25 The World of Tim Frazer – tv serial
26 Paul Temple Intervenes – radio serial
27 Passport To Danger! – radio serial
28 Bat Out of Hell – tv serial
29 Send For Paul Temple Again – radio serial
30 Mr Hartington Died Tomorrow – radio serial

31 A Man Called Harry Brent – tv serial
32 Paul Temple and the Gregory Affair – radio serial
33 The Female of the Species (contains The Girl at the Hibiscus and Introducing Gail Carlton) – radio series
34 The Doll – tv serial
35 Paul Temple and the Sullivan Mystery – radio serial
36 Five Minute Mysteries (contains Michael Starr Investigates and The Memoirs of Andre d'Arnell) – radio series
37 Melissa – tv serial
38 Paul Temple and the Madison Mystery – radio serial
39 Farewell Leicester Square – radio serial
40 A Game of Murder – tv serial
41 Paul Temple and the Vandyke Affair – radio serial
42 The Man From Washington – radio serial
43 Breakaway – The Family Affair – tv serial
44 Paul Temple and the Jonathan Mystery – radio serial
45 Johnny Washington Esquire – radio series
46 Breakaway – The Local Affair – tv serial
47 Paul Temple and the Gilbert Case – radio serial
48 Cocktails and Crime (An anthology of the lighter side of Francis Durbridge)
49 Tim Frazer and the Salinger Affair – tv serial
50 Paul Temple and the Lawrence Affair – radio serial
51 One Man To Another – a novel
52 Tim Frazer and the Melynfforest Mystery – tv serial
53 News of Paul Temple – radio serial
54 Operation Diplomat – tv serial
55 Paul Temple and the Conrad Case – radio serial
56 The Passenger – tv serial

Murder At The Weekend – the rediscovered newspaper serials and short stories

Also published by Williams & Whiting:
Francis Durbridge: The Complete Guide
By Melvyn Barnes

Titles by Francis Durbridge to be published by Williams & Whiting

Kind Regards From Mr Brix – a novel

Paul Temple and the Alex Affair

Paul Temple and the Canterbury Case (film script)

Paul Temple and the Geneva Mystery

Paul Temple: Two Plays For Radio Vol 2 (Send For Paul Temple and News of Paul Temple)

The Face of Carol West – a novel

The Knife – tv serial

The Yellow Windmill – a novel

INTRODUCTION

Francis Durbridge (1912-98) began his career in 1933 as a prolific writer of sketches, stories and plays for BBC radio. They were mostly light entertainments, but a talent for crime fiction became evident in his early radio plays *Murder in the Midlands* (1934) and *Murder in the Embassy* (1937). He continued to write plays and serials for BBC radio for many years, using his own name and occasionally the pseudonyms Frank Cromwell, Nicholas Vane and Lewis Middleton Harvey, but in 1938 he had the brainwave that was to define his career.

Durbridge's creation of the dream team of novelist/detective Paul Temple and his wife Steve, given the success of his serial *Send for Paul Temple*, led to sequels spanning thirty years that resulted in an enormous UK and European fanbase. In total there were twenty-eight Paul Temple mysteries, of which seven were new productions of earlier cases.

In the mid-twentieth century radio detectives were extremely popular, with Paul Temple's rivals including Dick Barton (by Edward J. Mason), Philip Odell (by Lester Powell), Dr. Morelle (by Ernest Dudley), P.C. 49 (by Alan Stranks) and Ambrose West (by Philip Levene). In fact in the 1940s, in addition to the Temples, Durbridge wrote radio dramas featuring investigators called Anthony Sherwood, Johnny Cordell, Amanda Smith, Gail Carlton, Michael Starr, André d'Arnell and Johnny Washington, and he even wrote a radio serial featuring the legendary Sexton Blake.

But he proved to be more than a radio dramatist when in 1952, while continuing to write for radio, he embarked on a long sequence of BBC television serials that achieved enormous viewing figures. And while his reputation from 1938 onwards was based on the regular radio exploits of the Temples, it was his parallel television career that firmly established his name in popular culture – with gripping serials such as *Portrait of Alison, My Friend Charles, The Scarf, The World of Tim Frazer, Melissa, A Man Called Harry Brent* and *Bat out of Hell*. His popularity on the small screen was phenomenal, with the result that for all his serials from 1960 the BBC gave him the unprecedented accolade of the "Francis Durbridge Presents" screen credit before the title sequence of each episode.

In fact he proved to be a multi-media playwright, with his radio career lasting until 1968 being overlapped by his television serials from 1952 to 1980 and overlapped again by his career as a stage dramatist from 1971 in the UK and even earlier in Germany. The latter saw him change his style from the "whodunit" form, and he became known for intriguing twist-after-twist plays including *Suddenly at Home, Murder with Love* and *House Guest*.

His radio serial *Paul Temple and the Margo Mystery* was first broadcast on the BBC Light Programme in eight thirty-minute episodes from 1 January to 19 February 1961 and repeated from 20 July to 7 September 1961, since when it has been repeated many times on BBC Radio 7 and its successor BBC Radio 4 Extra. As with many of the Paul Temple serials, the BBC later marketed a recording on audiocassettes and CDs (BBC Audio, 2004), which is also included in the CD box set *Paul Temple: The Complete Radio Collection: The Sixties 1960-1968* (BBC, 2017). From the Francis Durbridge files in the BBC Written Archives, incidentally, it appears that he originally planned to call this serial *Paul Temple and the Stewart Case* although Margo sounds much more intriguing!

James Thomason (1911-97) made his first appearance as Sir Graham Forbes of Scotland Yard, the role he subsequently reprised in the 1963 revival of *Paul Temple and the Jonathan Mystery* and the 1968 *Paul Temple and the Alex Affair*. Peter Coke (1913-2008) appeared as Temple for the eighth time, having taken over the role for *Paul Temple and the Gilbert Case* in 1954, and he remained for three more appearances until the concluding *Paul Temple and the Alex Affair* in 1968. Undoubtedly Coke and his co-star Marjorie Westbury (1905-89) are regarded as the definitive pairing of Paul and Steve Temple with their eleven serials, although Westbury excelled numerically as Steve with her twenty-two appearances overall. Before Coke, Marjorie Westbury had partnered Barry Morse in *Send for Paul Temple Again* (1945), Howard Marion-Crawford in *A Case for Paul Temple* (1946) and Kim Peacock on nine separate occasions.

The "Britishness" of the Temple radio serials is arguably the reason they acquired a huge European following, with translated versions broadcast in the Netherlands from 1939, Germany from 1949, Italy from 1953 and Denmark from 1954. *Paul Temple and the Margo Mystery* was broadcast in Germany as *Paul Temple und der Fall Margo* (23 February – 13 April 1962, eight episodes), translated by Marianne de Barde and John Lackland and produced by Eduard Hermann, with René Deltgen as Temple and Annemarie Cordes as Steve; in the Netherlands as *Paul Vlaanderen en het Margo mysterie* (30 September – 18 November 1962, eight episodes), translated by Johan Bennik (pseudonym of Jan van Ees) and produced by Dick van Putten, with Jan van Ees as Vlaanderen and Eva Janssen as Ina; and in Italy as *Margò* (19 – 30 June 1967, ten episodes), translated by Franca Cancogni and produced by Guglielmo Morandi, with Aroldo Tieri as Temple and Lia Zoppelli as Steve.

Paul Temple and the Margo Mystery was novelised, but long after its original radio broadcast. Published in the UK by Hodder & Stoughton in February 1986, it later appeared in German as *Der Hehler* and also as *Paul Temple und der Fall Margo*, in Italian as *Delitto a tempo di rock*, in Dutch as *Het Margo-mysterie*, in Danish as *Margo mysteriet* and in Norwegian as *Paul Temple og Margo-mysteriet*. Even later still, lovers of UK audiobooks were provided with a set of audiocassettes read by Michael Tudor Barnes (ISIS Audiobooks, 2002) and a set of CDs read by Toby Stephens (AudioGO, 2011).

Melvyn Barnes
Author of *Francis Durbridge: The Complete Guide* (Williams & Whiting, 2018)

This book reproduces Francis Durbridge's original script together with the list of characters and actors of the BBC programme on the dates mentioned, but the eventual broadcast might have edited Durbridge's script in respect of scenes, dialogue and character names.

PAUL TEMPLE AND THE MARGO MYSTERY

A serial in eight episodes

By FRANCIS DURBRIDGE

Broadcast on BBC Radio

1st January – 19th February 1961

CAST:

Paul Temple . . . . .Peter Coke
Steve, his wife . . . . .Marjorie Westbury
Sir Graham Forbes . . . . . . .James Thomason
Charlie .James Beattie
Superintendent Raine . . . . .Simon Lack
Mike Langdon . . . . .Tommy Duggan
Dr McCarthy . . . . .Duncan McIntyre
Tony Wyman . . . . Jon Rollason
Linda Kelburn . . . . .June Tobin
Stewardess . . . . Sara Nash
Telephone Operator . . . . . . .Mary Wimbush
Larry Cross . .. . Hugh Manning
George Kelburn . . . . .Julian Somers
Dr Jenkins . . . . .Peter Wilde
Ted Angus . . . . .Tom Watson
Elsie Jackson . . . . .Dorit Welles
Jane . . . . Janet Morrison
Fred Harcourt . . . . .George Merritt
Waiter . . . . Peter Wilde
Barmaid . . . . Janet Morrison
Dr Benkaray . . . . Mary Wimbush
Mrs Harcourt . . . . .Beatrice Kane
Bill Fletcher . . . . William Eedle
Mrs Fletcher . . . . .Joan Matheson

Bank Clerk . . . . .Nigel Anthony
Police Sergeant . . . . Nigel Anthony
Bank Manager . . . . .Haydn Jones
Hotel receptionist . . . . Peter Watts
Fiona Scott . . . . .Armine Sandford
Fortune-teller . . . . .Kathleen Helme
Vicar . . . . .Peter Wilde
Det Insp Burton . . . . .Douglas Storm
Ken Sinclair . . . . Peter Wilde
Prison Governor . . . . Peter Pratt
Midge Harris . . . . .Frank Partington
Boy . . . . .June Tobin
Waiter . . . . .Nigel Anthony
Mrs Perkins . . . . Janet Morrison
Man .Nigel Anthony
Oscar . . . . Douglas Storm
Wally Stone . . . . Malcolm Hayes
Maid . . . . Eva Stuart
Det. Insp. Milton . . . . Kenneth Dight
Nurse . . . . .Eva Stuart
Airport Announcer . . . . Jon Rollason

EPISODE ONE

THE COAT

OPEN TO: A Door Opens.

CHARLIE: I've brought you some tea, Mrs Temple.

STEVE: Oh, thank you, Charlie. What time is it?

CHARLIE: Just gone 'arf past four.

STEVE: Half past four? I didn't think it was as late as that. Then in New York it'll be about half past eleven …

CHARLIE: Yes, I suppose it will. Five hours back … Do you think Mr Temple will be up yet?

STEVE: Well, I hope so, Charlie. He promised to telephone.

CHARLIE: When are you expecting him home, Mrs Temple?

STEVE: Sometime next week.

CHARLIE: I'll bet you'll be glad.

STEVE: That's the understatement of the year, Charlie. It seems as if he's been away ages.

CHARLIE: Four weeks and a day. You know, I don't understand why you didn't go with him, Mrs Temple. You usually …

STEVE: Have you ever been to America, on a lecture tour, Charlie?

CHARLIE: No, can't say I have.

STEVE: Twenty-two towns in four weeks! That's not my idea of fun and …

STEVE is interrupted by the telephone ringing.

CHARLIE: There we are! That'll be Mr T!

STEVE picks up the receiver.

STEVE: (*On the phone*) Hello!

OPERATOR: (*On the other end of the line*) Mayfair 5101?

STEVE: Yes …

OPERATOR: Mrs Temple speaking?

STEVE: Yes – speaking …

OPERATOR: One moment, please. We have a call for you …

There is the sound of background static noises.

OPERATOR: Go ahead, New York …

TEMPLE: (*On the other end of the line*) Hello? …

STEVE: Paul? Is that you, darling?

TEMPLE: Hello, Steve! How are you?

STEVE: Oh, I'm fine, Paul. Looking forward to next week!

TEMPLE: I've got some news for you. I've finished my tour and I'm flying back tomorrow night.

STEVE: (*Delighted*) Tomorrow … Oh, Paul! Wonderful, darling!

TEMPLE: I'm due at London Airport at 11.15 – that's Thursday morning.

STEVE: I'll be there!

TEMPLE: There's no need to meet me, Steve.

STEVE: You try and stop me! What's the flight number?

TEMPLE: BA 784 … It's a BOAC flight …

STEVE: (*Delighted*) Due in at 11.15. Okay, sweetie!

TEMPLE: (*Amused*) What do you mean – okay? I'm the one who should sound American. (*Laughing*) All right, Steve – see you Thursday morning.

STEVE: Goodbye, Paul!

TEMPLE: Goodbye, dear.

STEVE: Have a good trip!

STEVE replaces the receiver.

CHARLIE: (*Smiling*) Now, Mrs Temple – what about this nice cup of tea?

STEVE: (*Excited*) You drink it, Charlie. I'm having a dry Martini!

FADE IN of music.

CROSS FADE music to the noise of a jet plane.

STEWARDESS: Can I get you anything to drink, Mr Temple?

TEMPLE: No, I don't think I will, thank you very much.

LANGDON: (*From the near background; an educated American voice*) Well, I'd certainly like something. Whisky on the rocks, please.

STEWARDESS: Yes, sir.

LANGDON: (*To TEMPLE*) May I sit here for a moment?

TEMPLE: Yes, by all means.

LANGDON: These jets are pretty fantastic, aren't they?

TEMPLE: Yes, they certainly are.

LANGDON: I've just flown in from California. Five hours, coast to coast. My name's Langdon, by the way. Mike Langdon. We met in Hollywood, Mr Temple.

TEMPLE: Did we?

LANGDON: You don't remember?

TEMPLE: I'm so sorry, but I've met so many people during the past few weeks, that I …

LANGDON: (*Laughing*) Yes, of course. I was at that cocktail party the film people gave you – me and two hundred others.

TEMPLE: (*Amused*) Yes, that was quite a party, wasn't it?

LANGDON: It sure was.

TEMPLE: Are you in the film business, Mr Langdon?

LANGDON: No; I'm with a publishing firm in New York, Talbot & Ryder. It's only a small firm, but we do very nicely. How did the lecture tour go, Mr Temple?

TEMPLE: Oh, very well – but it was a bit wearing, at times.

LANGDON: I'll bet! Our authors hate 'em. Still, they're first rate publicity.

TEMPLE: Is this your first trip to Europe?

LANGDON: No. I've been over many times before. I was in Paris two weeks ago. (*A pause*) Mr Temple, have you heard of a young man called Tony Wyman?

TEMPLE: No, I don't think so. Should I have done?

LANGDON: Well, I understand he's fairly well known in your country. He's a pop singer.

TEMPLE: Tony Wyman? No, I'm sorry; is he a friend of yours?

LANGDON: (*A little laugh*) No; and I doubt whether he'll turn out to be one, either. Mr Temple, I've got quite a problem on my hands and I'd sure like to talk about it. Is that okay by you?

TEMPLE: (*Amused by LANGDON's frankness*) Why – yes – go ahead.

LANGDON: About two years ago my firm was taken over by an Englishman called George Kelburn. If you don't know Kelburn personally, you've probably read about him.

TEMPLE: Yes, I've heard of Kelburn. He's a north country chap; reputed to be a millionaire.

LANGDON: That's right. Well, when Kelburn took our firm over he made me the Number One boy. He's a blunt, ruthless sort of guy, but we've always got on well together.

TEMPLE: Is he older than you?

LANGDON: Yes, he's about sixty; maybe sixty-two or three, I'm not sure.

TEMPLE: Go on, Mr Langdon.

LANGDON: Well, Kelburn's first wife died some years ago and he married again – a woman a lot younger than himself. He has a daughter, Julia, by his first wife. Julia's twenty-one – young, attractive, and hopelessly spoilt.

TEMPLE: Not an unusual story.

LANGDON: No, I suppose not, but – Well, to cut a long story short, Julia's got herself tangled up with a nightclub singer called Tony Wyman, and she's told dear old Papa that she intends to marry the guy.

TEMPLE: And Kelburn's against it?

LANGDON: Against it? Kelburn's going to stop that marriage if it's the last thing he does.

TEMPLE: Yes, but – how do you fit into all this, Mr Langdon? If you're just a business associate of Kelburn's …

LANGDON: (*Interrupting TEMPLE*) That's just the point, I don't fit into it! But Kelburn sent me an S.O.S., and there was nothing I could do about it.

TEMPLE: You mean, he wants you to try and influence her to …

LANGDON: Exactly! Julia and I have always got on well together, so he wants me to talk to the kid and try to persuade her to throw the boyfriend over.

TEMPLE: Do you think you've got much chance?

LANGDON: None. I've got no special influence with the kid, and according to all accounts she's nuts about this guy Tony Wyman.

TEMPLE: You seem to be in quite a spot.

LANGDON: You can say that again. Well, you're used to other people's troubles, Mr Temple! What would you do if you were in my shoes?

TEMPLE: (*Laughing*) Frankly, I don't know what I'd do.

LANGDON: If I refuse to help Kelburn he'll put me on the spot businesswise – there's no doubt about that, I know Kelburn. On the other hand, if I get mixed up in it and make a mess of things, which is more than likely, it isn't going to do me any good either.

TEMPLE: And how does Kelburn's wife react to all this?

LANGDON: Oh, Linda takes the point of view that Julia's twenty-one and she'll do what she likes, anyway.

TEMPLE: I see.

LANGDON: This whole business has turned up at a very awkward moment, so far as I'm concerned. I've had a hectic time just lately – been in ten countries in two months, and right now I'm ready for a holiday, not a first class family squabble.

TEMPLE: Well, there's no point in anticipating trouble, Mr Langdon. Perhaps when you get to London you'll find the situation has straightened itself out.

LANGDON: I certainly hope so.

TEMPLE: Anyway, I'm in the phone book. If you feel I can help you at any time, give me a ring.

LANGDON: (*Pleased*) Well, now that's very kind of you, Mr Temple. I do appreciate it, sir. I certainly do!

FADE the noise of the aircraft.

CROSS FADE to background noises of London Airport.

LANGDON: (*Approaching*) There you are, Temple! I see you got through the Customs all right.

TEMPLE: Yes, thanks. But I'm still trying to find my wife. We appear to have missed each other …

LANGDON: Is there anything I can do?

TEMPLE: No, thanks. I'm just going across to the other building to see if she's there.

FADE SCENE.

FADE UP of a telephone ringing.

The receiver is lifted.

CHARLIE: (*On the phone*) Hello? Mayfair 5101 …

We hear the person at the other end pressing button "A"; the coins drop.

TEMPLE: Is that you, Charlie?

CHARLIE: Mr Temple? Where are you?

TEMPLE: I'm at the airport. Is Mrs Temple with you?

CHARLIE: Why no! I thought she'd be with you, Mr Temple. She left here two hours ago.

TEMPLE: Did she take the car?

CHARLIE: Yes – the little runabout.

TEMPLE: You're sure she knew the time and place?

CHARLIE: Yes, she knew the time and place all right. She's been talking about nothing else for the past twenty-four hours.

TEMPLE: I see. Did she say whether she had any calls to make?

CHARLIE: No, but I don't think she had. (*After a moment*) I hope there hasn't been an accident …

TEMPLE: (*Quietly*) Yes, I hope so too, Charlie. I'll see you later.

CHARLIE: Very good, sir.

CHARLIE replaces the receiver.

FADE IN music.

FADE DOWN music.

A doorbell is ringing.

After a moment the door is opened.

FORBES: Good evening, Charlie.

CHARLIE: Good evening, sir. Mr Temple's expecting you.

The front door closes.

FORBES: Any news?

CHARLIE: No, sir, I'm afraid not. In here, Sir Graham …

CHARLIE opens the drawing room door.

TEMPLE: Come in, Sir Graham! It's very kind of you to come at a moment's notice …

FORBES: (*Interrupting TEMPLE*) My dear fellow, I'd have got here sooner, only I was on my way home when your message came through.

RAINE: I understand there's no news, Mr Temple?

TEMPLE: No, I'm afraid not.

FORBES: This is Superintendent Raine, Temple. I don't think you've met before?

TEMPLE: No, I don't think we have.

TEMPLE and RAINE shake hands.

TEMPLE: How do you do, Superintendent?

RAINE: How do you do?

TEMPLE: Sit down and I'll get you a drink.

FORBES: No, no, don't worry about drinks! Temple, tell me: have you checked the hospitals?

TEMPLE: I've checked every hospital within thirty miles of the airport. It took me the best part of the afternoon.

RAINE: I understand you found Mrs Temple's car?

TEMPLE: Yes, it was in the car park at the airport. The attendant remembered her arriving – about half an hour before my plane was due. She left her coat in the back of the car, so she couldn't have intended to go much further than the lounge, or maybe the restaurant.

RAINE: I take it Mrs Temple didn't leave a note for you, sir, or anything which might …

TEMPLE: No; I've been through the place pretty thoroughly and apart from a telephone message there's nothing – absolutely nothing.

FORBES: What was the telephone message?

TEMPLE: It was on the pad upstairs. It simply said: "Tell P." – which is obviously me – "about L."

FORBES: Who's L?

TEMPLE: I don't know. But I don't think it's important, Sir Graham. According to Charlie, the message was written several days ago.

RAINE: Well, I'm sorry, Mr Temple, but it looks as if we shall have to face the facts. Your wife's obviously been picked up by someone. Now the question is …

RAINE is interrupted by the ringing of the telephone. TEMPLE picks up the receiver.

TEMPLE: (*On the phone*) Hello?

There is a pause, then we hear the pressing of Button "A"

at the other end of the line and the dropping of coins into a box.

MAN's VOICE: (*On the other end of the line*) All right … Go ahead … Talk to him now …

TEMPLE: Hello? … Hello, who is that? …

STEVE: (*On the other end: weakly*) Is that you, Paul?

TEMPLE: Steve! Is that you, Steve?

STEVE: (*Still distant; weakly*) Paul, can you hear me?

TEMPLE: Steve, where are you?

STEVE: Don't worry, dear … There's nothing to worry about …

TEMPLE: Yes, but Steve, where are you speaking from?

STEVE: I'm … perfectly all right …

TEMPLE: Steve, listen! There was a man on the phone, I heard his voice … Who was it?

STEVE: (*With a note of desperation in her voice*) Paul, don't try and …

TEMPLE: (*Urgently; interrupting STEVE*) Darling, please tell me … Where are you?

STEVE: (*Weakly*) Oh, Paul …

The line suddenly goes dead.

TEMPLE: Oh, my God!

FORBES: What's happened?

TEMPLE: The line's gone dead.

RAINE: Replace the receiver, Mr Temple, in case she tries to ring back!

FORBES: Temple, you said something about a man … Was there someone with Steve?

TEMPLE: Yes, I heard a voice just as I picked up the telephone. It sounded to me as if someone was with Steve and was telling her to …

TEMPLE is interrupted by the ringing of the telephone again.

He immediately picks up the receiver.

TEMPLE: (*On the phone*) Hello?

FORBES: Take it easy, Temple …

TEMPLE: Hello?

STEVE: (*Still tense; on the other end of the line*) Paul …

TEMPLE: (*Trying to control his anxiety*) Steve, where are you speaking from?

STEVE: … I don't know the number …

TEMPLE: Darling, look at the dial …

STEVE: It's a call box …

TEMPLE: Well, where is it?

STEVE: (*Dazed and confused*) Paul, I'm trying to concentrate, but …

TEMPLE: Is there anyone with you?

STEVE: No … not now, darling …

TEMPLE: Well, where's the telephone box, Steve?

STEVE: It's at Euston … It's near the station … (*Near to tears*) Please come and fetch me, darling … I'll wait for you in the station … near the bookstall …

TEMPLE: (*Desperately*) I'll be there in five minutes!

TEMPLE replaces the receiver.

FORBES: (*Quickly*) What's happened?

TEMPLE: She's at Euston Station!

FORBES: Right! Come on, Temple! (*To RAINE*) Get through to the Yard – we'll see you at the station!

FADE IN background noises of Euston Station.

FADE UP of SIR GRAHAM's voice.

FORBES: She's over there, Temple!

TEMPLE: (*Rushing forward*) Steve!

FADE IN of STEVE.

STEVE: (*Dazed; bewildered*) Paul! Paul … Oh, darling!

TEMPLE: Steve, thank God we've found you!

FORBES: Are you all right, Steve?

STEVE: Yes, Sir Graham, I'm just – just a little tired, that's all.

TEMPLE: What happened? How did you get here? Who was that man I heard …

FORBES: (*Quietly; aside*) Wait a moment, Temple. I think perhaps we'd better get her home and let a doctor see her before we start asking too many questions.

TEMPLE: Yes, of course! You're absolutely right, Sir Graham! Come along, darling …

START FADE.

RAINE: Let me help you, Mrs Temple.

COMPLETE FADE of station background, etc.

FADE IN SIR GRAHAM's voice.

FORBES: You know, Temple, this really is an extraordinary affair. I've never come across a case quite like it before. No ransom – no mysterious notes – no threats – no blackmail. Nothing.

RAINE: And no motive either, sir – so far as we can see.

TEMPLE: They must have had a motive! Whoever they are, they must have had a reason for picking Steve up like that!

FORBES: I agree, Temple. But what was the reason? After all, it isn't as if you're mixed up in a case at the moment, or even helping us over …

SIR GRAHAM is interrupted by a knock on the door.

The door opens.

McCARTHY: May I come in, Mr Temple?

TEMPLE: Yes, of course, Doctor. What's the verdict?

McCARTHY: Nothing to worry about – nothing at all. But there's no doubt Mrs Temple has had quite a shock, and, in my opinion, she's either been drugged or even possibly hypnotised.

TEMPLE: Hypnotised!

McCARTHY: However, the main thing is, there's nothing for you to worry about, Mr Temple. What your wife needs now is rest, and plenty of it! I've given her a sedative; she'll probably sleep most of tomorrow morning.

TEMPLE: Thank you, Doctor.

McCARTHY: I'll look in during the afternoon, or give you a ring tomorrow evening.

TEMPLE: Thank you.

McCARTHY: And, Superintendent …

RAINE: Yes, Doctor?

McCARTHY: My patient can't answer any questions – not at the moment, at any rate.

RAINE: Very well, Doctor.

McCARTHY: So hold your horses until tomorrow. (*Smiling*) And that goes for you too, Mr Temple. Good night!

TEMPLE: Good night, Doctor!

START FADE.

McCARTHY: It's all right, I can let myself out. Good night, Sir Graham!

FORBES: Good night, Doctor.

FADE SCENE.

FADE IN of a radio quietly playing music in the near background.

STEVE: (*Sleepily*) Paul … Why are you sitting over there?

TEMPLE: I'm listening to the radio and watching you, darling.

STEVE: Well – what time is it?

TEMPLE: (*Amused*) What time do you think?

STEVE: Oh, I don't know. (*Stretching herself*) About half past nine …

TEMPLE: It's a quarter past three …

STEVE: (*Sleepily*) A quarter past … (*Suddenly awake*) A quarter past three!

TEMPLE: (*Laughing*) Yes, darling. You've had quite a nice little nap …

STEVE: How long have I actually been …

TEMPLE: Since ten o'clock last night. The doctor gave you a sedative.

STEVE: Good heavens! You shouldn't have let me sleep like this! (*Sitting up in bed*) Oh, Paul – you look wonderful! How lovely to see you again!

STEVE kisses TEMPLE.

STEVE: Did you have a nice trip?

TEMPLE: Yes; I did – but it's the last trip I'm making without you, Mrs T.

STEVE: (*Laughing*) You can say that again!

TEMPLE: How do you feel?

STEVE: I'm perfectly all right now. There's no need to look so anxious.

TEMPLE: Do you feel well enough to talk?

STEVE: Yes, of course.

TEMPLE: What happened yesterday, Steve?

STEVE: (*Thoughtfully*) Well, now – let me think … I'm not sure where to begin …

TEMPLE: Suppose we begin at the very beginning. You set out to meet me at the airport, just as you planned …

STEVE: Yes, that's right. I arrived there with plenty of time to spare and parked the car. A man in unform, one of the airport officials, came up to me … checked the number of my car, and asked if I was Mrs Temple. He told me your plane had arrived ahead of schedule and you were waiting for me in the V.I.P. lounge.

TEMPLE: Would you recognise this man again?

STEVE: I doubt it.

TEMPLE: Go on, Steve.

STEVE: He asked me to follow him to another car just outside the car park. I thought he was taking me to another building some distance away. In the back of the car was a woman wearing an air hostess's uniform. I sat beside her and the man climbed into the driving seat and we drove off. We'd been going for about a minute when the woman suddenly pushed a pad over my face and I felt a sudden jab in my right arm.

TEMPLE: A hypodermic needle …?

STEVE: Yes – I'm afraid I don't remember anything else, about the journey, I mean. When I came to, I was in a darkened room – I felt absolutely awful – everything was going round and I wanted to be sick. After a while a man came into the room and gave me a drink – I don't know what it was, but it certainly made me feel better.

TEMPLE: Was the man the phoney airport official?

STEVE: I couldn't see him very well, but I don't think it was. For one thing, his voice sounded different.

TEMPLE: And what did he say?

STEVE: He said there was nothing to worry about – that I wasn't in any danger – and later on they'd be releasing me.

TEMPLE: Did you ask him why they'd kidnapped you?

STEVE: Yes, and he said: "We did it as a warning, and to prove that it was possible, Mrs Temple."

TEMPLE: Go on …

STEVE: Well, he left me, and about two or three hours later another man came into the room. (*Thoughtfully*) I think this was the man at the airport, he was about the same height, and he sounded rather like him.

TEMPLE: But you're not sure?

STEVE: No; I can't be a hundred per cent sure. Anyway, this man also assured me that there was nothing to worry about and that they were going to send me home. About half an hour later they drove me down to Euston and let me make the telephone call.

TEMPLE: But didn't they give you any idea what this was all about – why they'd abducted you?

STEVE: Not the slightest. (*A shade surprised*) Don't you know, Paul?

TEMPLE: (*Puzzled*) I haven't a clue. I'm not investigating a case at the moment. I'm not mixed up in anything – you know that, Steve.

STEVE: If only I could remember more details … What the people looked like …

TEMPLE: Don't worry about it, Steve. You're all right, that's the main thing.

STEVE: Yes, well – you must have been pretty worried.

TEMPLE: Oh, not really, darling – I just went berserk.

STEVE laughs.

TEMPLE: By the way, I put your coat in the wardrobe.

STEVE: My coat?

TEMPLE: Yes; we found it in the back of the car when we collected it from the airport.

STEVE: (*Puzzled*) But I didn't take a coat with me …

TEMPLE: Yes, you did, Steve.

TEMPLE opens the wardrobe door.

TEMPLE: Here it is … (*A pause*) Well?

STEVE: That's not my coat …

TEMPLE: But it is, Steve! It was in the back of the …

STEVE: (*Interrupting TEMPLE*) I don't care where it was! It's not my coat!

TEMPLE: (*Quietly*) Are you sure, dear?

STEVE: I'm positive. (*After a pause*) Is there anything in the pockets?

TEMPLE searches the pockets of the coat.

TEMPLE: No, nothing …

STEVE: There should be a maker's name on the back of the collar somewhere …

TEMPLE: Yes, I'm just looking for it … Ah, here we are! (*A pause; quietly*) Margo …

FADE IN of music.

FADE music.

FADE IN of a piano being played: a Chopin nocturne.

A door opens.

CHARLIE: Superintendent Raine would like to see you, sir.

STEVE stops playing the piano.

TEMPLE: (*Rising*) Hello, Superintendent! Come along in!

STEVE: Good evening, Superintendent.

RAINE: Good evening, Mrs Temple. You look better than you did a week ago.

STEVE: Yes, I'm fine now, thank you very much.

RAINE: I just happened to be passing and I thought I'd drop in and have a word with you.

TEMPLE: Glad to see you.

RAINE: Well – we don't seem to have got very far during the past week. We've made enquiries about the coat, but we've drawn a blank. We've failed to find the owner, or even the shop where it was bought from.

STEVE: What about the makers?

RAINE: We can't even locate the makers. According to all accounts, there isn't a coat firm called Margo – not in this country, at any rate.

TEMPLE: I see. Did you check with the airport people?

RAINE: Yes; and we've had no luck there, I'm afraid. I suppose you haven't had any bright ideas, Mr Temple?

TEMPLE: No, I'm afraid I haven't, except that …

RAINE: Well?

TEMPLE: Well, I think the people who kidnapped Steve were labouring under the delusion that I was just about to start a case of some kind.

RAINE: And you think the Mrs Temple incident was a warning to keep out?

TEMPLE: Yes, I do.

RAINE: Well, that's a possible explanation, I suppose – but what's the case?

TEMPLE: (*Smiling*) You tell me; I never interfere in anything, without an invitation. What's your biggest headache at the moment?

RAINE: Oh, our biggest headache is The Fence – trying to find out who the devil he is. But we've had that headache for some time now. I doubt whether we'll ever solve it.

STEVE: What do you mean – The Fence?

RAINE: Well, you know what a fence is, Mrs Temple?

STEVE: Yes – a man who receives stolen property.

RAINE: That's right. Well, during the past twelve months there've been several robberies. I mean, really big stuff. The two jewellers in Leicester Square …

STEVE: Yes …

RAINE: The fur warehouse in Bond Street …

TEMPLE: Lord Renton's place in Eaton Square …

RAINE: Yes, that's right. Well, it's our opinion that these particular jobs were all done …

STEVE: (*Interrupting RAINE*) … by the same gang!

RAINE: (*Laughing*) No, Mrs Temple. Nothing quite as simple as that. We think – in fact, we know – that the various jobs have been done by different people. We feel pretty confident, however, that the stolen property – the swag, if you like – was, in every case, handled by the same person.

TEMPLE: The Fence?

RAINE: Yes. So far we've failed to find out who this fence is – or where he operates from. But sooner or later we've got to find him, because, at the moment, he's indirectly responsible for most of the crime in this country.

TEMPLE: Really?

RAINE: Still, we've no reason for thinking – no proof, as it were – that Mrs Temple's experience had anything to do with The Fence.

TEMPLE: (*Thoughtfully*) No; I agree, Superintendent.

RAINE: (*Suddenly*) Oh, but – there was one thing I wanted to ask you.

TEMPLE: Yes?

RAINE: The day Mrs Temple disappeared you said something about a note – a telephone message – which was on the pad by the side of the bed.

TEMPLE: Yes, of course! I forgot all about that! (*To STEVE*) There was a note, Steve. It said: "Tell P. about L."

STEVE: Oh, that was Linda Stafford. She telephoned one morning and said she wanted to see you – seemed awfully disappointed when I said you were in New York.

TEMPLE: Who's Linda Stafford?

STEVE: She's a journalist – (*Laughing*) – or rather she was several years ago. We used to see quite a bit of each other when I worked in Fleet Street. Then she left and married a man called Kelburn.

TEMPLE: (*Surprised*) Kelburn? George Kelburn?

STEVE: Yes, I think so.

TEMPLE: Very wealthy. North country. She's his second wife.

STEVE: That's him. Anyway, when I said you were in New York she said she'd get in touch with you later. I thought nothing of it at the time, but a couple of days later I bumped into Linda at Freeman & Bentley's and naturally, I mentioned the telephone call, and to my amazement she said she hadn't phoned.

RAINE: She said she hadn't?

STEVE: That's right, Superintendent. She said she certainly had no wish to contact Paul about anything.

RAINE: That's very odd.

TEMPLE: It certainly is.

STEVE: Darling, why were you surprised when I mentioned the name Kelburn?

TEMPLE: Well, coming over on the plane a man called Langdon introduced himself to me. He works for George Kelburn. Apparently Kelburn's having trouble with his daughter and he's asked Langdon to try and sort it out.

RAINE: (*Significantly*) Yes, I've heard of Miss Kelburn. Julia, by name.

TEMPLE: That's right.

RAINE: Always in the newspapers. She must be quite a handful, that young lady; I don't envy Mr Langdon his assignment. Well, I'll be making a move. Glad you're feeling better, Mrs Temple.

STEVE: Thank you.

START FADE.

TEMPLE: Let me know if there is any news about the coat.

RAINE: Yes, I will indeed, Mr Temple.

COMPLETE FADE.

FADE IN the sound of a typewriter.

A door opens.

The typewriter stops.

STEVE: I think I'm going to bed now, Paul.

TEMPLE: Yes, all right, dear. I've just got a couple of letters I want to finish. Oh, Steve … How well do you know Linda Kelburn?

STEVE: We used to see quite a bit of each other in the old days, but we were never close friends.

TEMPLE: What's she like?

STEVE: Oh, attractive, I suppose; a little too self-centred for my liking. She's looking quite a bit older these days.

TEMPLE: Aren't we all? Were you surprised when she married Kelburn?

STEVE: Quite frankly, I'd never heard of him. She used to be quite friendly …

STEVE breaks off as the door opens.

TEMPLE: What is it, Charlie?

CHARLIE: Are you in or out, Mr Temple?

TEMPLE: At a quick glance, I should say we're in.

CHARLIE: Well, there's a Mr Langdon would like to see you. Looks like a Yank to me.

TEMPLE: Yes – he is a Yank, as you so elegantly put it, Charlie. Show the gentleman in.

CHARLIE: Yes, sir.

STEVE: Langdon? Is this the man you met on the plane?

TEMPLE: Yes.

STEVE: Did you ask him to call?

TEMPLE: Not in so many words, but I said if I could be of use any time, I'd be pleased to see him.

CHARLIE returns with MIKE LANGDON.

CHARLIE: Mr Langdon, sir.

TEMPLE: Hello, Langdon! Do come in! I don't think you've met my wife.

LANGDON: I haven't had that pleasure. Hello, Mrs Temple!

STEVE: How do you do, Mr Langdon?

TEMPLE: Can I get you a drink?

LANGDON: No, thank you, Temple. I've already had more than my share this evening. (*With a sigh*) Which isn't surprising, considering.

TEMPLE: Why? Is the Kelburn business getting you down?

LANGDON: It certainly is.

TEMPLE: You've seen Julia, I take it?

LANGDON: Yes, half a dozen times. It's hopeless – she has every intention of doing precisely what she wants.

TEMPLE: And what about the young man she's keen on – Tony Wyman?

LANGDON: I went to see Wyman last night.

STEVE: Where – at The Hide and Seek?

LANGDON: That's right, Mrs Temple.

START FADE.

LANGDON: I arrived at the club at about half past twelve and Wyman was just finishing his act. I'd already telephoned the manager to say that I wanted to have a word with him …

COMPLETE FADE.

CROSS FADE to TONY WYMAN singing; he is just finishing a number.

There is applause, and the sound of teenage voices, as the number finishes.

The applause FADES DOWN.

FADE IN of WYMAN: he has a distinct Cockney accent and is very sure of himself.

WYMAN: Are you the character who's been asking for me, mister?

LANGDON: (*Pleasantly*) Yes, that's right. Sit down and have a drink, Mr Wyman. My name's Langdon. I'm from New York.

WYMAN: You an agent?

LANGDON: No, as a matter of fact I'm a publisher.

WYMAN: A publisher? Oh, I see. Do you want to buy my life story? Two of the boys are cooking it up …

LANGDON: No, I don't want to buy your life story. We don't publish that kind of book. I want to talk to you about Julia Kelburn.

WYMAN: (*Surprised*) Julia Kelburn?

LANGDON: Yes. I understand that you're in love with her and you want to get married.

WYMAN: Who told you that?

LANGDON: Why – Julia. Besides, it's in all the newspapers.

WYMAN: Do you believe everything you read in the papers? That's strictly for the birds, Mr – What did you say your name was?

LANGDON: Langdon …

WYMAN: Strictly for the birds, Mr Langdon.

LANGDON: Look, I don't get this. Julia said you were unofficially engaged.

WYMAN: It's so unofficial I haven't heard of it. Look, I don't dig that love mush. Now what's this all about? You've got a proposition, let's have it.

LANGDON: Kelburn wants you to leave his daughter alone. He says if you promise not to see her again, he'll pay you five thousand pounds.

There is a pause, then suddenly TONY WYMAN starts to laugh.

It is a high-pitched laugh.

WYMAN: I thought Kelburn was a business man.

LANGDON: He is. He's a millionaire.

WYMAN: Well, tell him he's nuts! I wouldn't marry his daughter if she was the last piece on earth and he offered me fifty thousand. That kid of his gets in my hair. She sticks around the place night after night. She's a flippin' nuisance – not only to me, but to everyone else.

LANGDON: But Julia gave me the impression that you were in love with one another. She said you …

WYMAN: Look, pal, I knock up two hundred nicker a week here. I'm on the gogglebox every fortnight. I got two records in the Top Ten. I got all the blondes and brunettes I want – so why should I get married? Tell me, why should I get married? What am I missing?

LANGDON: (*Lamely*) Kelburn's a wealthy man. I thought perhaps …

The orchestra starts up again.

WYMAN: Lolly? Who worries about lolly? I got more lolly than I know what to do with. Tell Mr Kelburn he can keep his five thousand nicker, and that goes for his daughter too!

START FADE.

LANGDON: I'll deliver the message, Mr Wyman.

COMPLETE FADE.

FADE IN STEVE's voice.

STEVE: … What a charming young man!

LANGDON: Yes; I wasn't exactly enthralled by Master Wyman!

TEMPLE: Do you think he was telling the truth?

LANGDON: (*Puzzled*) I don't know, Temple. He sounded convincing and yet it just doesn't add up. Everyone I've spoken to swears he's got his eye on her. Temple, I know this is a bit of a cheek, but do <u>you</u> think you could make one or two enquiries for me?

TEMPLE: About Tony Wyman?

LANGDON: Yes.

TEMPLE: (*After a moment*) All right, Langdon, we'll get on the grapevine and see what we can do.

LANGDON: (*Pleased*) That's mighty kind of you. I appreciate it; I really do.

TEMPLE: Then how about changing your mind and having a drink?

LANGDON: There's nothing I'd like better!

COMPLETE FADE.

FADE IN of a bedroom clock chiming the hour.
It is three o'clock.
A pause.

TEMPLE: Are you awake?

STEVE: Yes, dear …

TEMPLE: It's three o'clock … can't you get to sleep?

STEVE: I keep thinking it must be pretty awful having a daughter like Julia Kelburn.

TEMPLE: Yes …

STEVE: Paul, do you think Linda <u>did</u> telephone me and she was lying when she said …

STEVE is interrupted by the ringing of the telephone.

STEVE: (*After a moment*) Who on earth can that be – at this time of the morning?

TEMPLE: It's probably a wrong number.

TEMPLE lifts the receiver.

TEMPLE: (*On the phone*) Hello?

LINDA: (*On the other end of the line*) Is that Paul Temple?

TEMPLE: Yes, speaking.

LINDA: (*Softly; as if afraid that she is being overheard*) This is Mrs Kelburn …

TEMPLE: Who?

LINDA: Mrs Kelburn … Linda Kelburn …

TEMPLE: Oh, good evening – or – good morning, Mrs Kelburn.

LINDA: (*A note of desperation in her voice*) Mr Temple, I'm sorry to disturb you at this time of night, but – I've got to see you. It really is important.

TEMPLE: Well – what is it you want to see me about?

LINDA: About – about Julia … my step-daughter.

TEMPLE: What about Julia?

LINDA: (*Softly; tensely*) When can I see you, Mr Temple? Will nine o'clock be all right? I've got your address so …

TEMPLE: (*Interrupting LINDA*) Look, Mrs Kelburn, I'm quite prepared to see you, but first of all I must know what this is all about.

LINDA: I've told you. It's about my step-daughter … Julia …

TEMPLE: Yes, I know, but – what about Julia?

There is a pause.

LINDA: She's going to be murdered.

FADE IN music.

FADE music.

TEMPLE is having breakfast; he is pouring himself a cup of coffee.

The door opens.

TEMPLE: Hello, Steve! You're nice and late this morning!

STEVE: Yes, I know. I didn't get to sleep until five o'clock.

TEMPLE: It's not surprising. We didn't stop talking until half past four. I'll pour you some coffee.

STEVE: No; I don't want any coffee, dear. I'll just have the orange juice. What time is it, anyway?

TEMPLE: Twenty past nine.

STEVE: My word, we are late …

TEMPLE: Yes – and so's your friend Linda Kelburn. She said she'd be here by …

The door bell rings in the background.

TEMPLE: This will be her now.

STEVE: Do you want me to stay?

TEMPLE: Yes, of course. I've got a hunch she only telephoned me because she knew that you …

The door opens.

TEMPLE: Yes, Charlie?

CHARLIE: Superintendent Raine would like to see you, sir.

RAINE enters.

RAINE: Excuse me! Mr Temple, may I have a word with you?

TEMPLE: Yes, of course! All right, Charlie.

RAINE: (*A shade breathless*) Good morning, Mrs Temple.

STEVE: Good morning, Superintendent.

The door closes.

TEMPLE: (*Tensely*) Something's happened! What is it, Raine?

RAINE: We picked a girl out of the river – about two hours ago. She'd been strangled. It was George Kelburn's daughter.

STEVE: Oh, Paul! …

TEMPLE: Julia Kelburn?

RAINE: Yes. But that isn't everything.

TEMPLE: What do you mean?

RAINE: The dead girl was wearing a coat. There was a name on a label stitched inside the collar. (*A moment*) We've seen that name before.

STEVE: (*Softly; almost frightened*) Margo …?

END OF EPISODE ONE

EPISODE TWO

CONCERNING TED ANGUS

OPEN TO:

FADE IN the voice of SUPERINTENDENT RAINE.

RAINE: We picked a girl out of the river – about two hours ago. She'd been strangled. It was George Kelburn's daughter.

STEVE: Oh, Paul! …

TEMPLE: Julia Kelburn?

RAINE: Yes. But that isn't everything.

TEMPLE: What do you mean?

RAINE: The dead girl was wearing a coat. There was a name on a label stitched inside the collar. (*A moment*) We've seen that name before.

STEVE: (*Softly; almost frightened*) Margo …?

RAINE: Yes, Mrs Temple – Margo.

TEMPLE: (*Quietly*) I see. (*Thoughtfully*) About a week ago Steve was kidnapped by persons unknown and then suddenly released. We don't know why this happened, our only clue in fact was a coat found in Steve's car. Inside the coat was the name Margo.

RAINE: And we tried to trace the name but failed. This morning however we came across the name again – on Julia Kelburn.

TEMPLE: M'm.

STEVE: Well, there's one person who won't be surprised by the murder, Superintendent. That's Julia's step-mother – Linda Kelburn.

RAINE: (*Surprised*) Why do you say that, Mrs Temple?

TEMPLE: Mrs Kelburn telephoned and made an appointment to see me at nine o'clock this morning. When I asked her why she wanted to see me she said it was about Julia who was going to be murdered.

RAINE: What time did Mrs Kelburn telephone you?

TEMPLE: About three o'clock this morning …

RAINE: (*Puzzled*) This is extraordinary – quite extraordinary!

TEMPLE: I agree. When I picked up the phone and …

RAINE: (*Interrupting TEMPLE*) No, you don't understand; I've seen Mrs Kelburn – about an hour ago. I went to the house in Eaton Square. She didn't say anything about telephoning you – on the contrary she seemed staggered by the news of the murder. If anything, I think she was even more shaken by the news than her husband.

TEMPLE: She never mentioned the phone call?

RAINE: Not a word.

STEVE: How did Mr Kelburn react?

RAINE: He was pretty badly shaken of course, but I had the impression he'd been worried about his daughter for some time. She mixed with a pretty bohemian crowd, you know, Mrs Temple.

TEMPLE: Yes. She was friendly with a man called Tony Wyman.

RAINE: Yes, I'm checking on Mr Wyman. I've got an appointment to see …

RAINE is interrupted by the telephone ringing.

TEMPLE: Excuse me.

TEMPLE picks up the receiver.

TEMPLE: (*On the phone*) Hello?

LANGDON: (*On the other end of the line*) Paul Temple?

TEMPLE: Yes, speaking.

LANGDON: This is Mike Langdon, Temple …

TEMPLE: Oh, good morning, Langdon!

LANGDON: Temple, I've got some terrible news …

TEMPLE: We've heard about Julia Kelburn. The Superintendent's with me now.

LANGDON: Then I expect he's told you all the details?

TEMPLE: Well, yes. It's a pretty awful business, Langdon. It must have been a shock for you.

LANGDON: Yes, it was – a terrible shock. I never realised the poor kid was so mixed … But look, Temple – I want to ask you a favour …

TEMPLE: What is it?

LANGDON: Kelburn's determined that the person responsible for this shan't escape. He's anxious to make the fullest possible investigation – expense no object.

TEMPLE: Well?

LANGDON: He'd like to see you, Temple. He'd like you to call round this morning if possible.

TEMPLE: I see. (*After a moment*) Does that go for Mrs Kelburn, too?

LANGDON: What do you mean?

TEMPLE: Does Mrs Kelburn want me to call round?

LANGDON: (*Puzzled*) Why, yes, of course. I imagine so. She hasn't said otherwise …

TEMPLE: Tell Mr Kelburn I'll be there at twelve o'clock.

LANGDON: (*Pleased*) Right! Thanks a lot. I appreciate it. Be seeing you then.

TEMPLE: (*Quietly*) Yes. Goodbye, Langdon.

TEMPLE replaces the receiver.

RAINE: Excuse my asking, Mr Temple – but who's this man Langdon?

TEMPLE: He's one of Kelburn's right-hand men. I met him on the plane coming over from New York. Kelburn sent for him. He apparently thought Langdon might be able to reform his daughter. I understand he'd got her out of one or two little scrapes in New York.

RAINE: All the way from New York because Kelburn couldn't cope with his own daughter? Sounds a bit far-fetched.

TEMPLE: I don't know. We never knew Julia Kelburn. We don't know what her father was up against. However, Langdon's main job was to try and buy off Tony Wyman.

RAINE: That's interesting. What happened?

TEMPLE: Wyman told Langdon he couldn't care less about Julia.

RAINE: M'm. This chap Langdon … Is he about fifty, going bald, about medium height?

TEMPLE: That's right.

RAINE: He was hovering about when I interviewed Kelburn and his wife, but they didn't introduce me. They were pretty upset, of course.

STEVE: Naturally …

RAINE: (*Casually*) Would you say there's been anything between Langdon and Julia Kelburn?

TEMPLE: I don't think so; but I wouldn't know, of course. You'd better ask Langdon that question.

RAINE: Yes … Well, goodbye, Mrs Temple!

STEVE: Goodbye, Superintendent.

START FADE.

TEMPLE: You've no objection, I take it – if I go along and see Kelburn?

RAINE: Not the slightest, Mr Temple. Not the slightest. It's a free country – so they tell me …

COMPLETE FADE.

FADE IN GEORGE KELBURN's voice.
He has a slight Yorkshire accent and at the moment is obviously under an emotional strain.

KELBURN: … It isn't that I mistrust the police, Mr Temple. I just think that a case of this kind demands a more imaginative approach than the average police inspector is capable of …

TEMPLE: (*Interrupting KELBURN*) Mr Kelburn, I've worked with the police for many years, and I can assure you that the majority of men at Scotland Yard are shrewd, intelligent, and highly efficient.

KELBURN: Efficient, yes, maybe! But slow – slow. That's the trouble – damned slow! My daughter's been murdered, Mr Temple – my only child … I'll give anything to find the swine responsible for that murder. Just name the fee …

TEMPLE: You don't solve a case of this kind simply by paying someone a fat fee, Mr Kelburn.

The door opens.

TEMPLE: The whole problem is far too …

TEMPLE breaks off.

KELBURN: Oh, there you are, Linda! I was wondering where you'd got to. Mr Temple – may I introduce my wife?

TEMPLE: How do you do, Mrs Kelburn? I believe you know Steve …

LINDA: I do indeed. Is she well?

TEMPLE: Thank you, yes. She was looking forward to seeing you this morning.

LINDA: This morning?

TEMPLE: Yes. We were expecting you to call at nine o'clock as arranged, but obviously this business …

LINDA: I'm sorry, Mr Temple, but I don't understand.

KELBURN: Were you under the impression that my wife was coming to see you?

TEMPLE: I was indeed.

LANGDON: What gave you that impression?

TEMPLE: The fact that she telephoned me in the early hours of the morning and said she wanted to see me.

LINDA: (*Staggered*) I – I telephoned you?

TEMPLE: Yes.

LINDA: When?

TEMPLE: About three o'clock this morning.

LINDA: But that's nonsense!

KELBURN: I can assure you my wife didn't phone you, Mr Temple. We occupy the same bedroom. If she'd made a telephone call at that hour of the morning I'd certainly have known about it.

LINDA: What exactly am I supposed to have phoned you about?

TEMPLE: You told me that you suspected … (*He hesitates*)

LINDA: Suspected, what?

TEMPLE: … That your step-daughter was going to be murdered.

KELBURN: Good God!

LANGDON: Are you serious, Temple?

KELBURN: But this is ridiculous!

LINDA: (*Suddenly*) Wait a minute! This is the second time I'm supposed to have made a mysterious telephone call. I met your wife a couple of weeks ago and she had some strange story about having spoken to me on the phone – and my saying I wanted to see you.

TEMPLE: And you didn't want to see me?

LINDA: Of course not! I didn't even phone …

TEMPLE: (*Quietly*) Someone did … (*Changing the subject*) Mrs Kelburn, your husband has asked me to investigate this affair and I think perhaps you might be able to help me.

LINDA: How, exactly?

TEMPLE: Well, you can start by telling me where Julia bought her clothes from.

LINDA: I'm afraid I don't know where she bought her clothes from. She wasn't very fussy about her dress, you know.

TEMPLE: Could you find out?

LINDA: Yes, I suppose so.

TEMPLE: I'm interested in the coat she was wearing at the time of the murder. There was a label inside with the name "Margo" on it.

LINDA: Margo?

TEMPLE: Yes. Does that name mean anything to you?

LINDA: No, I'm afraid it doesn't. But I'll make enquiries, if you like?

TEMPLE: I'd be grateful if you would, Mrs Kelburn.

KELBURN: Mr Temple, surely there's something we can do – something just a little more progressive than enquiring about a coat?

LANGDON: Mr Temple knows what he's doing, George.

TEMPLE: You have my phone number, Mrs Kelburn, if you want to get in touch with me?

LINDA: (*Without thinking*) Yes, of course … (*Suddenly changing her mind*) No, I'm afraid I haven't.

TEMPLE: It's in the book. Now, if you'll excuse me, Mr Kelburn, I have a lunch appointment.

LANGDON: Have you got your car?

TEMPLE: No, but I can easily pick up a cab.

LANGDON: I'll drop you, Temple. I'm going into the West End.

START FADE.

TEMPLE: Oh, thank you, Langdon. Goodbye, Mrs Kelburn. I hope to hear from you.

FADE SCENE.

FADE UP background noises of a small restaurant.

WAITER: Would you like some more coffee, sir?

TEMPLE: No, thank you.

WAITER: Very good, sir.

STEVE: Well! You've had quite a morning! What did you make of Linda Kelburn?

TEMPLE: Oh, she seemed pleasant enough, in a brittle sort of way.

STEVE: Do you think she got on well with her step-daughter?

TEMPLE: Yes, I think she did – and heaven knows that couldn't have been very easy. According to what Langdon was telling me on the way here Julia was quite a handful.

STEVE: Yes, I can believe that. (*After a moment*) Paul, do you think the people who kidnapped me were responsible for the murder?

TEMPLE: Yes, I do. (*Quietly*) And I think I know why they kidnapped you, Steve.

STEVE: (*Surprised*) You do?

TEMPLE: Yes. While I was in America a report appeared in one of the Continental newspapers that said … Well, I've got it in my wallet. Read it for yourself, Steve.

TEMPLE takes his wallet out of his pocket and hands the newspaper clipping to STEVE.

There is a pause.

STEVE: This is all about that man Raine mentioned – The Fence.

TEMPLE: Yes.

STEVE: (*Looking at the newspaper clipping*) It says Scotland Yard have asked you to help them discover his identity and that you've cut short your American tour in order … (*Looking up*) Is this true, Paul?

TEMPLE: No, darling – it's just a newspaper story. Sir Graham and I had never even discussed The Fence.

STEVE: But you think that someone read this and …

TEMPLE: I think The Fence himself read it and believed it. Remember what that man said to you, Steve. "We did it as a warning and to prove that it was possible, Mrs Temple."

STEVE: (*Quietly*) Yes …

TEMPLE: From now on you've got to watch your step, dear. Get Charlie to answer the door. Don't go anywhere on your own if you can help it. Always leave a message as to your whereabouts. Don't act on any telephone calls without checking. Well – you know the routine.

STEVE: Yes, I know the routine.

FADE UP background noises of the restaurant.
FADE SCENE.

FADE IN background traffic noises.
FADE IN the sound of TEMPLE's car ticking over.
STEVE is driving.

TEMPLE: (*Irritated*) By Timothy, this traffic really is appalling.

STEVE: Relax darling! I don't mind driving.

TEMPLE: I'm delighted to hear it.

STEVE: This is always the worst bit, anyway.

TEMPLE: Ah! That's better. We're on the move now!

STEVE changes gear: the car moves forward.
A pause.

TEMPLE: (*Amused*) It's all right, Steve – your hat is on straight.

STEVE: My hat?

TEMPLE: Wasn't that why you were staring in the mirror?

STEVE: No. As a matter of fact I was looking at the car behind.

TEMPLE: (*Turning round*) The one driven by the young man in dark glasses?

STEVE: Yes. It was standing outside the house when I left, and it was behind me when I drove to the restaurant.

TEMPLE: Was it, by Timothy! You don't recognise the young man?

STEVE: No, I don't … But it's difficult with those glasses he's wearing.

TEMPLE: Yes. (*A sudden decision*) Steve, take the next turn on the left … Quickly, darling!

The car makes a quick turn.

STEVE: What's the idea, Paul?

TEMPLE: (*After a moment*) Yes, he's following us all right … Pull behind that lorry at the traffic lights. Get into the kerb if you can, Steve.

STEVE: All right. (*A moment*) What are you going to do?

TEMPLE: I'm getting out. You drive straight home, Steve. I'll see you there in about an hour.

STEVE: (*Puzzled*) Yes, but what are you going to …

TEMPLE: (*Getting out of the car*) Take care! See you later, dear!

The car door opens and closes as TEMPLE gets out.

FADE UP traffic noises.

FADE UP the opening and closing of a car door.

WYMAN: Here, what's the big idea, getting into my car like this?

TEMPLE: Keep going! I'll explain later.

WYMAN: Who the hell are you?

The sound of car horns in the near background can be heard.

TEMPLE: Drive on! People are getting impatient.

WYMAN: I don't give two hoots what people …

TEMPLE: Drive on! And there's no need to follow that car, I can tell you all you want to know about it.

WYMAN: What the devil are you talking about?

TEMPLE: I think you know what I'm talking about. You've been following that car. Now I suggest you drive into Regent's Park – we can have a little talk there …

WYMAN: I – (*Quietly*) Yes, all right, Mr Temple …

FADE SCENE.

FADE UP of a stationary car ticking over.

TEMPLE: I should switch the engine off, Mr Wyman.

WYMAN switches off the car engine.

WYMAN: You recognise me, then?

TEMPLE: Yes, I recognise you. Now what can I do for you? Why are you following us around?

WYMAN: I've read a lot about you in the papers, Mr Temple, and I thought … Well, I'm in dead trouble, see? And I thought maybe you could sort of give me a line … I hung around your house hoping to catch you, but I couldn't pluck up enough courage to …

TEMPLE: What's the trouble, Wyman?

WYMAN: It's the police, Mr Temple. They've put the wind up me. That Superintendent Raine, he didn't 'alf give me a proper going over. Practically accused me of doin' the murder.

TEMPLE: You mean Julia Kelburn?

WYMAN: Yes, and I never even knew she'd snuffed it, straight I didn't. That chap Raine was at me for the best part of an hour, but all I could tell him was that I finished at the club just after one and went straight home.

TEMPLE: Just how friendly were you with Julia Kelburn?

WYMAN: Depends on what you mean by friendly.

TEMPLE: How did you meet her?

WYMAN: Some of the gang – the reg'lars – brought her to the club one night. She was dressed all sloppy like with her hair all over the place. I thought at first she was one of them beatniks. But we got talkin' a bit and she seemed to go for me. Next time she come in, I hardly knew her … She was turned out like a flippin' film star.

TEMPLE: Did you know her father was well off?

WYMAN: Well, not at first – she never let on. But later she started throwing the lolly around and I guessed somebody had the dough. She wasn't a bad kid. I was fond of her in a funny sort of way, but – well, she started getting in my hair. Hanging around the club, meeting me in restaurants, waiting for me at the TV studios … You know how it is.

TEMPLE: No, I don't know how it is. You tell me.

WYMAN: Well, you know – she was a bit of a mixed up kid. Bit dotty, perhaps, I don't know. Spent quids with one of those psychiatrists.

TEMPLE: (*Interested*) Oh – who told you that?

WYMAN: She did. She used to visit a doc in Wimpole Street. Benkaray I think the name was. Yes, that's right – Dr Benkaray.

TEMPLE: Did you tell the Superintendent about this?

WYMAN: No; I didn't tell 'im any more than was necessary.

The sound of a car approaching is heard.

WYMAN: I know those flat-foots. When I was a kid in Bermondsey I … Hi, look at this car! He's coming straight for us!!!

TEMPLE: Get out, Wyman! Quick!!!!

TEMPLE throws open the car door and jumps out of the stationary car.

WYMAN: (*Trapped*) I can't open the ruddy …

There is a sudden crash as the oncoming vehicle deliberately smashes into WYMAN's car.

There is a cry of pain from the trapped WYMAN.

FADE IN of excited voices, the sound of a police whistle, etc.

FADE noises down.

FADE SCENE.

FADE UP on the opening of a door.

JENKINS: Ah, there you are, Mr Temple!

TEMPLE: How is Wyman, Doctor?

JENKINS: He'll be all right. Got rather a nasty cut above his right eye and he's shaken up quite a bit, but I've given him a sedative. It must have been quite a spectacular little crash.

TEMPLE: It was – and a deliberate one too.

JENKINS: Lucky you managed to get clear.

TEMPLE: It was a near thing.

RAINE: (*Approaching*) Hello, Mr Temple! Are you feeling all right now?

TEMPLE: Yes, I'm fine. I was dead lucky.

JENKINS: You both were! If there's nothing more, Mr Temple, I'll get back to the ward.

TEMPLE: I'm much obliged, Doctor. Will Wyman be discharged?

JENKINS: Yes. In about an hour or so, I should say.

RAINE: Then I'll get a statement from him later. Thank you, Doctor.

TEMPLE: Well – what about the other chap, the driver?

RAINE: He's at the Station. Got off with a few bruises and a cut cheek.

TEMPLE: Who is he?

RAINE: A tough little Scot – name of Ted Angus.

TEMPLE: (*Thoughtfully*) Ted Angus …

RAINE: Yes. Do you know him?

TEMPLE: No, I don't think so.

RAINE: I've been onto Glasgow. They knew him up there, but they've never been able to get anything on him. I'm afraid we'll only be able to hold him for an hour or two.

TEMPLE: What's he do for a living – if anything?

RAINE: He's done all sorts of things. Barker in a fairground – travelling salesman – Wall of Death rider … According to Glasgow he's suspected of being mixed up in one or two smash and grab jobs, but he's always got clear. You know, I can hardly think it was you he was after. It was Wyman's car.

TEMPLE: Yes; maybe you're right. (*Suddenly*) I'd like to phone my wife – then perhaps I could have a word with Angus?

START FADE.

RAINE: Yes, of course. You can phone Mrs Temple from the station …

FADE SCENE.

FADE IN the voice of TED ANGUS: he has a distinct Scots accent.

ANGUS: I tell ye it was an accident, sir. The steering went completely … Couldn't ye see me trying to twist the wheel?

TEMPLE: I don't think you're telling the truth, Angus.

ANGUS: Here, d'ye think I run around crashing into people I've never seen?

TEMPLE: I think you might, if the money was big enough.

ANGUS: You're lucky there isn't a witness to hear ye say that! Who d'ye think ye are, anyway? Comin' in here an' insultin' an innocent man?

TEMPLE: My name's Paul Temple, and it's only by a stroke of luck that I'm here at all.

ANGUS: Oh, you're the writer feller. Now why should I want to do you any harm?

TEMPLE: That's what I'm asking you, Angus! Who told you to run me down?

ANGUS: Nobody – nobody at all.

TEMPLE: Then perhaps your instructions were to smash up Tony Wyman?

ANGUS: Tony Wyman? The laddie who sings on the telly? Why, I'm one of his fans!

TEMPLE: You were paid to crash into his car to scare him, weren't you?

ANGUS: This isn't one of your books, Mr Temple. Honest folk like me don't do that sort of thing. You've got it all wrong.

TEMPLE: You say you're honest – but you seem to have difficulty in proving it. What's your job?

ANGUS: I'm a car driver.

TEMPLE: Who's your boss?

ANGUS: I'm unemployed at the moment.

TEMPLE: Then what were you doing in that car?

ANGUS: Just driving it across London for a friend of mine – he owns a garage.

TEMPLE: What garage?

ANGUS: The Two Counties, at Mill Hill.

TEMPLE: Did you tell the police that?

ANGUS: Yes – and they checked it. They've checked everything. I tell you you're wasting your time, mister. It was just an accident.

TEMPLE: Accident or not, Angus – I'll give you one last word of advice. These people you're working for are ruthless …

ANGUS: (*Interrupting TEMPLE*) I keep telling you I'm not working for anybody!

TEMPLE: When you've served your turn, they'll ditch you, sure as fate – and they won't be too gentle about it either.

ANGUS: I can take care of myself, Mr Temple.

TEMPLE: I hope you can.

The door opens.

RAINE: Finished?

TEMPLE: Yes, I'm finished.

ANGUS: When are you letting me out of here?

RAINE: The sergeant will be along in a minute for a few more details, then you can go.

ANGUS: I should ruddy well think so! Treatin' me like a criminal!

RAINE: Come along, Temple.

TEMPLE: (*Turning*) Yes?

ANGUS: Have you heard how the kid is – what's his name – ?

TEMPLE: His name's Wyman. I thought you were a fan of his. He's very scared, Angus. You can tell your employer you made a good job of it.

The door closes.

RAINE: (*Softly; almost an aside*) What d'you make of him?

TEMPLE: He's about as straight as the Tower of Pisa. It's a pity you can't hold him, Raine.

RAINE: Yes, but we can't. He stuck to his story about the steering being faulty.

START FADE.

RAINE: And it might have been, of course – it was buckled to blazes …

COMPLETE FADE.

FADE IN the sound of a piano being played: a slow, depressing piece of music.

TEMPLE: By Timothy, Steve, you're in a depressing mood this evening!

The piano stops.

STEVE: Yes, I know. I keep thinking about that car accident. It might have been fatal, darling.

TEMPLE: Yes, well, it wasn't, Steve, so cheer up.

STEVE: I should have thought the police could have held that man Angus on some charge or other. We're always reading about people being detained by the police so I don't see …

The door opens.

TEMPLE: Yes, Charlie?

CHARLIE: I've found it, Mr Temple.

STEVE: What's that?

CHARLIE: The telephone number you wanted …

TEMPLE: Oh, good!

CHARLIE: Here we are, sir. It's in the book. (*Reading*) Dr Benkaray, 34a Wimpole Street …

TEMPLE: (*Also reading from the book*) M.C. Benkaray, 34a Wimpole Street … Yes, that's it … Thank you, Charlie.

CHARLIE: Anything else, Mr Temple?

TEMPLE: No, that's all right. Leave the book.

CHARLIE goes.

STEVE: What's all this about?

TEMPLE lifts the telephone receiver and dials the number.

TEMPLE: Tony Wyman told me that Julia Kelburn recently consulted a psychiatrist – a Dr Benkaray. I thought it might be quite an idea if I had a word with him.

STEVE: Why?

TEMPLE: Well, for one thing I'd like to know what she consulted him about … (*Suddenly; on the phone*) Hello?

ANGUS: (*On the other end of the line*) Welbeck 9291 …

TEMPLE: (*Slightly puzzled by the voice*) Dr Benkaray's house?

ANGUS: That's right.

TEMPLE: Can I speak to the doctor?

ANGUS: Who is it speaking?

TEMPLE: My name is Temple …

ANGUS: (*After a moment*) Right, hold on …

STEVE: What is it, Paul? What's the matter?

TEMPLE: I could swear that … The man on the other end, Steve – he sounded exactly like Ted Angus!

STEVE: But it couldn't have been, surely? I mean …

TEMPLE: (*Interrupting STEVE: on the phone*) Hello?

LARRY: (*On the other end of the line*) Who is that, please?

TEMPLE: Is that Dr Benkaray?

LARRY: No, this is Dr Benkaray's secretary. The doctor is out of town.

TEMPLE: My name is Temple. I'd like to make an appointment.

LARRY: Then I suggest you phone again towards the end of the month.

TEMPLE: But surely …

LARRY: (*Interrupting TEMPLE*) Any time after the 25th … I shall be pleased to make an appointment for you then.

TEMPLE: But I'm afraid that's too …

LARRY: (*Again interrupting TEMPLE*) Goodbye, Mr Temple.

LARRY replaces the receiver.

Realising he has been cut off, TEMPLE slowly puts down his receiver.

TEMPLE: Well, I'm blowed!

STEVE: What did he say?

TEMPLE: He cut me short and rang off. By Timothy, if he's the secretary – I wonder what the doctor's like?

The door opens.

STEVE: Yes, Charlie?

CHARLIE: There's a Mrs Kelburn called. She says she'd like to see Mr Temple.

TEMPLE: Show her in, Charlie.

CHARLIE: Yes, Mr Temple.

STEVE: Are you expecting Linda?

TEMPLE: No, but I told her to phone me if she had any information.

STEVE: What information could she have?

TEMPLE: I asked her to find out where Julia bought her clothes from. I thought perhaps … (*He stops*)

CHARLIE: Mrs Kelburn, sir.

STEVE: Hello, Linda!

LINDA: Hello, Steve. How are you?

STEVE: I'm fine, thank you.

TEMPLE: Mrs Kelburn, let me get you a drink.

LINDA: No, I won't, thank you, Mr Temple. I'm in rather a hurry. I'm dining with some people at Hampstead. Mr Temple, I've made one or two enquiries about Julia's clothes, and I've been through her wardrobe.

TEMPLE: Thank you.

LINDA: There's nothing with the name "Margo" on it, but I've discovered that most of her clothes – most of the respectable clothes, at any rate – were bought from a shop in Bond Street called Daphne Drake Ltd.

STEVE: Oh, I've heard of it. It's a very good shop.

LINDA: Yes, I think it is, although I don't go there myself.

TEMPLE: Did Julia have many clothes?

LINDA: Yes, she did, but she was a frightfully erratic sort of person. She'd probably wear nothing but jeans and a sweater for a month or so, and then suddenly buy herself half a dozen dresses and suits. There was no telling what she'd do. Unfortunately, it wasn't only her clothes that she was erratic about.

STEVE: What do you mean?

LINDA: Well – she wasn't exactly careful about her choice of friends, was she? Of course, the trouble was George wouldn't take her in hand. He wouldn't hear a word against her. Understandable, I suppose, but rather irritating at times.

TEMPLE: Did you try to take her in hand, Mrs Kelburn?

LINDA: No. It wasn't my job.

STEVE: But you were quite good friends?

LINDA: Yes – we were, considering. But the trouble really started when George got a bee in his bonnet about this Tony Wyman person and tried to lay the law down. It was too late – you just couldn't do that sort of thing with Julia. Tell her she couldn't have something, and she'd immediately want it.

TEMPLE: Yes, I can understand that.

STEVE: How is your husband, Linda?

LINDA: He's still very upset, of course – it's been a terrible shock to him, but the doctor's given him some dope. He was lying down when I left. I suppose there's no news, Mr Temple? The police have no idea who did it?

TEMPLE: No. At least, I certainly haven't heard anything, Mrs Kelburn.

LINDA: Well, I must be going.

TEMPLE: I'm very grateful to you for calling. You'll let me know if you come across anything you think might be of any importance?

LINDA: Yes, of course. I certainly will, Mr Temple.

STEVE: I'll show you out, Linda.

The door opens and closes.

FADE SCENE.

FADE UP of TEMPLE mixing himself a drink.

The door opens.

TEMPLE: I hope she enjoys her dinner.

STEVE: You don't like her, do you, Paul?

TEMPLE: No – but I'm glad she called. I wonder if this Daphne Drake place is worth investigating.

STEVE: Well, I can tell you one thing; the coat that was left in my car at the airport wasn't bought from Daphne Drake's.

TEMPLE: How do you know?

STEVE: It wasn't their style. They have much more expensive stuff than that. They have some really lovely things. (*After a moment*) You know, I think I ought to go along there tomorrow morning, Paul, and make a few enquiries.

TEMPLE: (*Laughing*) I know the sort of enquiries you'd make! Still, it's not a bad idea.

STEVE: Thank you, darling.

TEMPLE: But, Steve –

STEVE: Yes, dear?

TEMPLE: One dress – one only, remember …

STEVE starts to laugh.

FADE ON STEVE's laughter.

FADE SCENE.

FADE IN the voice of ELSIE JACKSON: a faintly artificial voice, just a shade too 'refined'.

ELSIE: … I think the dress is perfect, madam – I really do. And the colour's adorable. If you'd like to try it on again, Mrs Temple …

STEVE: (*After a moment*) No, I agree with you, it is a lovely dress. I'll take it.

ELSIE: Thank you, Mrs Temple. Shall we send it?

STEVE: Yes. I'll give you my address.

ELSIE: It might take a day or two because of the alterations – but it shouldn't be very long. Now, is there anything else I can show you?

STEVE: (*Hesitantly*) I don't think so. (*Suddenly*) Oh, a friend of mine has a coat I've been envying for sometime. (*With a little laugh*) She simply won't tell me where she bought it from, but there's a label inside the collar with the name "Margo" on it.

ELSIE: Margo?

STEVE: Yes. Would that be the manufacturer, or the retailer?

ELSIE: I really couldn't tell you, Mrs Temple. Margo? I'm sorry, but I've never heard the name before … Of course, we have some very nice coats, if … Yes, what is it, Jane?

JANE: Excuse me, Miss Elsie, the fitter says Dr Benkaray's coat is ready. She wants to know if the doctor's calling for it?

ELSIE: No, no, I promised her we'd post it to the Westerton address …

JANE: Very good, Miss Elsie.

START FADE.

ELSIE: Now, if you'll be good enough to come this way, Mrs Temple, I'll show you some of our coats. We have a small, but very lovely, selection …

FADE SCENE.

FADE IN background noises of a cocktail bar.
A piano is playing.

TEMPLE: Hello, Steve! I thought you were never coming! Did you buy up the whole shop?

STEVE: No, darling, I didn't.

WAITER: Can I get you anything, madam?

STEVE: I'd like a dry Martini.

TEMPLE: A dry Martini – and I'll have the same again.

WAITER: Yes, sir.

TEMPLE: Well, Steve?

STEVE: I've got some news for you, Mr Temple!

TEMPLE: About Margo?

STEVE: No. They've never heard of the name – at least, they say they haven't. But I'll tell you who they have heard of, Paul.

TEMPLE: Who?

STEVE: Dr Benkaray.

TEMPLE: (*Puzzled*) Dr Benkaray?

STEVE: Yes – she's a customer of theirs …

TEMPLE: She's a … Are you serious, Steve?

STEVE: I'm quite serious, darling.

TEMPLE: Well, I'm blowed! I took it for granted Benkaray was a man, I never thought … By Timothy, I must watch my step – I'm slipping, Steve! Go on, tell me what happened?

STEVE: Dr Benkaray bought a coat from Daphne Drake's and they were asked to post it to her – she's living in the country somewhere.

TEMPLE: Where, do you know?

STEVE: At a place called Westerton. I don't know the address.

TEMPLE: Westerton?

STEVE: Yes. Where is Westerton – the name seemed familiar?

TEMPLE: It's in Kent, about forty miles from here. Rather a nice little place. There's a very good pub there called The Red Hart. I used to know the landlord, a man called Harcourt.

STEVE: Oh, I remember The Red Hart! We stayed there one weekend, about six or seven years ago.

TEMPLE: That's right …

STEVE: Harcourt's a rather wizened-up little man with a bald head. He asked you to autograph one of your novels and you spilt the ink all over it …

TEMPLE: (*Laughing*) That's the chap.

STEVE: It's rather an odd place for a psychiatrist to live, isn't it? I should have thought she'd have lived in Town.

TEMPLE: She has a place in Town, in Wimpole Street. That's where I telephoned.

STEVE: Oh, yes, of course.

TEMPLE: (*Quietly*) Steve, I'm very interested in this Dr Benkaray, for several reasons. One: Julia Kelburn consulted her, and two: I still think it was that chap Angus who answered the telephone.

START FADE.

STEVE: Which means, I suppose, we're going to spend the weekend at Westerton?

TEMPLE: Yes, darling …

FADE SCENE.

FADE IN the voice of FRED HARCOURT.

FRED: (*Middle-aged: slightly country accent*) There you are, Mr Temple. A nice foaming tankard.

TEMPLE: Thank you, Mr Harcourt. Still brewing your own beer, I'm glad to see.

FRED: Ah, yes, that's our ace card. We get people from miles away – even from London – just to see what real beer tastes like.

TEMPLE: (*Laughing*) Yes. Talking of people from London – have you come across a Dr Benkaray in these parts?

FRED: You mean the lady doctor – who took Miller's Croft in Vine Lane?

TEMPLE: Yes, I should imagine that's the same person.

STEVE: She doesn't practice down here, does she?

FRED: No, Mrs Temple – at least, not with the locals. She's a specialist. Nervous diseases, I think - or something like that. Got a very nice place, they tell me; two cottages knocked into one. Everybody says how nice it is. Mrs Fletcher, one of my regular customers, used to be the Daily. Lovely place, she says it is.

TEMPLE: You haven't met the doctor?

FRED: No. Just seen her around in the village. Striking looking woman.

TEMPLE: Has she many friends – locally, I mean?

FRED: No, I reckon Mrs Fletcher knows her as well as most – although she doesn't work for her now. Hasn't been up there for almost a year. Always speaks well of the doctor, though, does Mrs Fletcher. Says she's a real lady.

STEVE: Where is Vine Lane?

FRED: It's about four miles from here. The cottage stands on its own. Wouldn't be another house for about a quarter of a mile.

STEVE: Sounds very lonely.

FRED: Oh, it is, Mrs Temple. But it's very pretty. There's a nice little wood and a stream running right across the end of the lane.

BARMAID: (*From the background*) Mr Harcourt!

FRED: (*Turning*) Coming, Maisie! Excuse me, Mr Temple.

TEMPLE: Yes, of course.

FRED: Oh, would you like me to put your car away, sir? We've got a private lock-up if you'd like one.

TEMPLE: No thanks, we shall probably go for a run after dinner.

FRED: Well, let me know what you think of the beer, sir.

A pause.

STEVE: Are you going to see this Mrs Fletcher?

TEMPLE: I might do later, darling, but it's a bit tricky. I don't want to attract too much attention. What do you think of the beer, Steve?

START FADE.

STEVE: Two of these and I should certainly attract attention – I should be spark out!

TEMPLE laughs.

FADE SCENE.

FADE IN a car travelling along a country lane.

It is going quite slowly.

STEVE: They certainly should be able to brew some good beer in these parts – I don't think I've ever seen so many hopfields.

TEMPLE: Yes … What's that sign say, darling?

STEVE: Where? Oh, I see … Vine … what is it? … Vine Lane.

TEMPLE: Yes, I thought it was.

The car slowly pulls in to the side and stops.

TEMPLE: I think we'll park on the grass verge here and take a little stroll.

STEVE: It's getting rather dark.

TEMPLE: Not very, darling – in any case, I've got a torch.

TEMPLE stops the car engine and opens the door.

TEMPLE: Do us good to stretch our legs.

TEMPLE and STEVE get out of the car.

We hear the sound of footsteps on the road.

STEVE: What is it you want to take a look at – the cottage?

TEMPLE: Yes.

STEVE: Well, don't expect me to tramp across fields in these shoes.

TEMPLE: (*After a moment*) Fred Harcourt was right – it is pretty lonely.

FADE DOWN the sound of the footsteps.

FADE IN of footsteps.

STEVE: Do you want to go any further, Paul?

TEMPLE: We'll just go as far as that tree, Steve, and then we'll turn back.

STEVE: It's funny we haven't seen the cottage.

TEMPLE: Yes … Wait a minute! I can see a light through the trees … Yes, there it is!

STEVE: It's still quite a long way away.

As STEVE speaks a MAN's voice can be heard calling from the near background.

TEMPLE: Yes, and it looks to me as if …

TEMPLE has heard the voice and stops talking.

STEVE: What was that?

TEMPLE: It was someone shouting. A man, I think …

STEVE: It came from over there, darling! I'm sure it …

TEMPLE: Ssh! Wait a minute, Steve.

There is a pause.

A MAN can now be heard calling: he is in obvious pain.

STEVE: Oh, Paul … Whoever it is – he's obviously in pain …

TEMPLE: Ssh!

The MAN's voice continues to be heard: the voice of a MAN in pain.

STEVE: It's over there – in the wood …

TEMPLE: Yes … Give me your hand, Steve.

STEVE: Have you got the torch?

TEMPLE: Yes …

FADE DOWN of the footsteps.

FADE IN of the footsteps and the noise of TEMPLE and STEVE pushing their way through the hedge growth.

TEMPLE: He must be somewhere around here because …

STEVE: (*Softly*) Oh, Paul! …

TEMPLE: (*Quietly*) By Timothy!

STEVE: Do you know him?

TEMPLE: Yes …

STEVE: Who is it?

TEMPLE: It's Ted Angus …

STEVE: Ted … Ted Angus?

TEMPLE: Yes … By Timothy, just look at him … He's really been beaten up, poor devil …

ANGUS: (*Weakly, in pain*) Don't hit me … Please don't hit me … Please don't …

TEMPLE: It's all right, Angus, no one's going to hurt you. This is Temple.

ANGUS: Who is it?

TEMPLE: Paul Temple. You remember – we met at the police station.

ANGUS: Oh yes … Yes, I remember. (*Tensely; making an effort*) Temple, listen …

TEMPLE: Yes, what is it?

ANGUS: Temple, this is important … Ask – ask Mrs Fletcher about … about …

TEMPLE: Go on, Angus, I'm listening …

ANGUS: Ask Mrs Fletcher about …

TEMPLE: (*Tensely; curious*) … About what? About Dr Benkaray?

ANGUS: No … Ask her about the coat …

END OF EPISODE TWO

EPISODE THREE

A CHANGE OF MIND

OPEN TO: The voice of TED ANGUS: he is in obvious pain.

ANGUS: Who is it?

TEMPLE: Paul Temple. You remember – we met at the police station.

ANGUS: Oh yes ... Yes, I remember. (*Tensely; making an effort*) Temple, listen ...

TEMPLE: Yes, what is it?

ANGUS: Temple, this is important ... Ask – ask Mrs Fletcher about ... about ...

TEMPLE: Go on, Angus, I'm listening ...

ANGUS: Ask Mrs Fletcher about ...

TEMPLE: (*Tensely; curious*) ... About what? About Dr Benkaray?

ANGUS: No ... Ask her about the coat ...

TEMPLE: The coat? What do you know about the coat, Angus?

ANGUS is now unconscious.

TEMPLE: Angus ... the coat ...

STEVE: It's no use, Paul – he's unconscious.

TEMPLE: Yes ...

In the background there is the hoot of an owl.

STEVE: What are we going to do? I don't think we ought to move him.

TEMPLE: No; we'll have to get a doctor right away.

STEVE: You mean – Dr Benkaray?

TEMPLE: She's probably the only one within miles.

STEVE: There was a call box at the end of the lane ...

TEMPLE: Yes, you go down to the box and ring the police. Give them all the details you know. Tell them to bring an ambulance as quickly as possible. Then take the car back to The Red Hart. I'll meet the police. They'll give me a lift back to the inn.

STEVE: Well – what are you going to do now? Try and get hold of Dr Benkaray?

TEMPLE: Yes.

STEVE: But do you think we should leave Angus here? He may be dying …

TEMPLE: He probably is, poor devil. But I'm afraid there's nothing we can do for him. Come along, darling, we haven't much time. I'll see you as far as the lane with the torch …

FADE UP the sound of the owl hooting.

FADE DOWN the hoot of the owl.

FADE IN heavy knocking on a door.

The distant ringing of a door bell.

LARRY: (*Off*) Hello? Who is that?

TEMPLE: (*Calling*) Open up!!! It's urgent!

LARRY: Who's there? What do you want?

TEMPLE: (*Calling through the door*) I tell you it's urgent! Open the door!

LARRY: (*Annoyed*) Wait a minute …

The door is unlocked and eventually opened.

TEMPLE: Is this Dr Benkaray's house?

LARRY: Yes – it is …

TEMPLE: I must see the doctor – it's urgent!

LARRY: The doctor isn't very well. She isn't receiving visitors tonight …

TEMPLE: Don't you understand? This is an emergency! There's a man very badly hurt, probably dying. Will you please do as I say and fetch the doctor!

LARRY: I've told you – she's lying down – she's not well …

In the background a door opens and DR BENKARAY comes into the hall.

She is a woman of about fifty: a slight mid-European accent.

BENKARAY: Larry, what is all this noise? What is going on here?

TEMPLE: Dr Benkaray?

BENKARAY: Yes – I am Dr Benkaray …

TEMPLE: My name is Paul Temple …

LARRY: (*Surprised*) Temple! You never said your name was …

BENKARAY: (*Interrupting LARRY*) There is something wrong, Mr Temple?

TEMPLE: Yes; there's a man in the wood at the back of your house. He's very badly injured – he was unconscious when I left him.

BENKARAY: Injured – in what way?

TEMPLE: It looks to me as if he's been beaten up.

LARRY: Beaten up? Are you trying to tell us that …

BENKARAY: Be quiet, Larry! I'll get my bag, Mr Temple. I'll be with you in a moment …

START FADE.

TEMPLE: Thank you, Doctor.

FADE SCENE.

FADE IN the voice of LARRY CROSS.

LARRY: Yes; he certainly has been beaten up.

BENKARAY: Could I take your torch for a moment, please?

TEMPLE: Yes, of course …

BENKARAY: Thank you …

BENKARAY is examining ANGUS.

LARRY: Good Lord! Just look at his head …

TEMPLE: Do you recognise him?

LARRY: No – no, Mr Temple. I've never seen him before.

TEMPLE: Do you know him, Doctor?

BENKARAY: No; and I'm afraid there's nothing I can do for the poor fellow. He's dead.

TEMPLE: Yes; I thought it was hopeless.

LARRY: But who is he? And how the devil did he get here?

TEMPLE: Have you heard anything suspicious this evening – any noise, for instance?

LARRY: No, not a thing. Have we, Doctor?

BENKARAY: I've been resting; it's doubtful whether I should have heard anything, anyway. Neither myself nor Mr Cross – who is my secretary, by the way – know this man, Mr Temple. Can you tell us who he is?

TEMPLE: His name is Ted Angus.

BENKARAY: But what was he doing here?

TEMPLE: I don't know. That's something the police will have to find out.

BENKARAY: Police?

TEMPLE: Yes – I sent my wife to telephone for them as soon as we found him.

BENKARAY: I see. And you, Mr Temple? What were you doing here?

TEMPLE: I was on my way to see you, Dr Benkaray.

BENKARAY: (*Surprised*) To see me?

TEMPLE: I tried to make an appointment to see you at your Wimpole Street address, but Mr Cross here refused to …

LARRY: (*Interrupting TEMPLE*) That's right! Of course! You telephoned …

TEMPLE: (*Enigmatically*) I telephoned.

BENKARAY: Why did you wish to see me, Mr Temple?

TEMPLE: I'm investigating the murder of Julia Kelburn. I think she was a patient of yours.

BENKARAY: Yes, she was – for a little while. She was a very sick girl, very sick.

TEMPLE: You mean – mentally?

BENKARAY: All the time she lived in great fear – a fear that dominated her.

TEMPLE: A fear of what, exactly?

BENKARAY: That is what I was trying to find out. I only saw her three times – perhaps four. I tried to get her to talk but always there was a barrier. I tried to break that barrier down, but it was no use …

TEMPLE: And what happened?

BENKARAY: What usually happens in a case of that kind? She failed to turn up for an appointment and I never saw her again.

TEMPLE: Dr Benkaray, you knew that Julia Kelburn had been murdered?

BENKARAY: Yes – it was in the newspapers.

TEMPLE: Then why didn't you inform the police that she had been a patient of yours?

BENKARAY: What was the point? I had nothing to tell the police.

TEMPLE: You could have told them about this phobia – about this fear of hers.

BENKARAY: Do you think the police would have attached importance to it?

TEMPLE: I think they might. Dr Benkaray, tell me: did Julia Kelburn ever come to see you down here?

BENKARAY: No; I don't see patients here – always in London. I bought this house so that I could get away from my patients and relax.

LARRY: Which brings us to an interesting question, Mr Temple. How did you know the doctor had a place down here?

Cars can be heard stopping in the distance.

TEMPLE: (*After a moment*) I made some enquiries.

BENKARAY: (*Suddenly*) There's someone coming …

TEMPLE: It's the police – probably the ambulance …

We hear the sound of approaching footsteps and voices.

LARRY: Yes, it's the police all right.

FADE UP of voices and footsteps.

FADE SCENE.

FADE IN TEMPLE and STEVE in their bedroom at The Red Hart: drinking coffee.

TEMPLE: Were they annoyed when you asked for coffee so late, Steve?

STEVE: Mrs Harcourt never lifted an eyebrow. She's rather a darling, Paul – even if she is a bit of a gossip.

TEMPLE: It was jolly good of them to send it up. It's just what I needed.

STEVE: Yes – it's been quite a night. (*A moment*) Paul …

TEMPLE: (*After drinking*) M'm?

STEVE: What did you make of Dr Benkaray?

TEMPLE: She's a curious, rather mysterious sort of individual. I certainly didn't like the character who calls himself Larry Cross.

STEVE: That's her secretary?

TEMPLE: Yes, but he doesn't look like a doctor's secretary – doesn't look like anybody's secretary! He's a tough egg if ever I saw one.

STEVE: Did you tackle them about Ted Angus answering the phone at the Wimpole Street address?

TEMPLE: No; because they both said they'd never seen Angus before.

STEVE: And what about the local police – did they know Angus?

TEMPLE: Well, the Inspector was inclined to be a bit cagey. I've an idea he's never tackled a murder case before. However, when we were at the station, I managed to have a word with him. He's going to get in touch with Sir Graham, so I imagine Raine or somebody else at the Yard will take over. (*He yawns*) By Timothy, I'm tired, Steve! I think that's about as far as we can get tonight, darling …

STEVE: Not quite.

TEMPLE: What do you mean?

STEVE: I've managed to glean a few odds and ends on my own …

TEMPLE: When?

STEVE: When I went into the kitchen to persuade Mrs Harcourt to make us coffee. I felt bound to let her indulge in a bit of gossip, and as it happened it paid off.

TEMPLE: (*Interested*) Go on, Steve …

STEVE: I asked her one or two questions about Mrs Fletcher.

TEMPLE: You mean the "Daily" – who used to work for Dr Benkaray?

STEVE: Yes. It seems that after leaving the doctor, Mrs Fletcher bought a garage at the far end of the High Street.

TEMPLE: A garage?

STEVE: Yes; she's a widow but she's got a son – a boy of about twenty-two or three. They've made quite a go of the garage. Her son's a good mechanic, and Mrs Fletcher works the pumps and sells accessories and so on. But what intrigues all the locals is where she got the money to buy the garage in the first place.

TEMPLE: Perhaps she borrowed it?

STEVE: A daily woman wouldn't find it easy to raise that sort of money. No, there's something very odd about it, Paul. According to Mrs Harcourt, the one thing Mrs Fletcher won't discuss under any circumstances – is where she got the money from.

TEMPLE: M'm. I expect the locals have some theory or other?

STEVE: The most popular theory is that Benkaray played fairy godmother and bought the garage for Mrs Fletcher – but no one knows quite why she should.

TEMPLE: (*Quietly*) I see.

STEVE: Did Dr Benkaray strike you as being the sort of woman who would do that sort of thing?

TEMPLE: I don't know; it's difficult to say. (*Thoughtfully*) You know, this is very interesting about Mrs Fletcher, Steve – very interesting. Especially when one remembers what Ted Angus said.

STEVE: Ask Mrs Fletcher about the coat …?

TEMPLE: Yes … (*Thoughtfully; to himself*) Ask Mrs Fletcher about the coat …

FADE IN music.

FADE DOWN of music.

FADE UP background noises of light traffic on the road outside The Red Hart.

MRS HARCOURT: Fred's just bringing your cases down, Mrs Temple.

STEVE: Thank you, Mrs Harcourt.

MRS H: I do hope you'll come and stay with us again.

STEVE: I hope so too. We've been very comfortable.

MRS H: You want to come in the spring, Mrs Temple. It's lovely round here when the orchards are in bloom.

STEVE: Yes, I'm sure it must be.

A car approaches and stops.

STEVE: Ah, here's my husband!

The car door opens.

MRS H: And here's Fred with the cases.

FRED: Ah, there you are, Mr Temple! I've brought your cases down.

TEMPLE: Thanks, Fred. Would you put them in the boot?

FRED: Certainly.

FRED opens the boot and puts the cases inside.

FRED: Mr Temple …

TEMPLE: Yes, Fred?

FRED: D'you think I could have a word with you before you leave?

TEMPLE: Yes, of course.

FRED: We'll go into my office, sir.

TEMPLE: Wait in the car, Steve; I won't be a minute.

STEVE: Yes, all right, darling.

FADE SCENE.

FADE IN FRED HARCOURT's voice.

FRED: I wanted you to take a look at this newspaper, Mr Temple.

FRED hands TEMPLE a newspaper from his desk.

FRED: There's a piece here about this girl that was murdered. It says you're taking an interest in the case.

TEMPLE: Yes, that's true.

FRED: Would you say that's a good photograph of her, Mr Temple?

TEMPLE: (*Looking at the newspaper*) Well – I never met Julia Kelburn, but this looks like a pretty good photograph, judging from the others I've seen. Why do you ask?

FRED: I've got a good memory for faces, Mr Temple. You sort of get the knack of it in this business.

TEMPLE: (*Interested*) You've seen this girl?

FRED: Yes; she spent the night here. It'd be about six months ago. I remember saying to the missus: "There's something strange about that girl," I said, "there's a sad look about her eyes."

TEMPLE: Have you got her name in the register?

FRED: That's another peculiar thing; she signed herself in as Julia Smith. I've got the register here …

TEMPLE looks vaguely at the register.

TEMPLE: Julia Smith … London … I wonder why she didn't give her real name?

FRED: That's what I said to the missus when I saw the newspaper this morning. If there'd been a man with her, well, you expect that sort of lark then … But she was on her own – though a man did call for her early next morning.

TEMPLE: Did you talk to her at all?

FRED: Only when she arrived. She stayed in her room all evening – sent down for four double whiskies – one at a time, of course. When I took 'em up, she looked to me as if she'd been crying. I'd half a mind to ask her if I could help her, but she didn't give me any opening.

TEMPLE: You say a man called for her next morning?

FRED: Yes, soon after seven it was. I had to get up early to make out the bill, and I remember the missus was upset because the girl wouldn't have any breakfast.

TEMPLE: Did you see the man who called for her?

FRED: Yes; but I can't remember him as well as the girl. He was medium height, I think. Wore rimless glasses and spoke with a bit of an American accent.

TEMPLE: Was he an American?

FRED: I don't know. Wouldn't like to say, for sure. We get a lot of smart Alecs down here at the weekends, and half of 'em try to talk like Yanks … Difficult to say whether this chap was a real American or not …

TEMPLE: What sort of terms were they on?

FRED: You might have thought he was her dad come to fetch her home …

TEMPLE: Well, thanks, Fred. I'm most grateful to you for telling me this; it might be very helpful.

FRED: If anything else comes back to me, Mr Temple, I'll let you know …

FADE SCENE.

FADE UP the noise of a car engine.
The car is travelling slowly.
TEMPLE is driving.

TEMPLE: You did say the garage was at the end of the High Street?

STEVE: That's what Mrs Harcourt said …

TEMPLE: Well, unless it's round the corner I shall begin to think we're driving the wrong way.

STEVE: Yes … Paul, that man you were telling me about – the man Fred Harcourt mentioned – he sounded to me like Mike Langdon.

TEMPLE: Yes. That's what I thought.

STEVE: Was Langdon over here six months ago?

TEMPLE: He could have been. He travels quite a lot.

STEVE: (*Suddenly*) Turn left, Paul! There's the garage!

TEMPLE: Ah, yes …

The car slows down.

STEVE: I suppose that's the son over there, at the petrol pumps.

TEMPLE: Yes. (*A pause*) Where's the office? Oh, I see – it's attached to the house. (*After a moment*) Steve, ask young Fletcher to fill her up and take a look at the oil … I'm going to have a word with his mother.

The car stops.

A door opens.

STEVE: Yes, all right.

BILL: (*From the background*) I shan't be a minute, sir!

TEMPLE: (*Calling back*) All right, no hurry. (*To STEVE: as he gets out of the car*) Keep him talking, Steve, if you can.

STEVE: Right …

FADE DOWN the noise of the car engine.

FADE SCENE.

FADE IN the sound of a door opening: the sound of a spring bell as the door opens.

TEMPLE: Good morning. Do you sell cigarettes?

MRS FLETCHER: Over this side, sir. (*She has a slight cockney accent and is in her mid-fifties*)

TEMPLE: Oh, yes! I'll have twenty of those, please – the filter tips …

MRS F: Thank you, sir.

MRS FLETCHER uses the cash register.

MRS F: Your change … Just driving down to the coast, sir?

TEMPLE: No, as a matter of fact my wife and I spent the night here – at The Red Hart.

MRS F: Oh, not a bad little pub.

TEMPLE: No; indeed. Mrs Fletcher, isn't it?

MRS F: (*Faintly surprised*) Yes, that's right.

TEMPLE: Fred Harcourt mentioned you.

MRS F: Oh …

TEMPLE: He said you used to work for Dr Benkaray.

MRS F: Oh, did he?

TEMPLE: Yes; I'd heard of Dr Benkaray and happened to mention her name. Incidentally, while you were working for the doctor did you come across a man called Ted Angus?

MRS F: (*Abruptly*) No, I didn't.

TEMPLE: You've heard the name before, I take it?

MRS F: I can read. It's in the newspapers.

TEMPLE: Yes. Angus was murdered last night – in the wood, not far from Dr Benkaray's place.

MRS F: Yes, I know.

TEMPLE: But you've never heard of Angus – not until you read about him this morning?

MRS F: No, I hadn't. Are you a newspaper man?

TEMPLE: No.

MRS F: Well, you ought to be – you're nosey enough for one!

The door opens and the bell rings.

BILL: Ma, could you … Hello, something wrong?

MRS F: This chap's askin' me a lot of questions, Bill. I don't know who he is but …

BILL: Well, I do! (*To TEMPLE; pleasantly*) You're Paul Temple, aren't you?

TEMPLE: That's right.

BILL: Thought so. Your photograph's on the back of a book I've been reading. It's all right, Ma – he's nothing to do with the newspapers.

MRS F: (*Puzzled*) Are you from the police, then?

TEMPLE: No, but I'm helping the police to investigate a murder case; Julia Kelburn …

BILL: Oh, I read about her! Bit of a hot number, wasn't she?

TEMPLE: She was a patient of Dr Benkaray's.

BILL: Go on … Was she? Didn't know that, did you, Ma?

MRS F: No, I didn't. But then the doctor has hundreds of patients.

In the background we hear the sound of a motor horn.

BILL: She was good to Ma, the doctor was.

MRS F: (*Wanting to get rid of BILL*) That's Tom Easton's van – go and see what he wants, Bill.

BILL: Okay.

The door opens and closes.

TEMPLE: Mrs Fletcher, I don't want to make a nuisance of myself, but it might be worth your while to tell me one or two things.

MRS F: What things?

TEMPLE: My wife and I found Ted Angus last night. He'd been beaten up. Just before he died he mentioned your name.

MRS F: (*Amazed*) Ted Angus did?

TEMPLE: That's right.

MRS F: You – you must be mistaken.

TEMPLE: No, I wasn't mistaken.

MRS F: Well – what did he say?

TEMPLE: He said: "Ask Mrs Fletcher about the coat."

MRS F: The coat? What coat? What was he talking about?

TEMPLE: I don't know. I was hoping you'd tell me.

MRS F: (*On edge*) I don't know what this is all about. I don't know anyone called Angus. It wasn't me he was referring to – must 'ave been another Mrs Fletcher.

TEMPLE: (*Pleasantly*) I see. Very well. I'm sorry to have troubled you.

MRS F: (*Stopping TEMPLE*) No; wait a minute! (*After a pause*) Have you said anything about this to the police or anyone?

TEMPLE: (*Still very pleasant*) No; not a word – and there's no reason why I should. Look – here's my card. If you should remember anything about Ted Angus or Julia Kelburn, just give me a ring.

MRS F: (*Surprised*) Julia Kelburn? I never set eyes on the girl. She was never in these parts.

TEMPLE: According to Fred Harcourt she was. Well, if you remember anything – give me a ring. It'll be worth your while, Mrs Fletcher, I assure you.

TEMPLE opens the door and the bell starts to ring again.
FADE on the sound of the bell ringing.
FADE SCENE.

FADE IN of TEMPLE's voice.

TEMPLE: What's the matter with Charlie? Where is he?

STEVE: Don't be impatient, darling!

TEMPLE: Ring the bell again, Steve.

STEVE presses the bell button and as she does so the door opens.

CHARLIE: Sorry, I was in the kitchen.

TEMPLE and STEVE enter the hall.

TEMPLE: Take one of the cases, Charlie.

CHARLIE: Yes, sir.

TEMPLE: The heavy one …

CHARLIE: Oh, very good, Mr Temple. (*Suddenly*) Oh, before I forget! You've got a visitor. He's in the drawing room.

TEMPLE: Yes – I was just looking at the hat and gloves …

CHARLIE: It's a Mr Kelburn, sir. He's been here about twenty minutes.

TEMPLE: (*Surprised*) Kelburn?

CHARLIE: Yes.

STEVE: Any other messages, Charlie?

CHARLIE: A Mr Langdon telephoned; twice, as a matter of fact. He said he'd ring back later.

TEMPLE: Yes, all right. Oh, and Charlie – I'm expecting Sir Graham Forbes. Show him into the drawing room when he arrives.

CHARLIE: Okay … Yes, sir.

A door opens.

TEMPLE: Hello, Kelburn! Sorry to have kept you waiting, only my wife and I have been …

KELBURN: (*Abruptly*) That's all right. I apologise for intruding like this.

TEMPLE: I don't think you've met my wife.

KELBURN: No, I haven't. Good afternoon, Mrs Temple.

STEVE: How do you do, Mr Kelburn?

KELBURN: (*Faintly aggressive; yet nervous*) Temple, there's no point in beating about the bush. I'll get straight to the point. I've changed my mind.

TEMPLE: Changed your mind? About what, exactly?

KELBURN: About the murder. About your investigation. I want you to withdraw from the case. Naturally, I'll pay any reasonable fee you decide to ask and any expenses which …

TEMPLE: Wait a minute! Why have you changed your mind, Mr Kelburn?

KELBURN: I've thought about this and decided that there's nothing to be gained by further private investigation. It can't bring Julia back.

TEMPLE: No, but it might result in the murderer being brought to justice.

KELBURN: (*Hesitantly*) Yes, well – it's Julia I keep thinking about. It can't bring my daughter back. Naturally, I appreciate you feel some disappointment in losing a profitable assignment.

TEMPLE: (*Irritated*) That's nothing to do with it. I make my money out of books, Kelburn – not other people's troubles. I'm working on this case simply because I became involved in it; there's no other reason.

STEVE: But, Mr Kelburn, surely you realise the police are bound to go on with their investigations?

KELBURN: Yes. Yes, I realise that. There's nothing I can do about the police, unfortunately.

STEVE: And they'll expect you to co-operate.

KELBURN: I've already told the police all I know. There's nothing else I can say or do which could possibly help them. I've given this matter a great deal of thought, Temple, and that's my decision.

TEMPLE: Very well, if that's your decision.

KELBURN: Now don't be stupid about the financial aspect. I don't expect people to work for nothing. Send your account to my office in …

TEMPLE: (*Interrupting KELBURN*) There won't be an account. I started this investigation partly on your behalf; I shall continue it entirely on my own.

KELBURN: (*Stiffly*) That's up to you, of course. But I can't undertake to give you any co-operation. In fact, I may be going abroad in the near future.

TEMPLE: Very well.

KELBURN: Sorry about this, Temple, but these decisions have to be taken.

TEMPLE: I only hope this is one you won't regret. I'll see you out.

KELBURN: Thank you. Goodbye, Mrs Temple. I'm glad to have met you.

STEVE: (*Faintly acid*) It's been a pleasure.

The door opens.

The telephone rings.

STEVE lifts the receiver.

STEVE: (*On the phone*) Hello?

LANGDON: (*On the other end of the line*) Mrs Temple?

STEVE: Yes …

LANGDON: This is Mike Langdon … Do you think I could have a word with your husband?

STEVE: Yes – hold on.

A pause.

TEMPLE: Who is it, Steve?

STEVE: It's Mr Langdon …

TEMPLE: (*On the phone*) Hello, Langdon! Sorry I was out when you called earlier.

LANGDON: That's okay. I just wanted you to know I'm going back to the States at the end of the week.

TEMPLE: I see.

LANGDON: But I'd like to see you again, if possible, before I leave.

TEMPLE: Yes, of course. Where are you now?

LANGDON: In Eaton Square.

TEMPLE: Then why not come round straight away?

LANGDON: Thanks – that suits me fine.

TEMPLE: Then I'll expect you in about half an hour.

LANGDON: Right! Goodbye.

TEMPLE: Goodbye, Langdon.

TEMPLE replaces the receiver.

STEVE: What did he want?

TEMPLE: He's going back to New York at the end of the week and he wants to see me before he leaves.

STEVE: Well, having just met his employer I feel quite sorry for your American friend, although I imagine Langdon can take care of himself.

The door opens.

TEMPLE: Yes, I think he can … What is it, Charlie?

CHARLIE: Sir Graham, sir.

FORBES enters with SUPERINTENDENT RAINE.

TEMPLE: Hello, Sir Graham! Come along in, Superintendent.

FORBES: Hello, Steve!

STEVE: Hello, Sir Graham … Good afternoon, Superintendent.

RAINE: Good afternoon, Mrs Temple.

STEVE: (*To TEMPLE*) I'm just going to see about some tea, Paul.

TEMPLE: Yes, all right.

The door opens and closes.

FORBES: Temple, was that Kelburn we saw getting into his car?

TEMPLE: Yes.

RAINE: He appeared to be in rather a tizzy.

TEMPLE: Yes, I think he is. He asked me to withdraw from the case, Sir Graham. He says he doesn't want me to make any further investigations.

FORBES: Why should he ask you to do that?

TEMPLE: He didn't say why; but I got the impression he was frightened.

FORBES: Frightened – of what?

TEMPLE: I don't know.

RAINE: You mean – you think someone's bringing pressure to bear on him?

TEMPLE: Yes – or he's just plain frightened. Perhaps he knew Ted Angus …

FORBES: Yes, that's just what I was thinking, Temple.

RAINE: Tell us about Ted Angus, Mr Temple. What exactly happened, last night?

TEMPLE: Well, Steve and I went down to Westerton. You know why – I told you on the phone about Steve's visit to the dress shop and Dr Benkaray.

RAINE: Yes.

TEMPLE: Well, after dinner we went for a drive. I wanted to take a look at Dr Benkaray's place. We parked the car and walked through the wood towards the house. Suddenly we heard a noise; it was Ted Angus – he'd been beaten up.

RAINE: Then what happened?

TEMPLE: Steve went for the police and I fetched Dr Benkaray.

FORBES: Did she recognise Angus?

TEMPLE: She said she'd never seen him before – and that went for the secretary, too.

RAINE: The secretary?

TEMPLE: Yes – a dead pan character called Larry Cross.

RAINE: Did the doctor ask you what you were doing in the wood?

TEMPLE: Yes, she did. I said I was on my way to see her and that I wanted to question her about Julia Kelburn.

FORBES: How did she react to that?

TEMPLE: She wasn't particularly helpful. She said that Julia had some kind of a complex and during two or three brief interviews she'd failed to get to the bottom of it.

RAINE: In other words – she stalled?

TEMPLE: Yes.

RAINE: Well, we know Miss Kelburn's trouble. We probably know why she consulted the doctor.

TEMPLE: What do you mean?

FORBES: Julia Kelburn was a drug addict.

TEMPLE: How did this come out?

FORBES: Medical report on the post-mortem. Incidentally keep this to yourself, Temple.

TEMPLE: Yes, of course. I'm not completely surprised.

FORBES: No – we weren't.

TEMPLE: Have you told Kelburn?

RAINE: Not yet. As soon as I've got a few more details from the doctor I'll make an appointment to see him.

TEMPLE: (*Thoughtfully*) I wonder if Kelburn knows and that's why he wants me to drop the case.

FORBES: Yes, it's a possibility. Let's face it, no one likes that sort of publicity.

TEMPLE: No …

RAINE: I'll check on this Dr Benkaray, Mr Temple – see what her background is. I'll let you know what we find out.

TEMPLE: Thank you, Superintendent. Incidentally, I meant to ask you – what about young Wyman? Is he all right now?

RAINE: Yes, he went back to work last night. I dropped in on him just as he was finishing his act.

TEMPLE: Well?

RAINE: He didn't say much; but I got the impression he thought that Angus had smashed into his car deliberately. That kid's scared, Mr Temple – if we could get on the right side of him I think he'd talk.

FORBES: Yes, that's my impression.

The door opens and STEVE returns.

TEMPLE: He's at The Hide and Seek, isn't he?

RAINE: That's right – in Leicester Square.

TEMPLE: What time does he come on?

RAINE: About eleven-thirty.

STEVE: What's all this about The Hide and Seek?

FORBES: We're talking about Tony Wyman, Steve.

STEVE: Oh, yes – how is he, Sir Graham?

FORBES: He's all right now – he's back at work.

STEVE: If you can call it work!

RAINE: It's work all right, Mrs Temple. You should have seen him last night – the sweat was pouring off him.

FORBES: I'd like you to have another talk with him, Temple. Tonight, if possible.

TEMPLE: Yes, it might be quite an idea. I'll get Charlie to book a table.

STEVE: I take it I'm in on this, Paul?

TEMPLE: Yes, of course. You can wear your new dress.

STEVE: I can't – it hasn't arrived yet.

CHARLIE enters pushing a tea trolley.

STEVE: Ah, here's Charlie with the tea!

FORBES: I don't think we can stop for tea, Steve. You see …

STEVE: Nonsense! Everything stops for tea in this house! Sit down, Superintendent – make yourself at home.

RAINE: (*Sitting down; with a look at FORBES*) Er …

FORBES: (*Laughing*) Sit down, Raine.

START FADE.

TEMPLE: Charlie, ring The Hide and Seek in Leicester Square and book me a table for this evening. Tell them I want it near the floor.

STEVE: (*Pouring out tea*) Not too near the floor, darling …

COMPLETE FADE.

FADE UP the sound of a typewriter.

There is a knock and a door opens.

The typewriter stops.

CHARLIE: Mr Langdon to see you, sir.

TEMPLE: Come in, Langdon.

LANGDON: It took me a little longer to get here than I thought.

The door closes.

TEMPLE: Sit down. Can I get you a drink?

LANGDON: No, I won't have a drink, if you don't mind. Temple, I wanted to see you about Kelburn.

TEMPLE: Oh? What about Kelburn?

LANGDON: Well, quite frankly, I'm baffled. At one time he was quite determined to find out who murdered Julia, but now – I'm very sorry, Temple, but I'm afraid he wants you to withdraw from the case.

TEMPLE: Yes, I know.

LANGDON: You know?

TEMPLE: Yes, Kelburn's been here. Langdon, tell me: why d'you think he's changed his mind? Has something happened?

LANGDON: Well, it all seems to date from a letter he received this morning. I noticed him change colour the moment he read it.

TEMPLE: Did he tell you what was in the letter?

LANGDON: No; he simply sent for me in the middle of the morning and told me he'd changed his mind about your investigating the case. I argued with him of course, but it was no use. It never is, once he's made up his mind. I'm sorry, Temple …

TEMPLE: That's all right, don't worry about me. But tell me; have you noticed anything else about Kelburn?

LANGDON: What do you mean?

TEMPLE: Has his attitude changed in other directions – towards his wife, for instance?

LANGDON: (*Thoughtfully*) Yes, I think it has. Up to a couple of days ago they seemed to get on very well together – neither of them was very demonstrative but they appeared to enjoy each other's company. But on Monday night I happened to go downstairs fairly late to collect a book I was reading … (*He hesitates*)

TEMPLE: Go on …

LANGDON: Well – they were in the drawing room and rowing like fury. I only heard the tail end of it, but boy, it was a humdinger of a row! I heard Kelburn say: "If you go on like this you'll finish up the same way as Julia."

TEMPLE: … Finish up the same way as Julia? …

LANGDON: Yes. That kind of shook me. Whether he meant Linda would finish up in the river, or whether he … Well, I don't know what he meant. But one thing I do know – I shall be mighty glad to get away from the Kelburn family and back to New York.

TEMPLE: Yes, I can imagine that. (*Pleasantly casual*) Langdon, tell me: when were you last in England?

LANGDON: About six months ago. I came over to talk with Kelburn about a printing process.

TEMPLE: You didn't by any chance visit a pub called The Red Hart – at Westerton?

LANGDON: Westerton? No, no, I don't think so. Where is that?

TEMPLE: It's in Kent – about forty miles from London.

LANGDON: No, I've never been there. Might have passed through it, but I don't remember the place. Why do you ask?

TEMPLE: (*Completely dismissing the matter*) Oh, nothing. I wondered, that's all.

FADE SCENE.

FADE IN the sound of a dance orchestra and a crowded dance floor.

FADE the orchestra and noise to the background.

STEVE: There's no sign of Tony Wyman.

TEMPLE: No …

STEVE: It's nearly forty minutes since he finished his act.

TEMPLE: Yes. I wonder if he got my note?

STEVE: Well, if he didn't, I suppose … (*She breaks off*) Isn't this Wyman – coming across the floor?

WYMAN: (*Approaching*) Sorry to have kept you, Mr Temple. I had to make two telephone calls and then my agent popped in and I couldn't get rid of him. He's still waiting for me, as a matter of fact, so I can only spare you a couple of minutes.

TEMPLE: That's all right, Wyman. Sit down. Oh, I don't think you know my wife.

WYMAN: (*Sitting down*) No, I don't. Hello!

STEVE: We enjoyed your act.

WYMAN: Thanks; but it wasn't so hot tonight. Wasn't feeling too good.

STEVE: I expect you're still feeling a bit shaky.

WYMAN: Yes, I am. The doc says I'm okey, but blimey, I don't feel it!

TEMPLE: I suppose you read about the man who crashed into us – Ted Angus?

WYMAN: Yes …

TEMPLE: He was murdered …

WYMAN: (*Tensely*) Yes; I know.

TEMPLE: Angus smashed into your car quite deliberately – he was out to get one of us. I think it was you, Tony.

WYMAN: Thanks – you've made my night!

TEMPLE: You were going to tell me something just before the accident. What was it?

WYMAN: I don't remember.

TEMPLE: But you must remember, because …

WYMAN: (*Tense; on edge*) I've told you – I don't remember!

TEMPLE: Was it about Dr Benkaray?

WYMAN: I've never heard of Dr Benkaray.

TEMPLE: Now don't be stupid, Tony – it was you who told me about her. Incidentally, Ted Angus was found two hundred yards from the doctor's cottage. Did you know that?

WYMAN: (*Obviously surprised*) No; no, I didn't.

TEMPLE: Well, he was.

WYMAN: (*Nervously*) Look, Mr Temple, my manager's told me to keep my mouth shut. He says I've done too much talking and I think he's right. I don't know anything about this bloke Angus – about Dr Benkaray – about Julia Kelburn – about nothin'. I just know nothin'.

TEMPLE: All right, Tony – but if you get into trouble …

WYMAN: (*Worried*) What d'you mean trouble?

TEMPLE: If you get into trouble – the sort of trouble that manager of yours can't get you out of – give me a ring.

WYMAN: I don't know why you should talk to me like this, Mr Temple. I shan't get into trouble. I keep my nose clean – always have done. I shan't get into trouble.

TEMPLE: I hope you're right, Tony.

WYMAN: Good night, Mrs Temple. Glad you liked the act.

STEVE: Goodbye …

A pause.

TEMPLE: Well – what do you make of him, Steve?

STEVE: My word, he's a frightened young man if ever I saw one.

FADE UP of the dance orchestra and the background noises.

FADE DOWN the orchestra and noises completely.

FADE IN the noise of a London taxi: it is travelling rather slowly.

STEVE: This taxi seems to be taking ages, Paul … I wish you'd brought the car.

TEMPLE: Yes, so do I now. By Timothy, this traffic's unbelievable.

STEVE: Yes, isn't it? One o'clock in the morning and yet there seems to be … Hello?

The taxi pulls up.

STEVE: Why is he slowing down?

TEMPLE: Traffic lights …

A pause.

STEVE: … You know, I've been thinking about Tony Wyman. It seems quite fantastic to me that a girl like Julia Kelburn should … (*She breaks off*) What is it, Paul?

TEMPLE: … The people in that car … on the right, Steve …

STEVE: Where?

TEMPLE: The sports car … (*Quickly*) Don't let them see you!

STEVE: Who is it?

TEMPLE: It's Mrs Kelburn and Larry Cross …

STEVE: Who's Larry Cr … Oh, the doctor's secretary!

TEMPLE: Yes … (*Quietly*) Don't let them see you, Steve …

STEVE: (*Suddenly excited*) Paul, that man – the one you say is Larry Cross …

TEMPLE: Yes?

STEVE: I've seen him before … Yes, I'm sure I have … He was at the airport, darling …

TEMPLE: At the airport?

STEVE: Yes; he was the man in the uniform. The man I told you about – the airport official. He had a moustache then, but it's the same man …

TEMPLE: Are you sure, Steve?

STEVE: … I'm positive, I know I was in a pretty bad state that night, Paul … but I'm sure I'm right …

TEMPLE: (*Quietly*) We're moving … Sit back, Steve.

STEVE: What are we going to do? Shall we tell the driver to follow them?

We hear the sound of the sports car racing away.

TEMPLE: What – in this taxi? (*Amused*) Don't be silly, darling …

FADE UP the noise of the taxi.

FADE SCENE.

FADE IN TEMPLE knocking on the front door.

The door opens.

STEVE: I expect he's in bed.

The door closes.

CHARLIE: (*Approaching*) No, I'm not, Mrs Temple. I was just making myself a nice cup of tea. Would you like a cup, sir?

TEMPLE: No, thank you. I'm more in the mood for a whisky and soda. What about you, Steve?

STEVE: What's this box, Charlie? Oh, it's my dress – from Daphne Drake's!

CHARLIE: Yes; a young lady delivered it just after you left. I'll take it upstairs, Mrs Temple.

STEVE: Yes, put it in the dressing room.

TEMPLE: Are you going to have a nightcap, Steve?

STEVE: Yes, pour me a brandy, darling – just a tiny one. I'm going to try my dress on.

TEMPLE: (*Laughing*) What – at this hour of the morning?

STEVE: I'll be down in a minute. And pour yourself a stiff one, Paul – you'll need it when I tell you what I paid for the dress.

TEMPLE enters the drawing room.

He starts to mix the drinks.

The telephone rings.

A slight pause.

TEMPLE lifts the receiver.

TEMPLE: (*On the phone*) Hello?

We hear the sound of coins dropping and button "A" being pressed.

MRS F: (*On the other end of the line*) Mr Temple?

TEMPLE: Yes – speaking. Who is that?

MRS F: (*Hesitantly*) It's – It's Margo …

TEMPLE: (*Surprised*) Margo?

MRS F: (*Tensely*) Mr Temple, don't let your wife open the box …

TEMPLE: Which box? Do you mean the one from the dress shop …

MRS F: Yes! Don't let her touch it! Whatever you do don't let her touch it, Mr Temple!

TEMPLE immediately drops the receiver and rushes towards the door.

TEMPLE: (*Calling out*) Steve! Steve!! Steve, don't open the box …

Suddenly, from upstairs, there is a loud explosion – followed by a desperate scream from STEVE.

END OF EPISODE THREE

EPISODE FOUR

BILL FLETCHER'S STORY

OPEN TO:

TEMPLE: Steve! Steve!!! Steve, don't open the box …

FADE IN the sound of an explosion and a scream from STEVE who is upstairs in the bedroom.

FADE SCENE.

FADE IN the quick opening of a door.

TEMPLE: Steve … Darling – are you hurt?

STEVE: No … No, I don't think so. I … (*A relieved little laugh*) No, I'm all right … I seem to be all in one piece anyway …

CHARLIE rushes into the room.

CHARLIE: Mrs Temple – for heaven's sake, what happened?

TEMPLE: Bring some brandy, Charlie!

CHARLIE: But what happened?

TEMPLE: Bring the brandy!

CHARLIE: Okey-doke …

TEMPLE: Sit down, darling.

STEVE: Oh, Paul, just look at the dressing room …

TEMPLE: Never mind the dressing room – sit down, Steve.

STEVE sits down on the bed.

STEVE: Gosh! (*Starts to laugh; a shade nervously*) Things do happen to the Temples, don't they? Never a dull moment!

TEMPLE: (*Quietly*) Tell me what happened, Steve.

STEVE: I took the parcel into the dressing room and started to undo it there. I heard you shouting and went into the bedroom. I'd got as far as the door when the thing exploded. Thank goodness you shouted, Paul!

TEMPLE: (*Grimly*) Yes …

STEVE: But why did you shout?

TEMPLE: A woman telephoned – she warned me about the parcel …

STEVE: A woman? Which woman?

TEMPLE: She said her name was Margo – but I'm pretty sure it was Mrs Fletcher.

STEVE: Mrs Fletcher? … Well – whoever it was, thank goodness she telephoned!

TEMPLE: Yes. Let's go downstairs, darling. We'll clear this mess up later …

FADE SCENE.

FADE IN on STEVE's voice.

STEVE: … But, Paul, I can't for the life of me think why anyone at Daphne Drake's should do a thing like that! After all, they'd be the first to be questioned.

TEMPLE: (*Thoughtfully*) Yes … Let's think back a bit, Steve. It was Linda Kelburn who sent us to Daphne Drake's in the first place because she said that Julia bought most of her clothes there.

STEVE: Yes, that's right. But surely you don't think Linda had anything to do with tonight?

TEMPLE: I wouldn't be too sure. After all, what was she doing with Larry Cross, Dr Benkaray's so-called secretary? And why did she make two telephone calls to us and then flatly deny that she made them? No, there's something very odd about Mrs Kelburn, Steve.

STEVE: Mm.

TEMPLE: Let me get you another brandy, darling.

STEVE: No, thank you, dear.

TEMPLE: If I remember rightly, you said you bumped into Linda when I was in America?

STEVE: That's right – twice.
TEMPLE: Twice?
STEVE: Yes.
TEMPLE: I didn't realise that. What happened?
STEVE: Well, I met her at Harridge's on the Saturday morning – the day after you left. We had coffee together. About three weeks later she phoned and said she wanted to see you.
TEMPLE: And you said I was in the States?
STEVE: That's right. A few days later I bumped into her again and naturally I mentioned the phone call. You know what happened – she said she hadn't made it.
TEMPLE: Yes. (*Quietly*) Steve, the first time you met her, in Harridge's – what did you talk about?
STEVE: Oh – old times – Fleet Street – the usual gossip. She said she'd read a book of yours and didn't think it was very good.
TEMPLE: Charming.
STEVE: (*Laughing*) It turned out you hadn't written it. I was delighted.
TEMPLE: And nothing particular happened on that occasion – nothing unusual, I mean?
STEVE: No, nothing, darling. (*Casually; an afterthought*) Oh – she asked me to post a letter for her …
TEMPLE: Post a letter?
STEVE: Yes. I happened to mention I was going up to the fourth floor to buy some stamps. She said she had a letter she'd forgotten to post and would I post it for her.
TEMPLE: Who was the letter to?
STEVE: (*Laughing*) Oh, Paul, I don't remember. I don't even know whether I looked at it.

TEMPLE: Had it a threepenny stamp?

STEVE: Yes, I think so. (*A pause*) Paul, what are you thinking about?

TEMPLE: What's that, Steve?

STEVE: I said: What are you thinking about?

TEMPLE: I was just thinking … I was just thinking I'd have another brandy, darling …

FADE SCENE.

FADE IN of SIR GRAHAM's voice.

FORBES: … But who did you see, Raine? Was it the proprietor, or just the woman who runs the shop?

RAINE: I think she's the manageress, Sir Graham. They called her Miss Elsie …

TEMPLE: That's the woman who attended to Steve.

RAINE: Yes, that's right. Anyway, she had a pretty plausible explanation, I must admit. Apparently, they were going to deliver the parcel themselves and then at about 4pm a young woman called and said she had been asked by Mrs Temple to collect the dress. Naturally, they thought the woman was bona fide, otherwise …

TEMPLE: … She wouldn't have known about the dress in the first place.

RAINE: Exactly.

FORBES: So they handed it over …

RAINE: Yes – and then, of course, the girl apparently switched parcels.

FORBES: Well, it sounds feasible, I must admit.

TEMPLE: Did you get a description of this girl?

RAINE: Well, I did my best, but they were all pretty vague. I suppose that's understandable; it's a very busy shop. They thought she was about twenty-seven or eight – average height – dark coloured hair. No distinctive features.

FORBES: (*Irritated*) No distinctive features! Ye gods, the times we hear that one! You know, I don't think we'll get anywhere with this investigation until we find the motive – and I don't mean the motive for what happened last night – but the motive for the murder.

TEMPLE: I agree, Sir Graham.

RAINE: Well, surely the most likely lead is the fact that Julia Kelburn was a drug addict.

TEMPLE: Yes, I agree – that could be a very useful lead. I suppose you've consulted the narcotics people …?

RAINE: Oh, they're on to it, Temple – they've been briefed. But they haven't come up with anything – not yet, at any rate.

FORBES: What about this doctor – Benkaray?

RAINE: I saw her yesterday. I went down to Westerton to have a word with the local people. Dr Benkaray seems to be genuine; she's been practising in Town for the last ten years. But I didn't get much information out of her about Julia Kelburn; she was very cagey.

TEMPLE: Did you meet her secretary, Larry Cross?

RAINE: Yes, I did. Now he's a tough egg, if ever I saw one. Doesn't look a bit like my idea of a doctor's secretary.

TEMPLE: Nor anyone else's. We saw him last night, by the way, when we were returning from The Hide and Seek. He was with Mrs Kelburn.

FORBES: (*Surprised*) With Linda Kelburn?

TEMPLE: Yes, they were in a sports car together. Cross was driving. Incidentally, Steve thinks that Cross was the man who spoke to her at London Airport – the phoney B.O.A.C. official.

RAINE: (*Surprised*) You mean – she recognised him?

TEMPLE: Yes, but don't do anything; not yet, Raine.

There is a knock and the door opens.

TEMPLE: Steve may be mistaken and we don't want …

SERGEANT: Excuse me, sir. Mr Kelburn to see you.

FORBES: Oh, yes. Show him in, Sergeant.

SERGEANT: Yes, sir.

The door closes.

RAINE: Did you send for Kelburn, Sir Graham?

FORBES: Yes, I did. I think it's only fair we tell him about this new development.

RAINE: You mean the drugs?

FORBES: Yes. He's a right to know, and in any case he may be able to help us.

The door opens.

SERGEANT: Mr Kelburn, sir.

FORBES: Come in, Mr Kelburn. My name is Forbes. I think you've met Superintendent Raine and Mr Temple.

KELBURN: Yes, I have.

FORBES: Please sit down.

KELBURN: I'd rather stand, if you don't mind. I didn't expect to find you here, Temple.

TEMPLE: I had an appointment with Sir Graham. I'm just about to leave.

KELBURN: There's no reason for you to leave – so far as I'm concerned. What is it you want, Sir Graham?

FORBES: Certain information has reached us concerning your daughter – we thought it only fair that … that you should be made aware of it.

KELBURN: What information? What are you referring to?

FORBES: I'm afraid it's been established, Mr Kelburn, that your daughter took drugs.

RAINE: (*Bluntly*) She was a drug addict …

KELBURN: (*Quietly*) Oh …

TEMPLE: You don't seem very surprised?

KELBURN: (*After a moment*) No – no, I'm not.

TEMPLE: You knew?

KELBURN: Yes.

RAINE: How long have you known, sir?

KELBURN: About two or three days. I … I think perhaps I will sit down, Sir Graham, after all.

FORBES: Yes, of course.

A pause.

KELBURN: That's why I tried to stop your investigations, Temple. I didn't want you to find out about Julia. I thought if you found out about her taking drugs, then the press would get onto it and – well … the whole unsavoury business would be revived again – the murder and everything.

RAINE: Who told you your daughter was a drug addict, sir?

KELBURN: (*Irritated*) I do wish you wouldn't use that phrase, Superintendent! No one told me. I - I just sensed it.

RAINE: (*Dubiously*) Just sensed it?

KELBURN: Yes.

TEMPLE: Mr Kelburn, part of the time Julia mixed with people of her own class, the sons and daughters of fairly wealthy parents …

KELBURN: Yes …

TEMPLE: But at other times she used to associate with quite a different type of person; the arty-crafty crowd, people on the fringe of the underworld …

KELBURN: Nonsense!

TEMPLE: It isn't nonsense, it's true. Your daughter took drugs, therefore she got the drugs from somewhere. Now the point is – from where? None of her respectable friends would peddle the stuff, so it's my guess …

KELBURN: (*Angrily*) No one's interested in your guesses, Temple!

TEMPLE: On the contrary, I'll make a guess that will interest you – interest you very much.

KELBURN: (*Curious in spite of himself*) What do you mean?

TEMPLE: I don't believe you just sensed that your daughter took drugs; that's absurd! My guess is – someone told you – someone wrote you a letter about Julia and told you quite frankly that she was a drug addict. (*A moment*) Well – am I right?

KELBURN: (*Quietly*) Yes.

TEMPLE: Who wrote the letter?

KELBURN: A girl – a very old friend of Julia's. (*A pause*) Fiona came to the house quite often; she was a nice girl, highly respectable, and she intensely disliked Julia's more tacky friends.

She was always trying to persuade Julia to live a more useful life, to – well – settle down. After the murder Fiona wrote me a letter, Temple, saying that I'd made a mistake in asking you to investigate the case. She said you were bound to discover that Julia had taken drugs and the inevitable consequences of such a discovery would be weeks of unsavoury publicity.

TEMPLE: And you believe that?

KELBURN: Of course – it's the truth. Temple, be honest – you know damn well it's the truth! Once the newspapers get hold of a story like this, they just never let go.

RAINE: Who is this girl, Fiona? What's her surname, Mr Kelburn?

KELBURN: I'm sorry, I'm not prepared to divulge that.

RAINE: But you must divulge it! We've got to question the girl, we've got to ask her …

KELBURN: No one's questioning her! No one's seeing her! Whatever happens, I'm not having Fiona subjected to a police cross examination. The girl wrote me the letter simply out of kindness and I haven't the slightest intention …

FORBES: (*Interrupting KELBURN*) Mr Kelburn, I see your point of view and I appreciate it, but you don't understand – you've got to tell us who this girl is. We're investigating a murder case.

KELBURN: I'm sorry, Sir Graham, I've made up my mind about this. If it hadn't been for Temple here, I wouldn't even have told you about the letter.

RAINE: (*Irritated by KELBURN's manner*) I suppose you know that it's an offence to withhold information from the police, sir?

KELBURN: Yes, I know.

START FADE.

KELBURN: But I'm still going to withhold it, Superintendent …

SCENE FADE.

FADE UP of a telephone ringing.

STEVE lifts up the receiver.

STEVE: (*On the phone*) Hello?

TEMPLE: (*On the other end of the line*) Steve? …

STEVE: Hello, darling!

TEMPLE: How are things?

STEVE: Oh, fine. The man's been from the decorators, Paul, and he says as we're having the dressing room redecorated the bedroom should be completely …

TEMPLE: (*Laughing*) Yes, all right, Steve. Look – I want you to meet me with the car in about an hour. I shall be at the Club.

STEVE: Where are we going?

TEMPLE: Down to Westerton – but we shan't be staying the night, dear.

STEVE: All right, I'll pick you … (*She stops; cautiously*) Paul …

TEMPLE: Yes?

STEVE: There's a book by the side of your bed – you were reading it last night …

TEMPLE: (*Puzzled*) Yes?

STEVE: What's it called?

TEMPLE: Now why on earth should … Good for you, Steve! Don't take any chances!

STEVE: What's it called?

START FADE.

TEMPLE: It's a novel: "Advise and Consent".

STEVE: (*Relieved*) See you in about an hour, darling …

FADE SCENE.

FADE IN the sound of TEMPLE's car.
STEVE is driving.

STEVE: … But what happened when Kelburn refused to tell them who wrote the letter?

TEMPLE: Nothing, darling. What could Sir Graham do? Raine got rather pompous, of course, but it didn't get him anywhere.

STEVE: But surely he'll have to tell them who this Fiona person is, sooner or later. After all, Kelburn may be right – perhaps she is a very nice girl – but she may be able to help the police in their investigations.

TEMPLE: I agree; but I doubt very much whether Kelburn will change his mind – in his present mood, at any rate.

A pause.

STEVE: What's in the envelope, Paul?

TEMPLE: M'm? Oh, some photographs. They were taken for me yesterday and delivered to the Club.

STEVE: Photographs of what?

TEMPLE opens the envelope.

STEVE: Oh – Mike Langdon?

TEMPLE: Yes. Not bad, either, considering they were taken in the street without his knowing.

STEVE: I suppose you're going to show them to Fred Harcourt at The Red Hart?

TEMPLE: Yes. I want to know whether Langdon really was the man who called for Julia Kelburn that morning.

STEVE: Well, I think he was … I've got a sort of intuition about Mr Langdon …

TEMPLE: (*Laughing*) I was wondering when that good old intuition would start to work …

STEVE: You can laugh! But I've been right before …

TEMPLE: Yes – well, you get that intuition of yours to work on Mrs Fletcher – tell me how she fits into the picture …

STEVE: (*Slowly; puzzled*) I wish I could. I just can't make head or tail of Mrs Fletcher; but by golly, if it was her on the phone last night, I'm more than grateful to her.

TEMPLE: It was Mrs Fletcher all right; I'm sure.

STEVE: Are you going to try and see her while we're in Westerton?

TEMPLE: Yes, I am. For one thing, I want to ask her who … (*Suddenly*) Turn right here, Steve …

The cars slows down and turns.

STEVE: (*Puzzled*) Is this the way to Westerton? I thought …

TEMPLE: No, it isn't – but I've got a call to make first. You'll see a modern block of flats at the top of the hill – Monte Carlo Mansions – I want you to stop there.

STEVE: (*Laughing*) Who on earth lives at Monte Carlo Mansions?

TEMPLE: Who do you think? Mr Tony Wyman …

FADE UP the noise of the car.

FADE DOWN the car noise.

FADE IN of a doorbell ringing.

The ring is repeated several times and eventually the door is opened.

TEMPLE: Good morning!

WYMAN: (*Sleepily; unfriendly*) Oh, it's you! What's the big idea, waking me up at this hour of the morning?

TEMPLE: It's nearly twelve o'clock, Wyman.

WYMAN: All right, it's nearly twelve o'clock – so what?

TEMPLE: I want to talk to you. May I come in?

WYMAN: Well – it's not very convenient, but you can come in if yer want to.

TEMPLE: I want to.

The door shuts.

WYMAN: Now what's this all about? You're not goin' to ask me the same flippin' questions all over again, are yer? I'm a very busy man, Mr Temple.

TEMPLE: You look busy – especially in those pyjamas. (*Looking round the flat*) It's a very busy little flat.

WYMAN: Look – are you tryin' to be funny?

TEMPLE: (*With authority*) Why didn't you tell me about Julia?

WYMAN: What d'yer mean?

TEMPLE: Why didn't you tell me she took drugs?

WYMAN: Took – took drugs?

TEMPLE: Yes; and don't tell me you didn't know, because I shan't believe you.

WYMAN: I – I didn't know, honest I didn't.

TEMPLE: That's not what Fiona told me.

WYMAN: (*Surprised*) Fiona? You mean Fiona Scott?

TEMPLE: Who else?

WYMAN: But why should Fiona Scott tell you that I … Why, blimey, I only saw the girl once! Julia took me down to Brighton to see her one Sunday – and a stuck-up little thing she was, too! Hardly spoke a dozen words to me. I don't believe she told you that … Look, are you givin' me the run around? Tryin' to pin somethin' on me?

TEMPLE: No; strange though it may seem, I'm not trying to pin anything on anyone. Goodbye, Tony. You've been most helpful.

WYMAN: (*Surprised*) What d'yer mean – most helpful?

START FADE.

TEMPLE: What I say: most helpful. Don't trouble to see me out …

WYMAN: (*Puzzled*) Look – I don't get this …

COMPLETE FADE.

FADE UP of a car engine ticking over.

A car door opens.

STEVE: How was the boy genius?

TEMPLE: Slightly temperamental – but he told me what I wanted to know.

STEVE: Good. Where now – Westerton?

TEMPLE: Yes – but stop at the Fletchers' garage first.

The car drives away.

A pause.

STEVE: (*Smiling*) Fiona – what?

TEMPLE: What did you say?

STEVE: I said: "Fiona – what?", darling.

TEMPLE: (*Amused*) Fiona Scott – she lives in Brighton. So you know what I was up to.

STEVE: Don't be silly …

TEMPLE laughs.

FADE SCENE.

FADE UP the sound of the car.

STEVE: ... There's the garage – d'you want me to drive in or pull up here?

TEMPLE: Oh, I should drive in, darling. We need some petrol anyway. (*Suddenly*) Hello!

STEVE: What is it?

TEMPLE: That's Dr Benkaray over there, with Larry Cross. You'd better not drive in, Steve – pull up here.

The car slows down and stops.

TEMPLE: Stay in the car – I don't want Cross to know you've recognised him.

STEVE: Yes, all right.

TEMPLE: I shall tell Bill Fletcher I'm having trouble with the car – so don't be surprised if we come back and take a look at it.

FADE UP of TEMPLE walking towards the garage.

TEMPLE: Good afternoon. I'm afraid I'm having a spot of trouble with my car and I wonder if ...

BILL: Be with you in a minute, sir!

TEMPLE: Thank you.

BENKARAY: Good afternoon, Mr Temple.

TEMPLE: (*Pleasantly*) Oh, hello, Doctor!

BENKARAY: What are you doing in this part of the world?

TEMPLE: I'm on my way to the coast, and the wretched car's gone all temperamental. Is this chap any good?

BENKARAY: Yes – I think he's a good mechanic.

LARRY: We had a friend of yours down here yesterday, Temple – Superintendent Raine.

TEMPLE: Yes, so I believe.

LARRY: Asked a lot of damn silly questions. He seems to think there's a connection between the Ted Angus murder and the Kelburn affair. I can't imagine why.

TEMPLE: Well, perhaps you haven't got sufficient imagination, Mr Cross.

LARRY: What do you mean?

BENKARAY: Do you think there's a connection, Mr Temple?

TEMPLE: Yes, I do.

BENKARAY: Well, tell us – what is the connection? We're always keen to learn.

TEMPLE: (*With a laugh*) You should have asked the Superintendent that question.

BENKARAY: We did – but unfortunately he didn't enlighten us.

BILL: (*Approaching*) Nineteen and fourpence, Doctor.

BENKARAY: Charge it to my account, will you? Oh, and Bill …

BILL: Yes, Doctor?

BENKARAY: Ask your mother to telephone me when she gets back.

BILL: Yes, I'll do that.

A car starts.

LARRY: Goodbye, Temple.

TEMPLE: Goodbye. Goodbye, Doctor.

BENKARAY: (*Looking at TEMPLE*) Goodbye, Mr Temple. I expect we shall meet again sometime.

The car drives off.

BILL: Having trouble with your car, Mr Temple?

TEMPLE: (*Watching the doctor's car drive away*) What? Oh – no; I wanted to talk to you.

BILL: (*Surprised*) Talk to me? What about?

TEMPLE: About your mother.

BILL: (*After a moment*) Okay – let's go in the office.

Footsteps are heard.

A door opens and closes: the sound of a spring bell.

TEMPLE: Is your mother away?

BILL: Yes, she's up in Town, seeing my Aunt Gladys. Did you want her for anything special?

TEMPLE: I was anxious to talk to her.

BILL: Anything I can do?

TEMPLE: It's rather a personal matter.

BILL: Oh, I see.

TEMPLE: I heard Dr Benkaray ask you to get your mother to phone her. Are they close friends?

BILL: I suppose you could say that. Mother used to work up at her place, and when we moved down here the doctor became one of our best customers.

TEMPLE: Do you like the doctor?

BILL: She's been very good to mother.

TEMPLE: That wasn't what I asked you.

BILL: I'd sooner keep my likes and dislikes to myself, if you don't mind, Mr Temple.

TEMPLE: (*Smiling*) That's sensible of you. It's just that your mother did me a very great favour and I'd like to repay her.

BILL: (*Puzzled*) My mother did you a favour?

TEMPLE: Yes; an attempt was made on my life – and on my wife's – and your mother phoned and tipped me off. Otherwise I might not be here today.

BILL: This is news to me. Are you sure it was my mother who telephoned you?

TEMPLE: Yes, I'm pretty sure.

BILL: Well, Mother wouldn't expect any money, you know – even if she did do you a favour.

TEMPLE: I wasn't thinking of that. I had a feeling she was in some kind of trouble and it occurred to me that I might be able to help her in some way. I've a certain amount of influence, you know.

BILL: (*Quietly*) Yes, I know, Mr Temple. I've heard a great deal about you and I've always thought ... But how did you know my mother was in trouble?

TEMPLE: (*Quietly*) Bill, why don't you tell me about it? I give you my word, I'll treat the whole thing in confidence.

There is a pause.

BILL hesitates, then suddenly makes up his mind.

BILL: Well, it's like this, Mr Temple. When I was a lad we used to live at Little Weston, about two miles away. Dad died when I was sixteen, and Mother went out to work. There wasn't much money, but I got a job in the garage at Little Weston. When I was nineteen we came to live here. Mother got this job with Dr Benkaray and she managed to fix me up at Perrymount Engineering, helping to repair tractors and things. I always wanted a garage of my own, as long as I can remember, but there was never any money.

TEMPLE: Go on, Bill.

BILL: Well – we went on steadily enough, and then Mother started going to the doctor's afternoons as well as mornings, sometimes evenings as well. Then after about two years, she came home one night and said she'd finished at the doctor's and was buying this garage which had just come on to the market. She got it cheap enough, too, on account of putting down the ready.

TEMPLE: D'you think your mother saved enough money to buy the garage?

BILL: No, she couldn't have saved a quarter of it. I asked her where the rest came from but she'd never let on. Said she'd managed to raise a loan, and it was her business.

TEMPLE: I see.

BILL: But in spite of everything, Mr Temple, Mother isn't happy. I'm sure she isn't. Don't ask me why, but she isn't.

TEMPLE: You said she's in London at the moment?

BILL: Yes, she's always popping up to Town these days to see her sister – that's my Aunt Gladys. They've never been as friendly. In the old days Mother used to say they only met at weddings and funerals.

TEMPLE: You sound a bit suspicious of your aunt?

BILL: Oh no, it isn't that, but …

TEMPLE: Well, have you any reason for suspecting that your mother doesn't see your aunt when she goes up to London?

BILL: No, no, but – after one of these trips I saw a theatre programme sticking out of her handbag. It was from the Regency Theatre at Brighton.

TEMPLE: She could have gone to Brighton – it's not very far from London. Perhaps she took your aunt there.

BILL: Then why didn't she tell me about it? At one time she used to tell me everything …

TEMPLE: (*After a moment*) Of course, there may be a very simple explanation for all this. I don't know whether it's occurred to you, Bill?

BILL: What's that?

TEMPLE: Your mother might have fallen in love with someone.

BILL: Oh, no! It's not that, Mr Temple.

TEMPLE: How do you know?

BILL: She'd have told me if it was something like that. She's friendly with lots of chaps she meets at The Red Hart – we've had many a laugh over them. But she knows I wouldn't mind her marrying again – she had a rough time with my Dad and I've often told her she's entitled to a second chance if she meets the right man.

TEMPLE: I see. Well, if she isn't seeing your aunt she's obviously seeing someone on these trips of hers.

BILL: Yes.

TEMPLE: And you've no idea who it is?

BILL: No, I haven't. All I know is that after every trip she comes home looking more worried than ever.

TEMPLE: Has your mother received any strange telephone calls lately, or visitors, or …

BILL: Yes – she has! There was one chap – he came to the house late one night, about two months ago.

TEMPLE: Can you tell me anything about him?

BILL: Mother and he had a row. She thought I was asleep in bed, but when I heard voices I went to the top of the stairs. They were standing in the hall arguing with each other. I'd never seen the man before but I think he was an American because …

TEMPLE: An American?

BILL: Yes.

TEMPLE: Did you see the man – clearly, I mean?

BILL: Yes.

TEMPLE: Then you'd recognise him again?

BILL: I think so. Yes, I'm sure I would.

TEMPLE: Then take a look at these photographs …

TEMPLE produces the photographs from his pocket.

BILL: Yes – that's him! That's the chap all right …

TEMPLE: You're sure?

BILL: I'm positive! But how on earth did you get these photographs?

TEMPLE: Don't worry about the photographs, Bill – just tell me what happened.

BILL: Well – there was a row, a first class one – and the funny thing is, so far as I could make out it was all over a blinking coat …

START FADE.

TEMPLE: Over a coat?

BILL: Yes; Mother had a coat over her arm and she kept saying …

COMPLETE FADE.

FADE BACK into the voice of MRS FLETCHER.

MRS FLETCHER: … There's the coat, and I don't want anything more to do with it!

LANGDON: I don't think you realise what you're doing!

MRS F: Oh, yes I do! I know what I'm doing all right!

LANGDON: Somebody's got to take this to Margo!

MRS F: Well, it's not going to be me!

LANGDON: Now don't be darned awkward – it's got to be you!

MRS F: Let Julia take it for once.

LANGDON: You know perfectly well Julia can't take it! Brighton isn't safe for Julia. In any case, she refuses to have anything to do with it.

MRS F: And she isn't the only one!

LANGDON: I just don't understand this change of attitude. You've always done as you were told in the past.

MRS F: Yes – well, the past is the past. Let other people do the dirty work for a change!

LANGDON: But why? The set-up's just the same. Things haven't changed. You simply meet Margo in the usual place and hand over the coat. There's no risk attached to it – and plenty of dough.

MRS F: I tell you I'm not doing it! Now clear off – I don't want you to wake the boy up.

LANGDON: (*Quietly*) There'll be trouble – I suppose you realise that?

MRS F: All right – there'll be trouble.

LANGDON: If Benkaray gets to know about this …

MRS F: (*Angrily*) Tell the doc! Tell her! Go ahead – tell her …

LANGDON: You must be nuts! You know Benkaray! You know what'll happen if she thinks you're trying to break away …

MRS F: You can say two words to Dr Benkaray – just two words … Edgar Northampton …

LANGDON: (*Puzzled*) Edgar Northampton …?

MRS F: That's right!

LANGDON: And who the devil's Edgar Northampton?

MRS F: (*A short laugh*) Never you mind, but if Benkaray gets awkward mention that name.

She'll understand, if you don't. Now take the coat – I don't want it …

START FADE.

LANGDON: I hope you know what you're doing.

MRS F: I know what I'm doing all right …

COMPLETE FADE.

FADE BACK to TEMPLE with BILL FLETCHER.

TEMPLE: And then what happened?

BILL: The man left and I went back to bed. And I don't mind telling you I lay awake for two or three hours, trying to figure things out. And I'm no clearer about it now than I was then.

TEMPLE: Did you tell your mother what you'd heard?

BILL: No; I never mentioned it.

TEMPLE: You're quite sure you heard the name "Margo" mentioned?

BILL: Yes.

TEMPLE: And "Julia".

BILL: Yes.

TEMPLE: Did it occur to you that they were talking about Julia Kelburn?

BILL: (*Genuinely surprised*) Julia Kelburn? That's the girl that was murdered … No, I never thought of that.

TEMPLE: She was a patient of Dr Benkaray's.

BILL: Was she?

TEMPLE: Yes. So it's possible – quite possible – that your mother knew her.

BILL: Yes, I suppose … (*Suddenly*) Mr Temple, you don't think my mother had anything to do with the murder? …

TEMPLE: (*Interrupting BILL*) I don't think your mother committed the murder, Bill, if that's what you mean. But it's my guess – she knows who did.

BILL: (*Softly; distressed*) Oh, no! If my mother's got into trouble, Mr Temple, it's because of me. She always wanted me to have a good start in life – to have a garage of my own. Even when I was a kid she …

TEMPLE: Don't worry, Bill. We'll sort this out. Now tell me: I want to get this straight. You heard the man say to your mother: "You know Benkaray! You know what'll happen if she thinks you're trying to break away."

BILL: Yes.

TEMPLE: And your mother replied –?

BILL: "You can say two words to Dr Benkaray – just two words … Edgar Northampton …" But don't ask me what she meant, Mr Temple – because I haven't a clue! I don't know anyone called Northampton – never heard the name before.

TEMPLE: Are you sure?

BILL: I'm positive. (*Worried*) You believe me, don't you, Mr Temple?

TEMPLE: (*After a pause*) Yes, I believe you. Now listen …

START FADE.

TEMPLE: Try not to worry too much about this, Bill – and keep your eyes and ears open. If you see anything or hear anything, which you think might be of interest to me …

COMPLETE FADE.

FADE UP of footsteps.
The car door opens.

STEVE: Well! I thought you'd walked out of my life!

TEMPLE: Sorry, darling. I got caught up.

TEMPLE gets into the car and shuts the door.

STEVE: Did you see Mrs Fletcher?

TEMPLE: No; she's away.

STEVE: Where?

TEMPLE: (*His thoughts elsewhere*) I don't know.

STEVE: You look very thoughtful, Paul. Has something happened?

TEMPLE: I've had quite a talk to young Fletcher.

STEVE: What's he like?

TEMPLE: He's an innocent, hard working young man; but I'm afraid his mother's kept him in the dark about quite a lot of things. That's what's worrying him at the moment.

STEVE: Did he tell you anything about Dr Benkaray?

TEMPLE: Yes – and he also told me something about Mike Langdon.

STEVE: (*Surprised*) Langdon?

TEMPLE: Langdon was down here a little while ago. He tried to persuade Mrs Fletcher to take a coat to someone in Brighton – someone called Margo.

STEVE: Margo?!

TEMPLE: Yes; but oddly enough that doesn't interest me as much as the Brighton angle. Remember Tony Wyman told me that he met Julia Kelburn's friend – Fiona – at Brighton.

STEVE: Yes. You think Margo and this Fiona Scott might be one and the same person?

TEMPLE: I don't know; it's possible, I suppose. We'll skip The Red Hart, darling – and go down to Brighton.

STEVE: Yes, all right, Paul.

The car starts and drives away.
FADE OUT.

FADE IN the noise of the car.

STEVE: Have you any idea how long we'll stay in Brighton?

TEMPLE: Oh – probably two or three days.

STEVE: But we haven't any things with us, Paul. What are we going to do?

TEMPLE: We'll stop in the next town and telephone Charlie. He can bring some things down to us on the next train.

STEVE: Yes, that's a good idea.

TEMPLE: Have you got any money on you, Steve?

STEVE: (*Laughing*) About thirty shillings …

TEMPLE: Oh, dear. I've only got about six or seven pounds …

STEVE: We shall need more than that …

TEMPLE: Yes. What's the next town?

STEVE: I think it's Tenterhurst.

TEMPLE: Well – if you see a bank, pull up. Then you can go into a box and phone Charlie while I'm trying to cash a cheque.

STEVE: Right. Where shall I tell Charlie we're staying?

TEMPLE: Oh – what's that hotel on the front, Steve?

START FADE.

STEVE: The Palace, isn't it?

TEMPLE: That's right. Tell him we're at The Palace, darling …

COMPLETE FADE.

FADE TO a Bank interior.
Footsteps on a marble floor.

CLERK: Good afternoon, sir.

TEMPLE: Good afternoon. I have an account at your Shaftesbury Avenue Branch and I want to cash a cheque.

CLERK: I see, sir. Can I have your name, please?

TEMPLE: Temple – Paul Temple.

CLERK: Oh – how much did you want, Mr Temple?

TEMPLE: I've made the cheque out for fifty pounds.

CLERK: I see. Well – would you mind waiting while I have a word with the manager, sir?

TEMPLE: Not at all.

FADE UP and DOWN of the background noises of the Bank.

The door of the MANAGER's Office opens.

MANAGER: (*Middle-aged; rather fussy in manner*) Good afternoon, Mr Temple.

TEMPLE: Good afternoon.

MANAGER: Would you care to come into my office for a moment?

TEMPLE: Certainly.

FADE the background noises as the door shuts.

MANAGER: Do sit down.

TEMPLE: Thank you. I'm sorry if this is inconvenient, but my wife and I happen to be …

MANAGER: (*Pleasantly; interrupting TEMPLE*) Not at all, not at all, Mr Temple! It's what we're here for. I'm delighted to meet you.

TEMPLE: Thank you.

MANAGER: My daughter will be very thrilled when she hears about this. She enjoyed your last book enormously, Mr Temple. Never stopped talking about it.

TEMPLE: You're very kind.

MANAGER: How would you like this, Mr Temple? In fives?

TEMPLE: Thank you, that would do admirably.

MANAGER: Well, if you would be kind enough to sign this slip …

The door opens.

CLERK: You rang, sir?

MANAGER: Yes, Wilson. Here's Mr Temple's cheque. He wants fifty pounds in fives – and see if you can find some new notes.

CLERK: Very good, Mr Northampton.

The door closes.

MANAGER: I hope we shall have the pleasure of seeing you again in Tenterhurst, Mr Temple.

TEMPLE: I hope so too, Mr – er – Northampton?

MANAGER: Yes.

TEMPLE: (*Politely*) Edgar Northampton?

MANAGER: (*Obviously surprised*) That's right, Mr Temple …

END OF EPISODE FOUR

EPISODE FIVE

BREAKWATER HOUSE

OPEN TO:

CLERK: You rang, sir?

MANAGER: Yes, Wilson. Here's Mr Temple's cheque. He wants fifty pounds in fives – and see if you can find some new notes.

CLERK: Very good, Mr Northampton.

The door closes.

MANAGER: I hope we shall have the pleasure of seeing you again in Tenterhurst, Mr Temple.

TEMPLE: I hope so too, Mr – er – Northampton?

MANAGER: Yes.

TEMPLE: (*Politely*) Edgar Northampton?

MANAGER: (*Obviously surprised*) That's right, Mr Temple …

TEMPLE: I heard your name mentioned when I was getting some petrol at the garage in Westerton.

MANAGER: Oh, yes – we have a sub-branch there. Tuesdays and Fridays.

TEMPLE: Then I expect you know Mrs Fletcher and her son – they keep the garage in the High Street.

MANAGER: Fletcher? Let me think now … a tall, fair-haired woman?

TEMPLE: No; she's just average height, turning grey …

MANAGER: Ah, yes! I remember. We met at a garden fete about eight months ago. (*Smiling*) When she discovered I was a bank manager she was rather anxious to get my advice … Yes, of course; I remember the lady. How stupid of me …

TEMPLE: I expect people are always after free advice, Mr Northampton?

MANAGER: They are indeed. Still – advice costs nothing, as they say.

There is a knock and the door opens.

CLERK: Fifty in fives, sir.

MANAGER: Thank you, Wilson.

The CLERK leaves and the door closes.

MANAGER: There we are, Mr Temple. I'll just count them for you … Ten Fives …

TEMPLE: Thanks very much. I must be getting along; my wife's waiting for me in the car.

The MANAGER opens the door.

MANAGER: Any time you're passing, Mr Temple, we'll be delighted to see you.

In the background a telephone rings.

TEMPLE: Thank you.

MANAGER: Ah, excuse me … Goodbye.

TEMPLE: Goodbye.

The door closes.

FADE UP footsteps in the main hall of the bank.

LARRY: Oh, hello, Mr Temple!

TEMPLE: Good afternoon, Mr Cross!

LARRY: Had to dash over to cash a cheque for the doctor – only just made it before they closed.

TEMPLE: So did I.

LARRY: They gave you the V.I.P. treatment, I see – big welcome in the manager's office. Now I wonder what that means?

TEMPLE: It could mean I have a large overdraft.

LARRY: (*Smiling*) Yes – you're right there.

CLERK: Ten ones – five in halves, Mr Cross.

LARRY: Thank you. Oh – I'd like a new cheque book. Thirty open.

CLERK: Yes, sir.

TEMPLE: You find that sports car of yours expensive to run, Mr Cross?

LARRY: (*Puzzled*) Sports car?

TEMPLE: The cream one – the one I saw you in the other night with Linda Kelburn.

LARRY: Who's Linda Kelburn?

TEMPLE: She's George Kelburn's wife – Julia's step-mother.

LARRY: (*Amazed*) You saw me with Mrs Kelburn?

TEMPLE: Yes.

LARRY: Where?

TEMPLE: In Leicester Square.

LARRY: You certainly didn't. I don't know Mrs Kelburn – I don't know any of the Kelburns.

TEMPLE: Didn't you know Julia – the dead girl?

LARRY: No; why should I?

TEMPLE: She was a patient of Dr Benkaray's.

LARRY: So what?

TEMPLE: You're the doctor's secretary – surely you know her patients?

LARRY: Not all of them.

TEMPLE: I see.

CLERK: Your cheque book, sir.

LARRY: Thank you. Goodbye, Mr Temple.

TEMPLE: Goodbye.

LARRY: Oh – if you see me in that sports car again, stop me. I'd like to take a look at it!

TEMPLE: I'll bear that in mind, Mr Cross.

FADE SCENE.

FADE IN a background of light traffic.

A car door opens.

STEVE: Did you get the money?

TEMPLE: Yes.

STEVE: You've been ages.

TEMPLE: I've been talking to Larry Cross. He was cashing a cheque.

STEVE: Yes, I saw him going into the bank. I had a good look at him this time. I was right, Paul – he was the man I told you about; the man at London Airport.

TEMPLE: Yes, I'm not surprised. He's a nasty piece of work. (*Suddenly*) Well, come on, Steve! Brighton!

STEVE: All right, darling.

STEVE starts the car.

TEMPLE: Did you telephone Charlie?

STEVE: Yes; he's catching the four o'clock train.

TEMPLE: Good.

STEVE: What exactly are we going to do in Brighton, Paul? Look for that friend of Julia's – Fiona Scott?

TEMPLE: Yes. (*After a moment*) … Amongst other things …

FADE SCENE.

FADE IN the hall of a large seaside hotel.

RECEPTIONIST: Room 528, Mr Temple.

TEMPLE: Thank you.

RECEPTIONIST: I'll have your baggage sent up to the room, sir.

TEMPLE: I'm afraid we haven't any at the moment.

RECEPTIONIST: Oh – er – indeed, sir?

TEMPLE: My man's bringing our things down from London. Would you send him up to our room as soon as he arrives?

RECEPTIONIST: Yes, of course, Mr Temple. Your key …

TEMPLE: Thank you.

LANGDON: (*Approaching*) Good afternoon. Mr George Kelburn is expecting me.

RECEPTIONIST: Your name, sir?

LANGDON: Langdon.

RECEPTIONIST: Just a minute, sir.

TEMPLE: Hello, Langdon, this is a surprise!

LANGDON: (*Surprised*) Temple! Well – whadya know? Hello, Mrs Temple! Good to see you again!

STEVE: Good afternoon, Mr Langdon.

LANGDON: Well, this really is a pleasure. I'd no idea you'd be down here.

TEMPLE: We felt we needed a breath of sea air.

LANGDON: You're not the only ones. Kelburn's got the same idea.

STEVE: I thought you were going back to the States, Mr Langdon?

LANGDON: I was, Mrs Temple. I was due to leave this morning but Kelburn made me cancel.

TEMPLE: Why?

LANGDON: Well, there seems to be an awful lot of work to do and he just doesn't seem to be able to cope with it. I guess he's got too accustomed to having me around, that's about it.

TEMPLE: I'm sure you've been a great help, Langdon.

LANGDON: Yeah, I know, but he expects me to interfere in affairs which don't really concern me.

TEMPLE: Family affairs?

LANGDON: Yes. He keeps asking my advice about – well, about his wife for one thing.

TEMPLE: How do you mean?

LANGDON: They seem to have drifted apart these last few weeks. I wouldn't be surprised if they didn't split up. Only the other day Kelburn was asking my advice about getting a divorce.

STEVE: Don't tell me he'll expect you to handle that for him?

LANGDON: (*Laughing*) You'd be surprised what he expects me to handle, Mrs Temple.

TEMPLE: Is he interested in some other woman, do you think?

LANGDON: Gee, no! The boot's on the other foot, if anything. I've seen Linda out twice recently with another man.

TEMPLE: A tall, dark-haired, hatchet-faced man of about forty?

LANGDON: Yes – could be.

TEMPLE: I think you'll find he's Dr Benkaray's secretary.

LANGDON: Dr Benkaray? That's the doctor Julia consulted.

TEMPLE: That's right.

LANGDON: D'you know this character, then?

TEMPLE: I've met him.

LANGDON: When?

TEMPLE: During the course of my investigations. But how did Mrs Kelburn meet him – that's what I'd like to know?

LANGDON: Maybe she went with Julia one day, to the doctor's, I mean?

TEMPLE: That's certainly a possible explanation.

RECEPTIONIST: Excuse me, sir. Mr Kelburn says you may go up now. It's Room 219 – second floor.

LANGDON: Thank you.

START FADE.

TEMPLE: Will you be staying in London, Langdon?

LANGDON: That's up to Kelburn. But I can tell you this – the moment he gives the word I shall be heading back to New York.

COMPLETE FADE.

FADE IN of TEMPLE's voice calling to STEVE. She is on the balcony of their room.

TEMPLE: (*Calling*) Don't catch cold out on the balcony, Steve.

STEVE: (*From the background*) It's not cold – it's a lovely afternoon.

TEMPLE: (*Flicking pages of a telephone directory*) She's not in the phone book …

STEVE: (*Coming into the room*) What's that, Paul?

TEMPLE: Fiona Scott – she's not in the phone book. (*Putting the directory down*) I can't say I'm surprised. I didn't expect it to be that easy.

STEVE: Talking of surprises – were you surprised to see Langdon down here?

TEMPLE: Not really.

STEVE: Why?

TEMPLE: Because of what Bill Fletcher told me. Langdon tried to persuade his mother to bring a coat to Brighton; to deliver it to Margo.

STEVE: D'you think Margo and this girl – Fiona Scott – are one and the same person?

TEMPLE: (*Laughing*) You asked me that question before, Steve. I don't know. According to what Kelburn says, Fiona Scott is a highly respectable young lady who disapproved of Julia's more sensational friends.

STEVE: That's only what Kelburn says …

TEMPLE: Yes; but why should he say it if it isn't true?

STEVE: Yes, well, I know what I would do if I were investigating this case.

TEMPLE: (*Amused*) What would you do, darling?

STEVE: I should forget all about Fiona Scott and concentrate on Mike Langdon.

TEMPLE: And what about the other suspects? Larry Cross – Tony Wyman – Mrs Fletcher – Dr Benkaray – even Edgar Northampton.

STEVE: (*Surprised*) The bank manager? You don't think he had anything to do with …

TEMPLE: (*Laughing*) No, I don't – but Mrs Fletcher implied that he knew something about Dr Benkaray.

STEVE: What sort of a man was he?

The telephone starts to ring.

TEMPLE: Edgar Northampton? Oh – typical bank manager.

TEMPLE picks up the receiver.

TEMPLE: (*On the phone*) Hello …

FORBES: (*On the other end of the line*) Temple?

TEMPLE: Yes …

FORBES: Forbes here …

TEMPLE: Hello, Sir Graham! Are you speaking from London?

FORBES: Yes.

TEMPLE: How did you know we were down here?

FORBES: Charlie told me. What are you doing in Brighton anyway?

TEMPLE: Oh – we just thought we'd pop down here for a breath of sea air.

FORBES: I see. I thought perhaps you might be looking for a girl named Fiona Scott.

TEMPLE: (*Laughing*) How did you find out that name?

FORBES: What's more to the point – how did <u>you</u> find it?

TEMPLE: I had a talk to Tony Wyman. He apparently met her some little time ago.

FORBES: I see. Well, listen, Temple – we've got her phone number. Brighton 1930 …

TEMPLE: Brighton 1930 …

FORBES: Yes. But we haven't contacted her because we don't want to scare the girl. I thought you might phone her – unofficially, as it were – and get the lie of the land.

TEMPLE: Yes, all right, Sir Graham. (*Amused*) How did you get the number?

FORBES: We do find things out for ourselves occasionally. Keep in touch, Temple.

TEMPLE: Yes, all right.

FORBES: Love to Steve …

SIR GRAHAM rings off.

STEVE: What's the joke?

TEMPLE: That was Sir Graham.

TEMPLE starts dialling a telephone number.

TEMPLE: Charlie told him we were down here. He's given me Fiona Scott's phone number.

STEVE: I'll bet Raine found it. He'd make sure you weren't going to put one over on him.

TEMPLE: Yes … (*On the phone*) Hello? …

FIONA: (*On the other end of the line*) Brighton 1930 …

TEMPLE: Could I speak to Miss Fiona Scott, please?

FIONA: (*Hesitantly; a cultured soft voice*) Who is it speaking?

TEMPLE: My name is Temple – Paul Temple.

FIONA: This … this is Fiona Scott speaking.

TEMPLE: Oh, good afternoon, Miss Scott. I'm sorry to trouble you, but I understand from Mr Kelburn that you were a friend of his daughter's.

FIONA: Yes. Yes, I was.

TEMPLE: Well, as you probably know, I'm investigating …

FIONA: Mr Temple, please don't think me rude, but I don't want to have anything to do with this business. Julia's dead, and I feel …

TEMPLE: (*Interrupting FIONA*) Look, Miss Scott, I'm not trying to get you involved in this affair, please don't think that.

FIONA: Well – what are you trying to do?

TEMPLE: You knew Julia – you were a very close friend of hers. I think you were probably more fond of her than anyone else.

FIONA: Well?

TEMPLE: I think if we had a talk, you might be able to tell me little things about her that – well, that might be useful. Naturally, whatever you told me I should treat in the strictest confidence.

FIONA: (*After a moment*) I'm rather busy at the moment and I'm going over to Seadale this afternoon …

TEMPLE: Wouldn't it be possible for me to meet you at Seadale?

FIONA: Well, I'm staying with friends and …

TEMPLE: I could drive over tonight – or tomorrow morning – any time you like.

FIONA: (*A moment*) Well – let's say this evening then.

TEMPLE: Eight o'clock?

FIONA: (*Hesitantly*) Yes, I suppose that will be convenient – my friends live at Breakwater

House. It's about a mile outside the village, further along the coast.

TEMPLE: Thank you, Miss Scott. I'll see you this evening – and please don't mention this conversation to anyone.

FIONA: No, I won't. Goodbye, Mr Temple.

TEMPLE: Goodbye.

TEMPLE replaces the receiver.

STEVE: I gather we're going out tonight?

TEMPLE: (*Thoughtfully*) Yes.

STEVE: What did she sound like?

TEMPLE: Quiet – well spoken. She's visiting some friends at a place called Seadale.

STEVE: Seadale – that's further along the coast, about fifteen miles from here.

There is a knock and the door opens.

STEVE: Come in.

CHARLIE: Hello, Mrs Temple!

STEVE: Oh, hello, Charlie!

TEMPLE: You haven't wasted much time!

CHARLIE: No; wonderful train service! Just caught the old Belle as she was pulling out. Here's your case, Mrs Temple – and here's yours, sir.

STEVE: Thank you, Charlie. What's that small case?

CHARLIE: Oh, this! I brought the recorder down, Mr Temple. I thought I'd tape the phone calls while you were away, so you could hear them for yourself. Better than writing a message down.

TEMPLE: Much better, Charlie. Put it down over there. I'll plug it in.

STEVE: Have there been many calls?

CHARLIE: Only two important ones. Sir Graham rang, but he only wanted to know where you were.

The first call was from a woman – wouldn't give her name or anything – proper bag of mystery.

TEMPLE switches on the recorder.

STEVE: What time was this?

CHARLIE: Oh, about half past ten this morning …

TEMPLE: Here it is, Steve.

The voice of MRS FLETCHER FADE IN from the tape recorder.

MRS FLETCHER: (*On the tape*) Can I speak to Mr Temple?

CHARLIE: (*On the tape*) I'm afraid he's away at the moment. Who is that?

MRS F: Can you tell me where I can get in touch with him?

CHARLIE: Who is that speaking?

MRS F: You wouldn't know my name … Where is Mr Temple?

CHARLIE: He's gone down to Brighton for a few days with Mrs Temple …

MRS F: (*Obviously a little alarmed*) Why has he gone to Brighton – do you know?

CHARLIE: No, I'm sorry, I don't know.

MRS F: Is he going to Dreamland?

CHARLIE: (*Amused*) Don't ask me. Shouldn't think so: not Mr Temple's cup of tea. Look – if you leave your name …

MRS F: Where is Mr Temple staying?

CHARLIE: I'm sorry, I don't know.

MRS F: (*Obviously worried*) All right – I'll ring back later.

MRS FLETCHER replaces the receiver.

TEMPLE: Stop the recorder, Charlie …

STEVE: (*Puzzled*) Did you recognise the voice, Paul?

TEMPLE: Yes – it was Mrs Fletcher.

CHARLIE: Made me laugh when she mentioned Dreamland.

STEVE: Dreamland? Is that the funfair, over …

CHARLIE: That's right, Mrs Temple – over on the other side of the pier. Can't imagine you and Mrs Temple on the dodgems.

TEMPLE: (*Thoughtfully*) Can't you, Charlie? All right – let's hear the next one …

CHARLIE switches on the recorder again.

A pause.

CHARLIE: (*On the tape*) Hello?

LINDA: (*On the tape*) Can I speak to Mr Temple?

CHARLIE: I'm afraid he's away at the moment.

LINDA: Oh … Oh dear. Have you any idea when he'll be back?

CHARLIE: No; I'm afraid I haven't. Can I take a message?

LINDA: Will you be seeing Mr Temple?

CHARLIE: Yes, this afternoon. I'm going down to … see him.

LINDA: Well this is Mrs Kelburn. I'd like you to deliver a message for me.

CHARLIE: Okay – go ahead.

LINDA: Mr Temple saw me in a sports car the other night … I'm very anxious that he shouldn't mention this fact to anyone – particularly my husband.

CHARLIE: Oh – oh, I see. Well, I'll make sure he gets the message.

LINDA: Thank you. That's very kind of you. Goodbye.

CHARLIE: Goodbye.

TEMPLE stops the machine.

STEVE: Well, that ties up with what Mike Langdon said, doesn't it, Paul?

TEMPLE: You mean another man and the possibility of Kelburn getting a divorce?

STEVE: Yes.

TEMPLE: (*Thoughtfully*) Yes, but I can hardly believe Linda Kelburn's fallen for someone like Larry Cross.

STEVE: You never can tell. Women are peculiar creatures.

CHARLIE: (*Without thinking*) You can say that … Oh, I beg your pardon, Mrs Temple.

TEMPLE: You'd better get back to Town, Charlie. Are you all right for money?

CHARLIE: Yes – fine.

TEMPLE: Keep taping the phone calls. You know where we are if there's anything urgent.

CHARLIE: Righto! Goodbye, Mrs Temple. Don't eat too much rock.

STEVE: (*Laughing*) Goodbye, Charlie.

The door opens and closes.

STEVE: (*Puzzled*) Paul, why do you think Mrs Fletcher mentioned that fairground place – Dreamland?

TEMPLE: I don't know; but she obviously thought that was one of the reasons why we came here.

STEVE: But why on earth should she think that?

TEMPLE: We won't know until we visit the place.

STEVE: I can't wait for that!

TEMPLE: … Even then it might not be clear what she was getting at. You see, if there's someone there that she doesn't want us to …

TEMPLE is interrupted by a knock on the door.

TEMPLE: (*Calling*) Come in!

The door opens.

KELBURN: Can you spare me a minute, Temple?

TEMPLE: Yes, of course – come on in, Kelburn. You know my wife?

The door closes.

KELBURN: Yes – yes, I do. Good afternoon, Mrs Temple.

STEVE: … Good afternoon, Mr Kelburn.

TEMPLE: Do sit down.

KELBURN: I'd rather stand, if you don't mind. I'm very restless today, for some reason or other. Mrs Temple, I'd like to apologise for my rudeness the last time we met. I have rather an abrupt manner at times and it occasionally – well – gives the wrong impression.

STEVE: That's all right, Mr Kelburn.

KELBURN: The same applies to our last meeting, Temple. You were perfectly right, of course – no reason why you shouldn't continue your investigations if you feel like it. Quite understandable to want to keep on with a case once you've started it. Incidentally is that why you're down here in Brighton?

TEMPLE: No. My wife had a rather unpleasant experience just lately; we thought a change of air might do her good.

KELBURN: Yes, of course. Well, I'll tell you what I wanted to have a word with you about, Temple. It's rather a delicate matter. You'll treat this in confidence, of course?

TEMPLE: Yes, of course.

KELBURN: Well, I don't know whether Langdon mentioned this to you or not but … I'm afraid I'm having trouble with my wife.

TEMPLE: What kind of trouble?

KELBURN: She stays out late ... doesn't tell me where she's been, and – well – to be perfectly honest, I think she's having an affair with someone.

TEMPLE: Have you any idea who it is?

KELBURN: No, I haven't.

STEVE: Have you spoken to her about it, Mr Kelburn?

KELBURN: Yes, but she refuses to admit that there is anyone. But there is someone – I'm sure there is.

TEMPLE: Well – what do you want me to do?

KELBURN: I'd like you to make some enquiries for me, watch her, if possible. Oh, I know this isn't your usual line of country …

TEMPLE: (*Laughing*) It certainly isn't!

KELBURN: … But if I employed one of the usual agencies Linda would be onto it straight away, I'm sure she would.

TEMPLE: And you don't think she'd suspect me?

KELBURN: No, I'm positive she wouldn't. She might even confide in you. I'm convinced you're the man for this assignment, Temple.

TEMPLE: Does Mike Langdon agree with you?

KELBURN: Yes, he does.

TEMPLE: Well – I'll think about it.

KELBURN: (*Reverting to his old manner*) All right – but don't think about it too long. It's important. I won't mention a fee because the last time I mentioned money …

TEMPLE: (*Interrupting KELBURN*) I'll let you have a decision this evening. You'll be in the hotel, I take it?

KELBURN: Yes, I will. I'm dining here. Thank you, Temple.

STEVE: Mr Kelburn … Who do you think your wife is friendly with?

KELBURN: I told you, I don't know.

STEVE: But don't you suspect anyone?

KELBURN: No; she's got a large circle of friends. But according to Langdon she's been seeing rather a lot of Tony Wyman just lately, but whether he's the man or not I wouldn't know. I look forward to hearing from you, Temple.

TEMPLE: I'll see you tonight.

KELBURN: Goodbye, Mrs Temple.

STEVE: Goodbye.

The door opens and closes.

STEVE: (*Suddenly*) Paul, do you know what I think …

TEMPLE: No, darling, what do you think?

STEVE: I don't think Kelburn's worried about his wife. I think this is just an attempt to stop you investigating the murder.

TEMPLE: On the other hand, Linda is friendly with someone, remember. That's why she telephoned me, because she didn't want us to tell her husband about seeing her with Larry Cross.

STEVE: Yes, but I still don't think that's why he consulted you. For some reason or other Kelburn wants you to drop this case; if he can't get you to drop it, then he'll try and divert your attention on to something else.

TEMPLE: Meaning his wife?

STEVE: Yes.

TEMPLE: (*Thoughtfully*) M'm … could be. (*Suddenly*) Well, come along, Steve.

START FADE.

STEVE: Where are we going?

TEMPLE: Do you feel like a nice smooth ride on a roller-coaster?

STEVE: No, dear, I don't …

COMPLETE FADE.

FADE IN fairground noises.

The noise of a shooting gallery, a roller-coaster, dodgem cars, etc.

FADE the noises to the background.

STEVE: Paul, I'm exhausted! Can't we go back to the hotel?

TEMPLE: Just let's take a look over there – behind the shooting gallery.

STEVE: That's where we came in …

TEMPLE: No, that was on the other side, near the ghost train.

STEVE: Don't mention that ghost train!

FADE DOWN noises.

FADE UP noises.

STEVE: Paul, my feet are sending up an S.O.S.

TEMPLE: (*Laughing*) We shan't be long, Steve, but I don't want to leave here without exploring every … (*He stops*) By Timothy!

STEVE: What is it?

TEMPLE: (*Quietly*) Look at that sign … On the tent, near the shooting gallery …

STEVE: (*Reading*) Madame Margo – fortune teller … So that's what Mrs Fletcher meant!

TEMPLE: Yes!

STEVE: She thought you'd found out about Margo and that was the reason you'd come to Brighton …

TEMPLE: Because I'd discovered about the fortune teller?

STEVE: Yes.

TEMPLE: I think you're right, Steve. (*Tensely*) Now, listen …

Start FADE UP of fairground music.

TEMPLE: I want you to go in and have your fortune told. But I'll tell you what I want you to do …

FADE UP of fairground music.

Slow FADE DOWN of music.

FADE noises and music to the distant background.

We hear the sound of a curtain being noisily swept aside in the fortune teller's tent.

MARGO: (*Elderly; a faint Cockney accent*) I'm so sorry, madam – do come in. I was just having a cup of tea.

STEVE: I can wait.

MARGO: No, no … Please sit down, madam.

STEVE: You are Madame Margo?

MARGO: That's right dear. They all know me in Brighton. Been here for years …. Patronised by royalty.

STEVE: Royalty?

MARGO: His Royal Highness, Prince Castrola of Tian See. Nice young man, he was … But you never saw anything like his life line … Stood out like the M.1. …I had to tell him, dear … Well, I mean, he could see the break in the line himself … And sure enough, it came true only six months later … Now what sort of a reading did you want?

STEVE: I don't know. Which would you recommend?

MARGO: Looking at you, I'd say the palm, madam. Of course it's a bit more expensive, but it goes deeper – much deeper – if you know what I mean.

STEVE: Yes, you read the palm of a friend of mine and told her the most amazing story – it all came true. That's what made me so curious.

MARGO: Did I? I wonder if I remember her?

STEVE: I'm sure you would. You foretold a great tragedy in her life. And it happened, just as you said.

MARGO: (*Surprised and flattered*) Really? Of course, there's no getting away from the palm. It's all there. What happened to your friend?

STEVE: She was murdered.

MARGO: (*A change of tone; more serious*) Murdered?

STEVE: Yes. Her name was Julia Kelburn.

MARGO: Oh, yes. I think I read about the murder.

STEVE: But you don't remember Julia?

MARGO: No, I'm afraid I don't. But, of course, I see so many people, you know, especially in the height of the season.

STEVE: Yes, I suppose you do.

MARGO: Now, dear, if you'll just sit facing me … That's right …

MARGO switches on a light.

STEVE: Which hand do you want?

MARGO: Oh, both, dear … Under the light if you don't mind. That's it … (*A pause*) That's very interesting … Were you ever on the stage?

STEVE: No, I wasn't …

MARGO: You're married, and your husband's well known – famous, in fact … Got something to do with books and writing, is that right, dear …?

STEVE: Yes.

MARGO: (*After a moment*) It's an interesting hand. You travel a lot, don't you – er – Mrs …?

STEVE: Yes, we travel quite a lot.

MARGO: I can see a journey now; towards the end of the year – a sea voyage … (*Suddenly; catching her breath*) Oh … And there's danger, too, dear … You've got to be very careful; both you and your husband.

STEVE: (*A shade tense*) Why have we got to be careful?

MARGO: (*After a moment*) Because I can see an accident – a car accident …

STEVE: When is this – accident – likely to happen?

MARGO: I can't tell you. (*A pause*) It may be soon … very soon.

STEVE: Where is it going to happen?

MARGO: I don't know, but … (*She hesitates*)

STEVE: Go on …

MARGO: It seems to me your husband's driving … There's something here, in your palm … I can't tell what it is … it looks like a … dolphin.

STEVE: A dolphin? You mean a real dolphin?

MARGO: I can't tell … But watch out for it … When you see the dolphin be on your guard, dear … That's when the accident might happen …

Quick FADE IN of fairground music from the background.

FADE DOWN the music.
TEMPLE and STEVE are now walking toward their car.

FADE fairground noises and music during the following dialogue.

STEVE: … It was only when I mentioned Julia Kelburn that she seemed to be on her guard. I think she had a good idea then who I was.

TEMPLE: Yes, it sounds like it. D'you think she was expecting you?

STEVE: I don't know. The whole set-up was terribly phoney and normally I wouldn't believe a word she said, but there was a warning, Paul, about the car accident – I don't think there's any doubt about that.

TEMPLE: That's why I asked if you thought she was expecting you.

STEVE: It's difficult to say. But the thing that puzzled me is that reference to a dolphin. What did she mean – Watch out for the dolphin?

TEMPLE: I don't know. It could be a public house, I suppose, at a dangerous corner or crossroads.

STEVE: Yes, I never thought of that.

TEMPLE: Let's get back to the hotel. I don't want to be late getting over to Seadale.

STEVE: No.

TEMPLE: Tired?

STEVE: Yes – I am.

TEMPLE: Well, there's no need for you to come to Seadale, darling. I can see Fiona Scott by myself.

STEVE: Yes, of course you can.

A long pause.

STEVE: But you are not going to …

TEMPLE laughs.

FADE SCENE.

FADE IN the noise of the hotel lobby.

TEMPLE: 528, please …

The RECEPTIONIST passes TEMPLE his room key.

RECEPTIONIST: There you are, Mr Temple.

TEMPLE: Thank you.

RECEPTIONIST: Oh, and Mr Temple – Mr Kelburn left a message. He said when you came in would you care to join him in the American Bar?

TEMPLE: Thank you. Steve, here's the key … I'll be up in a few minutes.

STEVE: All right, darling.

FADE noise of the hotel lobby.

FADE IN to the background noise of the American Bar.

KELBURN: (*Calling*) Over here, Temple!

TEMPLE: (*Approaching*) Oh, hello, Kelburn! I got your message.

KELBURN: Sit down. What are you drinking?

TEMPLE: I don't think I'll have anything at the moment – thank you.

LANGDON: Won't you join me in a dry Martini?

TEMPLE: No, thank you.

KELBURN: Well – have you reached a decision about that problem, Temple?

LANGDON: Which problem is this?

KELBURN: About Linda. Mike told – I told you.

TEMPLE: Yes, I have. I'll help you, Kelburn.

KELBURN: Good!

TEMPLE: And I'll tell you why I'll help you. If, as you suggest, your wife is friendly with someone I think there's a chance that that person may be able to help me.

KELBURN: (*Puzzled*) Help you – with what?

TEMPLE: With my investigations. You see, I still intend to find out who murdered your daughter.

KELBURN: (*After a moment*) All right, go ahead. But just at the moment it's my wife I'm interested in. No one likes to be made a fool of, Temple. The moment you find out who Linda is playing around with …

TEMPLE: (*Interrupting KELBURN*) I'll let you know, Kelburn. Good night, Langdon – don't drink too many Martinis.

LANGDON: (*Amused*) I'll try not to.

FADE SCENE.

FADE IN the sound of TEMPLE's car.
TEMPLE is driving.

TEMPLE: By Timothy, this is a lonely part of the country. We haven't passed a car for ages.

STEVE: I hope we're on the right road.

TEMPLE: I expect we'll come to a signpost soon.

STEVE: By then it'll be too dark to read it.

TEMPLE: Cheer up, Steve!

STEVE: Oh, look! There's a cyclist …

TEMPLE: Where? Oh, yes – I see him …

STEVE: I think it's a parson …

The car stops.

VICAR: Oh, good evening.

TEMPLE: Good evening. We're looking for a place called Breakwater House.

VICAR: Ah, yes … Breakwater House … Now let me see … It's a little off the beaten track. Yes, I think it would be a better idea if you turned round …

TEMPLE: You mean, go back?

VICAR: That's right. You must keep a careful lookout for a turning on the left – rather a narrow lane.

TEMPLE: Have you any idea how far back it is?

VICAR: I should say very nearly a mile … it's just past a large, old-fashioned barn; you can't miss it.

STEVE: And Breakwater House is actually down the lane?

VICAR: Yes, about a quarter of a mile down the lane. There's rather a delightful arch at the entrance to the drive, with a stone dolphin at the top.

STEVE: A … dolphin …?

VICAR: Yes. Do look out for it; a beautiful piece of work; although I suppose it's rather on the dark side tonight, unfortunately. When you reach the drive go carefully … It's rather twisty, and the surface is very uneven.

TEMPLE: I'm much obliged.

VICAR: Not at all, not at all. I'm sure you won't have any trouble finding it. Goodnight.

STEVE: Goodnight.

TEMPLE: Goodnight – and thank you.

STEVE: Is there room to turn the car here?

TEMPLE: Yes, I think so.

STEVE: I should use that gateway, darling …

TEMPLE: Tell me if there's anything coming …

STEVE: All clear …

The car turns and continues back down the lane.

STEVE: (*After a moment*) Paul …

TEMPLE: Yes?

STEVE: You heard what he said about …

TEMPLE: Yes, I heard. Don't worry, darling; I'll take care …

FADE SCENE.

FADE back the noise of the car.

STEVE: We must be coming to the end of the lane …

TEMPLE: Yes, there's the gateway … By Timothy, it's a pretty formidable gate!

The car stops.

STEVE: It's wrought iron …

TEMPLE: Yes. Looks new to me …

STEVE: Just as well it's open – we'd have had a job to open it ourselves.

TEMPLE: Yes.

STEVE: There's the arch the vicar mentioned.

TEMPLE: Yes. Where's the torch? Ah, here it is … Let's have the window open.

A pause whilst TEMPLE winds down the car window.

TEMPLE: Yes – there's the dolphin … I'll shine the torch on it, Steve – so you can see it …

STEVE: Oh, yes – I can see it now … Take it easy up the drive, darling.

The car proceeds through the gate and up the drive.

STEVE: (*After a pause*) Slowly, Paul …

TEMPLE: Can't go much slower than this, Steve. I shouldn't think this drive has ever been repaired …

STEVE: We're coming to a sharp bend, I think … goes round to the left …

TEMPLE: This road's more suited to horses than …

TEMPLE brakes quickly.

The car stops suddenly.

STEVE: (*Alarmed*) What is it?

TEMPLE: Look! There's a rope – a steel rope – right across the drive!

The car door opens.

TEMPLE and STEVE get out of the car.

STEVE: Why are those bricks fastened to it?

TEMPLE and STEVE are now standing on the drive.

TEMPLE: They'd have smashed the windscreen to bits if we'd run into them at a good speed. Fortunately, I was crawling.

STEVE: The rope's fastened to a tree over there …

TEMPLE: (*Away from STEVE*) And to the top of a fence on this side … Hold on …

STEVE: What are you doing?

TEMPLE: I'm trying to unfasten it … No, it's no use … somebody's made quite a job of this.

STEVE: What are we going to do?

TEMPLE: Well, we can't take the car further down the drive because of the rope. I suppose we'd better go back to the hotel.

STEVE: Unless – we walk up to the house … That's what you'd like to do, isn't it?

TEMPLE: Yes. But if you're worried, Steve …

STEVE: No, I'm all right. Let's take a look at the house.

TEMPLE: Are you sure?

STEVE: Yes, I'm sure. Give me your arm, darling.

FADE UP of footsteps.

FADE the footsteps out, then in again.

STEVE: … You know, that fortune teller must have known we were coming here …

TEMPLE: – And what's more important, she knew there'd be an attempt to stop us.

STEVE: You mean – she knew about the rope?

TEMPLE: I don't know whether she knew about that, but she certainly knew something was going to happen.

STEVE: I wish I'd known about the state of the drive – I'd have worn some sensible shoes.

TEMPLE: I didn't know you'd got any.

STEVE: (*Laughing*) You know perfectly well what I mean.

TEMPLE: There's the house!

STEVE: Yes … (*A pause*) It's so dark, Paul – no light anywhere …

TEMPLE: Perhaps there are some at the back of the house …

STEVE: (*Her thoughts elsewhere*) Yes …

TEMPLE: What is it, Steve?

STEVE: Listen …

In the distant background can be heard the sound of the sea.

TEMPLE: It's the sea you can hear – it can't be far away.

STEVE: That's probably why they call it Breakwater House.

TEMPLE: Yes. Come along, Steve, let's take a look.

FADE UP the sound of footsteps.

FADE footsteps completely.

FADE IN of TEMPLE's voice.

TEMPLE: The place seems derelict …

STEVE: Yes, there's no one living here … But thank goodness it's not too dark …

TEMPLE: It's lighter away from the trees …

STEVE: Paul, the French window's open.

TEMPLE: Let's take a look …

A pause.

STEVE: It's open all right – nearly falling to pieces …

TEMPLE: Let's take a look inside … Give me your hand …

TEMPLE pushes open the French window and they enter the house.

FADE IN an echo.

STEVE: Paul, the house seems to be empty … There's no furniture at all.

TEMPLE: Not even a carpet …

STEVE: And just look at the wallpaper …

TEMPLE opens a door.

TEMPLE: This isn't any better either. By Timothy, just look at the place!

WYMAN: (*From upstairs; faintly*) Help … help!

STEVE: (*Quickly*) What was that?

TEMPLE: It came from upstairs … It sounded like a man's voice …

WYMAN: (*Calling; faintly*) Mr Temple, I'm upstairs … Help!!

STEVE: Paul, that sounds like Tony Wyman!

TEMPLE: Yes, it does …

WYMAN: (*Desperately; faint*) Mr Temple, help me … I'm upstairs!!

STEVE: It <u>is</u> Tony Wyman!

TEMPLE: Let's go upstairs … Keep hold of my arm …

FADE SCENE.

FADE UP of footsteps in a corridor.

STEVE: Where do you think the voice was coming from?

TEMPLE: I don't know … (*Calling*) Wyman! Tony, where are you?

A pause.

STEVE: There are so many rooms up here – must be a dozen or more …

TEMPLE: Let's have a look in here.

TEMPLE opens a door.

They enter the room.

A pause.

STEVE: What an enormous bedroom!

TEMPLE: By Timothy, it's as big as Hyde Park!

STEVE: He's obviously not in here.

TEMPLE: No … Is that a dressing room over there, Steve, or …

STEVE: (*Suddenly*) Paul … Someone's closing the door!

TEMPLE rushes towards the door but he is too late.

The door slams.

A lock clicks.

TEMPLE: Blast … (*Trying the door*) It's locked … Did you see who it was?

STEVE: No, I only saw the door move!

TEMPLE: What a stupid fool! I ought to have realised that someone was watching us!

TEMPLE bangs on the door.

TEMPLE: Open this door! Open this door!

STEVE: (*Anxiously*) Paul, it's pretty solid, isn't it? …

TEMPLE tries to force the door.

TEMPLE: Yes, it is …

STEVE: Do you think it was Tony Wyman we heard, and he deliberately got us upstairs so that he could …

TEMPLE: Wait a minute!

A slight pause.

STEVE: What is it, Paul?

TEMPLE: (*After a moment*) Do you smell petrol?

STEVE: (*Suddenly*) Yes! You're right … There is a smell of petrol and something burning …

TEMPLE: Someone's started a fire, Steve!

STEVE: (*Alarmed*) Oh, Paul!

TEMPLE throws his weight against the door again.

TEMPLE: We'll have to get this door open!

FADE IN the noise of the fire.

FADE UP the noise as the fire gradually increases.

END OF EPISODE FIVE

EPISODE SIX

MAINLY ABOUT WYMAN

OPEN TO: *FADE IN of STEVE's voice.*

STEVE: (*Suddenly*) Paul! You're right … There is a smell of petrol and something burning …

TEMPLE: Someone's started a fire, Steve!

STEVE: (*Alarmed*) Oh, Paul!

TEMPLE throws his weight against the door again.

TEMPLE: We'll have to get this door open!

TEMPLE continues to throw his weight against the door.

TEMPLE: (*Breathlessly*) It's no use I'm afraid …

STEVE: (*From the background*) Could we get out of this window?

TEMPLE: It's a good height from the ground. Is there anything underneath?

STEVE: No.

TEMPLE: Then we can't get out that way.

STEVE: Well, what are we going to do?

TEMPLE: Try the door again.

TEMPLE shakes the door again.

TEMPLE: If there were only some way of forcing the lock.

STEVE: Paul! There's a set of fire-irons over here … It's about the only bit of furniture in the room …

TEMPLE: Let me see …

STEVE: The poker … Couldn't you use it to force the door?

TEMPLE: It's certainly worth trying! Hold the torch, Steve. Now, if I can just get the end wedged into the mortice … Keep the torch steady, Steve.

STEVE: Sorry.

TEMPLE starts trying to force the lock with the poker.

TEMPLE: That's it … Let's hope the poker doesn't bend or snap …

The wood begins to splinter.

TEMPLE: I think it's going to work.

The wood continues to crack.

TEMPLE: Got it!

STEVE: Oh, good! Quickly, Paul, let's …

TEMPLE: Wait, Steve! Get behind the door … There may be someone outside. Now, steady – I'm going to open the door …

TEMPLE pushes open the door.

STEVE begins to cough.

STEVE: Oh! The smoke!

TEMPLE: (*Also coughing*) It's all right, there's no one there. Wait a second, to get our bearings.

STEVE: The staircase is on fire; we'll never get out that way!

WYMAN: (*Off*) Help! Help me!

STEVE: What was that?

TEMPLE: It's that voice again. I'm sure …

WYMAN: (*Off*) Help! Mr Temple – I'm in one of the rooms on this landing … Help me!

STEVE: It's Wyman, Paul! He's along this corridor somewhere …

TEMPLE: Careful, Steve … (*Coughing*) This confounded smoke …

WYMAN: (*Louder*) Temple, can you hear me? …

TEMPLE: I think he's in that room on the left … Keep behind me, Steve …

STEVE: Yes, all right.

TEMPLE pushes a door open.

TEMPLE: Anyone in here?

WYMAN: (*In the background; gasping for breath; distressed*) Temple, please come and help me …

STEVE: Paul, the torch … He's over in that corner …

TEMPLE: Wyman! What on earth are you doing here?

STEVE: He's tied to the chair … Oh, just look at …

TEMPLE: By Timothy, he'd had the same treatment as Ted Angus, by the look of things! Quickly, Steve, help me with these ropes … No, you hold the torch – I'll do it. Tony, try and lift your right arm so that we can …

STEVE: He's passed out! Look, they tried to gag him, Paul, but he's loosened it …

TEMPLE: We'll have to be quick, Steve.

STEVE: We can't leave him, Paul …

TEMPLE: No, of course not. As soon as I've untied this rope we'll try to get him downstairs.

STEVE: We'll never get him down the main staircase. You saw what it was like.

WYMAN: (*Dazed; semi-conscious*) Help me … Temple, don't let them …

TEMPLE: We are helping you, Tony … We're doing the best we can; but I can't get this … confounded rope … undone …

WYMAN groans.

TEMPLE: Wait a minute! … That's done it! That's cleared the rope …

STEVE: He's in a very bad way, I'm afraid.

TEMPLE: He certainly is.

WYMAN: (*Dazed*) Temple, there's a stone staircase at the back of the house … I think that's the best … way …

TEMPLE: All right, Tony. Show us where it is … Help me to lift him across my shoulder, Steve … That's it; have you got the torch?

TEMPLE lifts WYMAN from the chair.

STEVE: Yes. Are you sure you can manage, Paul?

TEMPLE: Yes – don't worry about me. Easy now … Hold on, Tony …

FADE UP the sound of the fire.

FADE the noises of the fire to the background.

TEMPLE: (*Coughing*) We'll soon be there, Tony … Hang on …

STEVE: This must be the door …

TEMPLE: Careful how you open it, Steve – stand behind it …

The door is opened.

STEVE: Yes, this is the stone staircase …

TEMPLE: You go first, Steve, and light the way.

STEVE: Yes, all right.

The sound of the fire recedes.

STEVE: Careful – they're rather narrow.

TEMPLE: I'll manage.

STEVE: There's a bend half way down.

TEMPLE: (*Breathing hard*) Yes, all right …

STEVE: … Can you manage, Paul?

TEMPLE: Yes, I can manage, but the poor devil's passed out again … We must get out into the open as quickly as we can …

TEMPLE painfully descends several stairs.

STEVE: … Can you see?

TEMPLE: Yes, I'm all right.

STEVE: Along here, Paul … I've found the door.

TEMPLE: Is it locked?

STEVE: No … only bolted … but I can manage it …

STEVE draws the bolts on the door.

STEVE: That's it …

A heavy door opens.

TEMPLE: (*Approaching; breathing hard*) Thank God for some fresh air …

STEVE: Can you put him down for a minute?

TEMPLE: Yes; I'll put him on the step.

TEMPLE puts WYMAN down on the step.

TONY is unconscious: moaning.

TEMPLE: All right, Tony. There's no need to worry – you're safe now. (*To STEVE*) We'll have to get him away from the building as soon as we can. The whole place is liable to collapse.

STEVE: I think we should get him to a doctor, Paul.

TEMPLE: That's easier said than done.

STEVE: Can't you feel the heat?

TEMPLE: Yes … I suppose we'd better move him … (*To WYMAN*) Tony, d'you think you can walk a few steps? … We've got to get away from the building …

WYMAN: (*Dazed; confused*) They're going to set the place on fire, Temple. You'll have to try and …

TEMPLE: Tony, listen! I want you to try and walk a few steps … put your arm over my shoulder – that's it …

STEVE: Quick, darling …

TEMPLE: Now off we go … Gently does it.

FADE UP the noise of the fire.

STEVE: Which way, Paul?

TEMPLE: To the right – that's where we left the car …

FADE IN the noise of the fire.

FADE DOWN the noise of the fire to the background.

STEVE: Here's an old garden seat …

TEMPLE: Yes, this'll do … Gently now … Easy … That's it …

WYMAN: (*Rambling*) They double-crossed me; they said that they were going to … (*His voice fades away*)

STEVE: It looks as if he's had a pretty nasty bang on the head.

TEMPLE: Yes. Can you stay with him, Steve, while I go for a doctor? There may be a phone box fairly near – or maybe I can telephone from one of the farms …

STEVE: Can't we get him to the car?

TEMPLE: No, I don't think so. It's the best part of half a mile down the drive.

STEVE: Yes, all right, Paul, I'll stay with him.

WYMAN: Temple …

TEMPLE: Yes, Tony? What is it?

WYMAN: You … you … Temple …

TEMPLE: Yes?

WYMAN: I've got to tell you … something …

TEMPLE: Yes, go on, Tony …

WYMAN: It's about – about Kelburn …

TEMPLE: Julia Kelburn?

WYMAN: No. No … Kelburn … You know … Kelburn.

TEMPLE: Yes, I know Kelburn. What about him?

WYMAN: … Kelburn … the fence … Don't let him get near … don't let him … touch … (*Weakly*) … the fence … (*His voice fades away*)

STEVE: He's passed out again.

TEMPLE: Yes. (*After a moment*) Steve, I think you'd better come with me. We obviously can't do anything for him until we get a doctor.

STEVE: (*Relieved*) Yes, all right.

TEMPLE: Help me lift his feet … (*After a pause*) I wish we'd got something to put under his head.

STEVE: Take my raincoat. I don't need it.

TEMPLE: Yes, all right …

STEVE takes off her coat and puts it under WYMAN's head.

STEVE: There … I think he's a little more comfortable anyway.

TEMPLE: Yes, I think he'll be all right for the time being. Have you got the torch?

STEVE: Yes, I've got it.

TEMPLE: Come on then, darling – this way …

FADE IN of footsteps on gravel.

FADE OUT of the footsteps.

STEVE: The fire seemed to start so quickly …

TEMPLE: It was the petrol. By Timothy, just look at it, Steve.

STEVE: Paul, what was Tony Wyman doing there?

TEMPLE: That's the biggest mystery of all … but somebody obviously resented his being there and gave the poor devil a heavy beating. I didn't like the look of him, Steve. I hope we can get a doctor, quickly.

STEVE: We still haven't seen Fiona Scott. I'm beginning to wonder if there is such a person.

TEMPLE: She was probably acting on instructions. Shine the torch, Steve … Ah, here's the rope – and the car …

STEVE: At last! Golly, shall I be glad to get these shoes off!

TEMPLE: Well, we shouldn't be long now …

The car doors open.

STEVE: You'll have to be careful backing the car down to the gates.

TEMPLE: I think I can manage.

The doors shut.

STEVE: Shall I get out and guide you?

TEMPLE: No, stay where you are for the present, Steve.

We hear the sound of the self-starter; the car doesn't start.

TEMPLE: That's funny … It should start on a warm night like this …

TEMPLE presses the starter again: the car still doesn't start.

TEMPLE: I've never had this trouble before.

The car door opens.

STEVE: What are you going to do?

TEMPLE: (*Outside the car*) Take a look under the bonnet. Pass me the torch, Steve.

STEVE: Here you are.

TEMPLE: Thanks …

Pause.

We hear the sound of the car bonnet being opened.

TEMPLE: Blast!

STEVE: What is it, darling?

TEMPLE: Someone's taken the rotor-arm. The car's useless.

STEVE: Are you sure?

TEMPLE: I'm positive.

STEVE: But what are we going to do?

TEMPLE: There's only one thing we <u>can</u> do. We'll have to walk to the road in the hope of finding somebody.

STEVE: Are you sure the car's hopeless?

TEMPLE: (*Irritated*) I'm positive … Come on, we'll have to walk down to the gate …

FADE SCENE.

FADE IN of footsteps again.

STEVE: How much longer?

TEMPLE: We'll soon be at the end of the drive.

STEVE: (*After a moment*) Paul …

TEMPLE: Yes?

STEVE: What's that place, over there?

TEMPLE: Where?

STEVE: Over on your left … Amongst the trees … It looks like a hut or something …

TEMPLE: Yes, it does. (*Curious*) Let's take a look at it …

FADE UP of the footsteps.

We hear the sound of branches being pushed aside.

FADE IN the noise of a small dynamo.

STEVE: What is this place?

TEMPLE: Well – it certainly isn't a hut or anything like that. Do you hear that noise?

STEVE: Yes. It's a motor of some kind.

TEMPLE: It's a dynamo. This is a small powerhouse, that's what it is. It must supply the current for the main building.

STEVE: You mean Breakwater House?

TEMPLE: Yes … There's a crack in the door … Let's see if we can see anything … Give me the torch, please.

STEVE: (*After a pause*) Well?

TEMPLE: … There's a lot of switches and things … Yes, that's what it is – a power-house. (*Dismissing the matter*) Come on, Steve – let's get back to the drive …

FADE DOWN the noise of the dynamo.

FADE IN of the footsteps again.

TEMPLE: I should think the fire is bound to attract attention by now.

STEVE: Seems to be dying down a bit.

TEMPLE: Are you all right, Steve?

STEVE: Well, I'll make it, if that's what you mean; but the next time I see a pair of shoes with stiletto … (*She stops*)

TEMPLE: What is it?

STEVE: Paul, look! The gates are closed … the wrought iron gates …

TEMPLE: (*Surprised*) By Timothy, so they are! Come on.

More footsteps: TEMPLE and STEVE reach the gate.

STEVE: Look at the padlock …

TEMPLE: That's very odd … a hefty padlock and chain …

STEVE: Now what do we do?

TEMPLE: I suppose I could try and climb over and …

STEVE: Oh, no, Paul! You couldn't possibly …

TEMPLE: (*Thoughtfully*) I must say, I can't see the point of this – unless it's just a delaying action. There must be some way out.

STEVE: What's on your side of the gate?

TEMPLE: A mesh wire fence. What about yours?

STEVE: The same. It looks fairly new – and quite strong.

TEMPLE: There must be a gap somewhere. Let's walk round and see if we can find …

STEVE: Paul! There's a car coming!

In the distant background a car can be heard approaching.

TEMPLE: Where?

STEVE: I saw the headlights catch the top of the trees …

A pause.

The sound of the car is heard again.

TEMPLE: Oh, yes. It seems to be coming up to the gates …

A pause.

The car draws level with the gates and stops.

STEVE: I expect it's someone who saw the fire.

The car doors slam.

TEMPLE: Hello, there!

LANGDON: (*Approaching*) Hello, Temple! I'm sorry we're late …

TEMPLE: (*Puzzled*) Why, hello, Langdon …

STEVE: (*Quietly*) Paul, Kelburn's there too.

KELBURN: Good evening, Temple. I'm sorry we're late but we had a devil of a job finding this place. Why on earth did you ask us to meet you here?

TEMPLE: I – asked – you – to meet me here?

KELBURN: Yes.

TEMPLE: When?

KELBURN: What do you mean – when? You sent me a note just as I was finishing dinner.

TEMPLE: And the note said …?

KELBURN: (*Irritated*) The note asked me to meet you here – tonight. It said you had some information for me about my wife – although why in heaven's name you should ask me to meet you at a God-forsaken place like this, I can't imagine!

TEMPLE: Kelburn, I didn't send that note – I didn't ask you to meet me here …

KELBURN: (*Surprised*) You didn't?

TEMPLE: No …

KELBURN: Then who on earth did?

LANGDON: Say, wait a minute! What's going on up the hill there? Is it a fire, Temple?

TEMPLE: Yes; and Tony Wyman's very badly hurt – he needs a doctor. It's urgent.

KELBURN: Tony Wyman – is he here?

STEVE: Yes …

KELBURN: (*Suspiciously*) Is that what you were going to tell me, Temple? That you'd discovered that Tony Wyman and my wife were having …

TEMPLE: I wasn't going to tell you anything! I've already told you, I didn't send that note …

KELBURN: Well, somebody did!

STEVE: Look, Mr Kelburn – Wyman's very seriously ill! He needs a doctor!

LANGDON: Where is he, Mrs Temple?

STEVE: He's up near the house – we had to leave him there.

LANGDON: I'll drive back into the village. Will you stay here with Mr and Mrs Temple, sir?

KELBURN: Yes, all right – but don't be long, Langdon.

TEMPLE: And phone the Fire Brigade …

LANGDON: Yes. I will.

LANGDON returns to his car.

During the following dialogue we hear the car drive away.

KELBURN: Can I join you, Temple, or is this gate locked?

TEMPLE: It's locked.

KELBURN: There must be a way through … Let's take a look at the fence …

TEMPLE: We've already looked at the fence …

KELBURN: (*Off*) Temple, come over here … It seems to sag just along there. Maybe if we lifted the wire I could crawl through.

TEMPLE: Yes, all right …

STEVE: (*Suddenly; alarmed*) Paul – wait!

TEMPLE: (*Turning*) What is it, Steve?

STEVE: Look, Paul! Here, where I'm shining the torch …

TEMPLE: A dead squirrel? It's been caught in the wire, by the look of things.

STEVE: Yes, but that wouldn't have killed it! Look at its coat – it's all scorched …

TEMPLE: (*Quickly*) Good Lord! Of course – it's been electrocuted! That means that the fence must be … (*Suddenly; shouting*) Don't touch that fence, Kelburn!

STEVE: Don't touch it, Mr Kelburn!!!!

KELBURN: Phew! That was a near thing, Temple. I was just going to lift it up …

STEVE: (*Quickly*) Paul, that's what Wyman meant – he must have known Mr Kelburn was coming here. He told us to warn him …

KELBURN: What do you mean, Mrs Temple?

STEVE: Tony Wyman told us to warn you about the fence. He said: Don't let Kelburn touch it …

KELBURN: (*Puzzled*) Wyman said that?

STEVE: Yes.

KELBURN: But how did Wyman know I was coming here? Did you tell him I was coming, Temple?

TEMPLE: I've told you, I <u>didn't know</u> you were coming!

KELBURN: Yes, of course. (*Thoughtfully*) I wonder if it was Wyman that sent that note?

TEMPLE: But if he sent the note, then obviously it was a trap to get you here.

KELBURN: That's what I mean!

TEMPLE: Then why did he warn you about the fence?

FADE IN of music.

FADE DOWN of music.

FADE IN of TEMPLE's voice.

TEMPLE: … Finally, we went back to the power-house and switched off the current …

FORBES: You had quite a night, Temple!

TEMPLE: We certainly did. Unfortunately, I still haven't been able to contact Miss Scott.

FORBES: That doesn't surprise me, after what happened.

TEMPLE: Which reminds me – how did you find her phone number?

FORBES: The Brighton police found it for us.

RAINE: Incidentally, Temple, the house is owned by some people called Delaware, who've been living in California for the past two years. They couldn't get the price they wanted for it, so it's been lying empty.

TEMPLE: I see.

FORBES: The thing that puzzles me, Temple, is why Tony Wyman went to the house. It's obvious he went there to meet someone – but who was it?

TEMPLE: I don't know, Sir Graham.

RAINE: Could it have been you, Temple?

TEMPLE: What do you mean, Superintendent?

RAINE: Well, from what you've told us, he obviously expected you. He called out to you – by name.

TEMPLE: Yes; he expected me all right. But that doesn't necessarily mean that's why he went to the house in the first place.

RAINE: I don't know; perhaps Kelburn wasn't the only person who received a note with your name on it.

FORBES: Yes, that's certainly a point, Raine. Incidentally, did you see the note, Temple?

TEMPLE: Yes; it was certainly signed with my name, but it wasn't my signature.

FORBES: I suppose you couldn't blame Kelburn for thinking it was. He wouldn't know your writing.

TEMPLE: No. Neither do I know his – or Langdon's.

FORBES: You mean …?

TEMPLE: It could have been written by either of them, just to explain away their presence at the house.

FORBES: Yes, that's true.

TEMPLE: Incidentally, what was the latest report on Wyman?

RAINE: Not very healthy, I'm afraid. They're worried about a heart condition.

FORBES: Hardly surprising when you consider he's had two attempts on his life in less than a week.

There is a knock and the door opens.

BURTON: May I come in, Sir Graham?

FORBES: Ah, yes! Come along in, Burton. Temple, this is Detective-Inspector Burton; Brighton C.I.D.

TEMPLE: Good morning, Inspector.

BURTON: Good morning, Mr Temple. I'm very pleased to meet you, sir.

RAINE: Any news of Fiona Scott?

BURTON: No trace of her, Superintendent. She left her digs after getting Mr Temple's phone call and she's simply vanished. We're still making enquiries.

BURTON puts an envelope down on the table.

BURTON: However, I thought this might interest you, sir.

FORBES: What is it?

BURTON: It's a report on some of the fingerprints we found at Breakwater House. One set quite obviously belongs to a man called Harris – Midge Harris. You remember Midge Harris, Superintendent – he was arrested …

FORBES: (*Surprised*) Midge Harris? Surely he's in Brixton at the moment?

RAINE: That's right, sir. He's awaiting trial. We pulled him in about three weeks ago – he was mixed up in the Regent Street smash-and-grab.

BURTON: That's the one where the loot's still missing?

FORBES: That's right, Inspector. Silver plate and jewellery – about two hundred and fifty thousand pounds' worth.

TEMPLE: But I remember Midge Harris. Short, red-haired little chap. He was one of the small-fry in that safe deposit affair; I put in a word for him.

FORBES: Yes; that's the chap.

TEMPLE: You say you picked him up about three weeks ago?

FORBES: Yes, that's right. You were in America, Temple. There was a smash-and-grab in Regent Street. We picked up Harris, and four witnesses – including the jeweller – identified him.

TEMPLE: I see. Then obviously he must have been in Breakwater House some time ago.

BURTON: Well, certainly before he was picked up – yes.

TEMPLE: Sir Graham, do you think I could have a word with Midge?

FORBES: Well – I don't see why not, if you think it'll serve any useful purpose.

RAINE: You're wasting your time, Mr Temple.

TEMPLE: Why do you say that?

RAINE: Midge won't talk – even if he knows anything. I had six hours with him the day he was arrested. He wouldn't tell me who his confederates were, where the stuff was hidden, or anything. He just wouldn't talk.

The telephone rings.

TEMPLE: I'd still like to see him, Superintendent.

FORBES lifts the telephone receiver.

FORBES: (*On the phone*) Hello ... Yes, speaking ... Just a moment, please ... (*To BURTON*) It's for you, Inspector.

BURTON: Thank you, sir. (*On the phone*) Hello? ... Yes ... Oh, hello, Sergeant ... When did it happen? ... I see ... Well, you know what to do – the usual drill ... Thank you for ringing.

BURTON replaces the receiver.

RAINE: What is it, Burton?

BURTON: Bad news I'm afraid, sir. Tony Wyman's dead. He died this morning without regaining consciousness ...

FADE SCENE.

FADE IN TEMPLE inserting his key in the door lock.

The door opens.

STEVE: (*Off*) Is that you, Paul?

TEMPLE: Where are you, Steve?

STEVE: (*Off*) In the drawing room.

TEMPLE takes off his coat.

TEMPLE: Pour me a glass of sherry, darling. I've had rather a hectic morning.

TEMPLE enters the drawing room.

STEVE: Is there any news of Tony Wyman?

TEMPLE: Yes, I'm afraid there is, Steve.

STEVE: He's dead?

TEMPLE: You don't sound very surprised.

STEVE: I could see he was in a pretty bad way when they put him in the ambulance.

TEMPLE: Yes, it's a pity we had to leave him on that seat. He must have been there over an hour. Might have just made all the difference.

STEVE: But what else could we do?

TEMPLE: I don't know, but I wish we could have revived him. Apart from anything else, there were so many things he could have told us.

STEVE: Yes; it would have been a great help to know what he was doing there. What does Sir Graham think?

TEMPLE: He's just as puzzled as we are.

STEVE: Paul, do you think Fiona Scott arranged to see Tony at Breakwater House?

TEMPLE: I don't know; it's possible, I suppose. I certainly think he had an appointment with someone.

STEVE: (*Significantly*) It could have been Kelburn.

TEMPLE: Yes, it could have been.

STEVE: Talking of Kelburn – his wife called round this morning.

TEMPLE: (*Surprised*) Linda? When was this?

STEVE: Just after you left.

TEMPLE: Go on, Steve – what happened?

STEVE: Well, it was about a quarter to eleven.

START FADE.

STEVE: Charlie had popped out to do some shopping. I was in your dressing room when the bell rang and it was two or three minutes before I answered it …

FADE BACK to a ringing doorbell.

After a pause the front door is opened.

STEVE: (*A shade breathless*) Why, Linda!

LINDA: Hello, Steve. May I come in?

STEVE: Yes, of course.

The front door closes.

STEVE: In here …

The drawing room door opens.

LINDA: (*Faintly nervous*) I happened to be passing, and I thought perhaps I … (*She stops; changes her mind*) No, that's not true. Steve, I want a word with your husband. I realise he probably hates being interrupted at work but …

STEVE: I'm sorry, but he's out, Linda – he's at Scotland Yard.

LINDA: (*Disappointed*) Oh. What time will he be back – do you know?

STEVE: No, I'm afraid I don't. It may not be until this evening.

LINDA: Oh dear. You – you've been away, haven't you?

STEVE: Yes, we went down to Brighton for a few days.

LINDA: Yes, I know – I telephoned. I – I left a message.

STEVE: We got the message, Linda – the same day. There was really nothing to worry about.

LINDA: (*Relieved*) Oh … Oh, good …

STEVE: I gather there's some trouble between you and your husband?

LINDA: That's putting it mildly. Things have been impossible just lately – quite impossible. He's so jealous, it just isn't true! Darling, may I have a cigarette?

STEVE: Yes, of course. There's some over there. Help yourself.

LINDA takes a cigarette and lights it.

LINDA: He's always imagining I'm having an affair with someone – with younger men.

STEVE: Do you have affairs with younger men, Linda?

LINDA: Now don't be idiotic! What do you take me for? George gives me everything I want. Why should I stick my neck out like that?

STEVE: Well, we did see you in a sports car with Larry Cross one evening.

LINDA: Larry Cross?

STEVE: Dr Benkaray's secretary. Paul and I saw you a couple of nights ago. The two of you were in a cream sports car …

LINDA: (*Puzzled*) A cream sports …? Yes, of course! I remember now! Oh, so his name's Cross, is it? I didn't know. I knew he was the doctor's secretary, of course, otherwise I wouldn't have accepted a lift from him.

STEVE: He was just – giving you a lift?

LINDA: That's right. I'd been to the cinema in Curzon Street and couldn't get a taxi. Suddenly he popped up and offered me a lift. I was delighted.

STEVE: But you didn't know who he was?

LINDA: I've told you, I knew he was the doctor's secretary but I didn't know his name.

STEVE: How did you know he was Dr Benkaray's secretary, then?

LINDA: Because I've been to see the doctor myself. This man – Larry Cross, did you say his name was? – makes the appointments.

STEVE: Why did you go and see Dr Benkaray, Linda?

LINDA: I say, what is this – an inquisition? If you must know, I was nervy – on edge – couldn't sleep. It's really not surprising after all I've been through just lately.

STEVE: Did you know that Julia consulted Dr Benkaray?

LINDA: (*Hesitating*) Yes – and that's how I came to go there myself. Julia raved about her.

STEVE: What was she treating Julia for – do you know?

LINDA: (*After a moment*) Yes; I know, but I swore I wouldn't … Well, I suppose now that Julia's dead there's no reason why you shouldn't know. Julia was taking drugs. Dr Benkaray was trying to cure her of the habit.

STEVE: I see. Linda, tell me: is it just since Julia died that things have become difficult between you and your husband?

LINDA: They've come to the surface more, if that's what you mean. Things have been particularly difficult, I suppose, since Mike Langdon arrived. I sometimes wonder if he puts ideas into George's head.

STEVE: Why should he do that?

LINDA: Well – he's seen me at The Hide and Seek once or twice, talking to Tony Wyman. By the way, I read about Tony this morning. Is he badly hurt?

STEVE: Yes, I'm afraid he is.

LINDA: Was he conscious when you found him?

STEVE: No, he'd been badly beaten up – he was unconscious most of the time. It was hopeless to try and question him, if that's what you mean.

LINDA: I didn't mean anything in particular. I – I just wondered how he was.

STEVE: Is that what you wanted to see Paul about – Tony Wyman?

LINDA: No, no, it was something quite different. I've already told you most of it.

STEVE: Then why not tell me the rest?

LINDA: It's just this, Steve: I happened to overhear a conversation between my husband and Mike Langdon. Mike was telling George that your husband was the best man to get the evidence for him.

STEVE: What evidence?

LINDA: Against me – for the divorce.

STEVE: (*Laughing*) But Paul doesn't go in for that sort of thing – you must know that!

LINDA: George has a way of persuading people.

STEVE: You mean – money?

LINDA: Yes.

START FADE.

STEVE: Well, don't worry, Linda – it would take more than money to persuade my husband to do something he doesn't want to do. Now, would you like a cup of coffee?

LINDA: Yes, I'd love one, Steve.

COMPLETE FADE.

FADE IN of TEMPLE's voice.

TEMPLE: … And what time did she leave?

STEVE: About twelve. She's a pretty complicated character, Paul. She always was – even in the old days.

TEMPLE: Is it a case of being complicated or simply – Linda first and the rest nowhere?

STEVE: She's certainly self-centred, but then, I should imagine her husband is too, from what I've seen of him.

TEMPLE: Yes. Why do you think she came here this morning?

STEVE: I think she wanted to know if Tony Wyman had told us anything.

TEMPLE: Yes, that's exactly what I thought. (*Suddenly*) What time are we having lunch?

STEVE: Just after one. Why – have you got an appointment?

TEMPLE: Yes, I'm seeing Ken Sinclair at three o'clock.

STEVE: Ken Sinclair? You mean the crime reporter on the Evening World?

TEMPLE: That's right.

STEVE: What are you seeing him about?

TEMPLE: Well, I'm interviewing a man called Midge Harris tomorrow afternoon and I think Ken may know something about him. Apparently Harris was arrested three weeks ago, but last night the Brighton police found several of his fingerprints at Breakwater House.

STEVE: But surely that's not possible; if Harris is in prison …

TEMPLE: The prints are old ones. Midge was obviously at Breakwater House some time ago.

STEVE: I see. Have the police questioned this man?

TEMPLE: Yes, but they can't get anywhere with him – he won't talk. That's why I'm seeing him.

STEVE: Well, what makes you think he'll talk to you?

TEMPLE: Once, a long time ago, I did him a favour. Besides, all the nice people talk to me – you know that, darling!

START FADE.

STEVE: (*Laughing*) Come along, let's have lunch!

COMPLETE FADE.

FADE IN to background chatter and noise of a small Fleet Street public house.

KEN: Hello, Temple!

TEMPLE: Hello, Ken!

KEN: It's good to see you!

TEMPLE: Nice of you to spare me half an hour.

KEN: Did you have a nice trip?

TEMPLE: Nice trip?

KEN: To the States.

TEMPLE: Oh, yes – yes, it was most exciting.

WAITER: Can I get you a drink, sir?

TEMPLE: I'd like a Scotch and soda, please. Ken, what are you drinking?

KEN: No; I'm fine, thanks. Well – what's it all about? What can I do for you?

TEMPLE: Ken, while I was in America there was a smash-and-grab in Regent Street. The police arrested a man called Midge Harris.

KEN: That's right.

TEMPLE: Give me the low-down. What exactly happened?

KEN: Well, whoever did the job got away with jewellery to the value of about a quarter of a million. Midge was in on it – there's no doubt about that, he was identified – but Midge was just one of the boys. He certainly wasn't the brains behind the set-up. You know Midge

Harris, he's as clever as paint, but he's small-time.

TEMPLE: Yes. Who do you think was behind it?

KEN: Why, this character they call The Fence. I don't think there's any doubt he was behind the operation. Let's face it, he's behind most of the crimes these days.

TEMPLE: (*Thoughtfully*) Yes …

KEN: You see, the whole point is – the boys know that the moment they've pulled a job the stuff will be taken off their hands and they'll be paid good money for it.

TEMPLE: But there's nothing new about this, surely – there have always been fences?

KEN: Yes, but not one like this: this chap's really got things organised. He operates on an international scale – will handle anything. But why are you interested in Midge Harris and The Fence? I thought you were investigating the Kelburn murder?

TEMPLE: I am.

KEN: You think there's a connection?

TEMPLE: There could be. Ken, tell me about Midge Harris. What's he been doing during the past two or three years?

KEN: He had a job with a transport firm for a time, but it was only a cover for his more nefarious activities; I'm sure of that. He's been living with a girl called Sally Jackson. Strange girl – she used to be an art student, then she started a ladies' hairdressers in Camden Town.

TEMPLE: Sally Jackson?

START FADE.

KEN: Yes.

TEMPLE: How long have they been together?

KEN: About three or four years. I don't quite know what she saw in Midge. She was a very much better class of person than he was …

COMPLETE FADE.

FADE IN of a door bell ringing.

MAN: They've been closed for a fortnight, mister.

TEMPLE: What do you mean – is Miss Jackson on holiday or something?

MAN: Don't ask me …

TEMPLE: Isn't there somebody living on the premises?

MAN: I suppose there must me – always a swarm of kids running in and out … Ring the bell again …

TEMPLE: This time I think I'll try the knocker.

We hear the sound of the door knocker.

There is a pause.

TEMPLE knocks again.

The door opens.

MRS PERKINS: Yes, what is it?

TEMPLE: I'm looking for Miss Sally Jackson.

MRS P: Then you'll 'ave to look a long way; she aint' 'ere.

TEMPLE: Have you any idea where I can find her?

MRS P: Gawd knows! Gone abroad, she 'as … You could try Paris or the Riviera …

TEMPLE: She hasn't left a forwarding address?

MRS P: No, all I know is she asked me to stop 'ere an' keep an eye on the place.

BOY: (*Off*) Ma … the kettle's boilin' …

MRS P: I'm comin'! Wish somebody'd take me to the Riviera, away from these blasted kids!

TEMPLE: Do you know when Miss Jackson is coming back?

MRS P: Not yet I 'ope, 'cos I got nowhere fixed … 'Ere, who are you, askin' all these questions? Not the police?

TEMPLE: No, as a matter of fact I'm a friend of Midge Harris's.

MRS P: Midge! Oh, 'im. Ain't got no more sense than what 'e was born with. Proper nit, 'e was, gettin' nabbed like that. Don't deserve a nice girl like Sal …

BOY: (*Off*) Ma! The kettle's on fire!

START FADE.

MRS P: All right, Sidney, I'm comin' … I'm comin'!

COMPLETE FADE.

FADE IN a door opening and closing.

TEMPLE: I'm sorry I'm late, Superintendent, but I've had rather a busy day.

RAINE: That's all right. I've spoken to the Governor – they're fetching Harris now.

TEMPLE: Good. Incidentally, I went to see a girl named Sally Jackson this morning.

RAINE: (*Smiling*) Midge's girl friend?

TEMPLE: Oh, so you know?

RAINE: Yes. She wasn't at home, of course.

TEMPLE: No, she was in the South of France, from what I can gather.

RAINE: That's near enough. Soon after we picked up Midge, Sally suddenly came into money and decided to travel.

TEMPLE: Where did she get the money from, do you know?

RAINE: Well, our bet is – someone took care of her in order to stop Midge talking …

The door opens.

GOVERNOR: Good afternoon, Superintendent.

RAINE: Ah, good afternoon, Governor! May I introduce Mr Temple …

The GOVERNOR and TEMPLE shake hands.

TEMPLE: How do you do, sir?

GOVERNOR: How do you do, Mr Temple? Delighted to meet you. Well, everything's ready, Superintendent. He's in the chaplain's room.

RAINE: How does he seem?

GOVERNOR: Oh – surly; I doubt whether he'll be very co-operative.

RAINE: No. Well – he's all yours, Temple. I wish you luck.

GOVERNOR: This way, Mr Temple.

The door opens.

FADE SCENE.

FADE IN the voice of MIDGE HARRIS.

HARRIS: … What's the big idea, Mr Temple? Why have you come to see me?

TEMPLE: Sit down, Midge. Make yourself comfortable.

HARRIS: There ain't no comfort in this place.

TEMPLE: Well, have a cigarette …

HARRIS: Wot you after, Mr Temple? Wot's the game?

TEMPLE: No game at all. I played straight enough with you last time, didn't I?

HARRIS: (*Dubiously*) Well …

TEMPLE: Light your cigarette and relax. Here …

HARRIS lights a cigarette with a lighter.
A pause.

HARRIS: (*Expelling smoke*) First I've had since they shoved me in this stinkin' hole.

TEMPLE: Yes; it was bad luck being picked up like that. I suppose you did do the job?

HARRIS: Is that what you've come to find out? The Beak said I done it.

TEMPLE: (*Pulling HARRIS's leg*) Well, if the Beak said you done it – you done it. (*Seriously*) No, it's nothing to do with that, Midge. I want your help over something else.

HARRIS: What?

TEMPLE: Someone tried to murder me the other night.

HARRIS: Murder you?

TEMPLE: Yes.

HARRIS: Go on – you're kiddin' …

TEMPLE: No, I'm not kidding. It happened near Brighton at a place called Breakwater House. (*Politely*) Have you ever been to Breakwater House, Midge?

HARRIS: No, I 'aven't.

TEMPLE: Now that surprises me, because they found your fingerprints there, in one of the rooms.

HARRIS: Who told you that?

TEMPLE: Superintendent Raine.

HARRIS: He's up the creek! How could my prints be at Breakwater House? I been stuck in this flippin' place for three weeks.

TEMPLE: I'm not suggesting that you were there recently, Midge, or that you had anything to do with the attempt on my life.

HARRIS: Then what are you suggesting?

TEMPLE: That you went to Breakwater House some little time ago and that the person who invited you there was the person who tried to murder me.

HARRIS: I don't know what you're talking about.

TEMPLE: I'm talking about Margo – alias The Fence.

HARRIS: (*Tensely*) I've never 'eard of anyone called Margo. I 'aven't been to Brighton for years.

TEMPLE: Then how do you account for the fingerprints?

HARRIS: (*Rattled*) I don't know; I can't account for 'em. I expect it's a frame-up – it usually is a ruddy frame-up.

TEMPLE: Midge, I don't want to scare you, but you're mixed up with a pretty slick bunch. Now, if I were you …

HARRIS: Well, you're not me, Mr Temple – so keep the flippin' advice to yourself!

TEMPLE: All right, Midge; if you won't talk, I'll have to have another word with your girl friend, that's all.

HARRIS: (*Puzzled*) My girl friend?

TEMPLE: Yes – Sally Jackson.

HARRIS: What d'yer mean – another word?

TEMPLE: I saw her yesterday afternoon, but she was so busy she could hardly spare time to talk to me.

HARRIS: (*Slowly; puzzled*) You saw her yesterday afternoon?

TEMPLE: Yes.

HARRIS: I don't believe you.

TEMPLE: All right …

HARRIS: Where did you see her? What was she doing?

TEMPLE: I've told you. She was in that hairdressing salon of hers, working like a slave.

HARRIS: You made a mistake – that wasn't Sal. She's got pots of money now; she's gone abroad somewhere.

TEMPLE: That's what you think!

HARRIS: What d'you mean?

TEMPLE: When she discovered I was a friend of yours she tried to borrow a fiver off me. That doesn't sound as if she's got pots of money, does it?

START FADE.

HARRIS: (*Hesitantly; worried*) I – I don't believe you.

TEMPLE: (*Pleasantly*) All right. Fair enough. You don't believe me, Midge.

COMPLETE FADE.

FADE IN of RAINE's voice.

The door opens.

RAINE: … That's all very well, Governor, but looking at it from our point of view, the attitude of the average criminal … Ah, here we are, Temple! Well – any luck?

TEMPLE: Not much, I'm afraid. He's a surly little devil, isn't he?

RAINE: Yes, and I wouldn't trust him as far as I could throw the … the … er … (*Lost for words*)

TEMPLE: You wouldn't trust him.

The GOVERNOR and RAINE laugh.

GOVERNOR: (*Closing the matter*) Well, is there anything else we can do for you, Superintendent?

RAINE: No, thank you, sir. You've been extremely helpful and we're very grateful to you for …

TEMPLE: (*Interrupting RAINE*) Yes, there is one small thing, Governor – if you'd be kind enough.

GOVERNOR: Anything to help, Mr Temple.

TEMPLE: During the next twenty-four hours a postcard will arrive for Harris – it'll have a little drawing in the right-hand corner. I want you to make sure he gets it, the moment it arrives.

GOVERNOR: (*Puzzled*) Yes, of course … But, may I ask, how did you find out about this postcard?

RAINE: Yes, how did you find out, Temple – and who's going to send it?

START FADE.

TEMPLE: I am, Superintendent.

FADE SCENE.

FADE UP of a doorbell ringing.

The door opens.

TEMPLE: Sorry, Charlie, I left my key in the study.

CHARLIE: That's all right, Mr Temple.

The door closes.

TEMPLE takes off his overcoat.

TEMPLE: Mrs Temple in the drawing room?

CHARLIE: No, she's out, sir. She went out about half an hour ago.

TEMPLE: Oh – where has she gone, do you know?

CHARLIE: No, she didn't say – but she seemed in quite a flap with … quite excited, Mr Temple.

TEMPLE: What do you mean – quite excited?

CHARLIE: Well, it was just after Mrs Temple made the phone call. She came into the kitchen and …

TEMPLE: (*Faintly alarmed*) What phone call? Who did Mrs Temple ring up?

CHARLIE: I don't know, sir. I don't know who it was – but about two minutes later Mrs Temple popped into the kitchen and said she was going out.

TEMPLE: But didn't she say anything else?

CHARLIE: Oh, yes, sir. She said: "I'm going out, Charlie, but if Mr Temple gets home before I get back just say …" (*Puzzled*) Then she said a very funny thing.

TEMPLE: Well – what did she say?

CHARLIE: She just said two words, Mr Temple.

TEMPLE: (*Tensely; trying to control himself*) What two words, Charlie?

CHARLIE: (*After a moment; puzzled*) Edgar Northampton …

END OF EPISODE SIX

EPISODE SEVEN

A TIME
TO WORRY

OPEN TO: FADE IN TEMPLE's voice.

TEMPLE: (*Alarmed*) What phone call? Who did Mrs Temple ring up?

CHARLIE: I don't know, sir. I don't know who it was – but about two minutes later Mrs Temple popped into the kitchen and said she was going out.

TEMPLE: But didn't she say anything else?

CHARLIE: Oh, yes, sir. She said: "I'm going out, Charlie, but if Mr Temple gets home before I get back just say …" (*Puzzled*) Then she said a very funny thing.

TEMPLE: Well – what did she say?

CHARLIE: She just said two words, Mr Temple.

TEMPLE: (*Trying to control himself*) What two words, Charlie?

CHARLIE: Edgar Northampton …

TEMPLE: Edgar Northampton?

CHARLIE: Yes. I don't know what she meant, Mr Temple. I've never heard of anyone called Northampton.

TEMPLE: (*Thoughtfully: to himself*) He's a bank manager. I've been rather puzzled as to how he fitted into the picture – it looks as if Steve's found out.

CHARLIE: (*Puzzled*) What picture, Mr Temple?

TEMPLE: What? Oh, sorry, Charlie – I was talking to myself. Now I'll tell you what I want you to do.

We hear the sound of a key in a lock.

The front door opens.

TEMPLE: I want you to go down to …

CHARLIE: Here's Mrs Temple now, sir!

TEMPLE: Steve! Where on earth have you been?

STEVE: (*Brightly*) Hello, Paul! Take my coat, Charlie, will you?

CHARLIE: Certainly, Mrs Temple.

TEMPLE: Steve, what the devil did you mean by …

STEVE: You look worried, Paul! Is anything the matter?

TEMPLE: Of course I'm worried! Leaving mysterious messages and disappearing like that …

STEVE: (*Laughing*) Come into the drawing room, darling, and I'll tell you all about it.

TEMPLE and STEVE enter the drawing room.

TEMPLE: Now, Steve – what's this all about? Where have you been?

STEVE: You remember what Mrs Fletcher said to Mike Langdon: "If Dr Benkaray gets difficult just say two words to her – Edgar Northampton" …

TEMPLE: Yes.

STEVE: Well, I've discovered what she meant.

TEMPLE: (*Interested*) What did she mean?

STEVE: Shall I start at the beginning?

TEMPLE: (*Exasperated*) I don't care where you start – providing you tell me what this is all about!

STEVE: (*Laughing*) Well, just over an hour ago I was in the study making out some cheques for the housekeeping accounts when the front doorbell rang.

START FADE.

STEVE: I don't think Charlie could have heard it because the bell continued to ring for some considerable time …

FADE BACK to the sound of a doorbell ringing.

The bell continues.

The front door opens.

MRS FLETCHER: (*Nervous; and a little tense*) Mrs Temple?

STEVE: Yes …

MRS F: I'd like a word with your husband, Mrs Temple. Do you think I could possibly … Oh, I beg your pardon – I don't think we've met. My name is Fletcher; I met your husband down at Westerton …

STEVE: Oh, of course, come in, Mrs Fletcher!

MRS F: Thank you.

The front door closes.

FADE IN STEVE and MRS FLETCHER entering the drawing room.

STEVE: I'm very sorry, but my husband isn't in just at the moment. I'm expecting him back, though, if you'd care to wait.

MRS F: Oh dear, I thought this might happen. I should have phoned, of course, and made an appointment.

STEVE: You can leave a message, Mrs Fletcher.

MRS F: Well, I … I wanted to see your husband personally, you see … (*Suddenly*) Mrs Temple, your husband called at the garage – he questioned my son, Bill.

STEVE: Yes, I know.

MRS F: Bill's a good boy, he's as straight as a die; he has nothing to do with this business – nothing at all …

STEVE: Do <u>you</u> know anything about it, Mrs Fletcher?

MRS F: That's not the point; it's my boy I'm concerned with – he's the one I'm worried about at the moment. Now, you tell Mr Temple to leave him alone! There's no reason for your husband, or anyone else, to question Bill.

STEVE: My husband has to question quite a lot of people who are not directly involved. He always works that way. That helps him to decide which people are really implicated.

MRS F: Yes, well, you tell him to leave Bill alone.

STEVE: All right, Mrs Fletcher, I'll do that. But I think you're making a great mistake.

MRS F: What do you mean?

STEVE: My husband likes your son – he's already told me that.

MRS F: Then why did he question him?

STEVE: He wanted to know what Bill knew about Dr Benkaray and your relationship with the doctor.

MRS F: (*Irritated*) That's no concern of your husband's.

STEVE: I think it is. Look, Mrs Fletcher, I don't know why you should feel particularly unfriendly towards my husband; he'd like to help you.

MRS F: Why? Why should he want to help me?

STEVE: Wasn't it you who warned us about the parcel from the dress shop?

MRS F: (*Hesitantly*) Yes, it was, but … Look, Mrs Temple, I must go now. I'm sorry if I've been rude.

STEVE: That's all right, Mrs Fletcher.

MRS F: I'm flying to Australia in two or three days' time, so I don't expect I shall see …

STEVE: Australia?

MRS F: Yes.

STEVE: Is your son going with you?

MRS F: No, I'm leaving him behind. I think he'll stand a better chance on his own. The garage business is all in order and I've made it over to him.

STEVE: I see.

MRS F: But in case Dr Benkaray and her crowd ever try to drag my son into anything, I wanted Mr Temple to know that Bill isn't that sort. He's straight as an arrow is Bill.

STEVE: What exactly are you suggesting they might drag him into, Mrs Fletcher? It would be as well for my husband to know, if you want him to keep a friendly eye on your son.

MRS F: (*Hesitantly*) They're mixed up in all sorts of things, Mrs Temple. Stolen property … drugs … All I ever did was to pass on messages or deliver packages that looked innocent enough. But I was a fool – I ought to have realised that they couldn't have paid that sort of money simply for running errands. I should have packed it in months ago.

STEVE: Have you ever met the person behind all this – the person they call Margo?

MRS F: Margo? The person who controls the outfit is The Fence, Mrs Temple. The name Margo is just for identification purposes.

STEVE: What do you mean?

MRS F: I'm sorry, but I can't give you any more information. Goodbye, Mrs Temple!

STEVE: (*Stopping MRS FLETCHER*) No, wait a moment! Tell me one thing, Mrs Fletcher, before you leave.

MRS F: Well?

STEVE: Do these people – the people you've been working for – know that you're going away?

MRS F: No, I don't think so.

STEVE: Well, supposing they find out and bring pressure to bear on your son?

MRS F: They won't do that, Mrs Temple. You see, if they try to get Bill involved I should go straight to the police. I've told them that.

STEVE: Yes, but they could – well – get rid of you.

MRS F: I've warned them about that, too. I've taken every precaution, don't you worry!

STEVE: What do you mean by – every precaution?

MRS F: I've got certain documents and tape recordings in a very safe place. If anything should happen to me they'll pass into the right hands. Bill will see to that all right.

STEVE: Well, if anyone should ever contact Bill after you've gone, I hope you'll tell him to get in touch with my husband right away.

MRS F: You can rely on Bill – he knows just what to do.

START FADE.

STEVE: Yes, well, I'm sorry, but I think you're making a mistake in running away, Mrs Fletcher …

COMPLETE FADE.

FADE IN of STEVE's voice talking to TEMPLE.

STEVE: … After she left I remembered what you'd told me about Edgar Northampton, and it suddenly dawned on me that the documents she'd referred to were probably in a deed box at his bank.

TEMPLE: Go on, Steve.

STEVE: I telephoned Reggie Whiteside …

TEMPLE: (*Surprised*) Our bank manager?

STEVE: Yes. I asked if he could see me. He was at a meeting, but I said it was a matter of life or death, so …

TEMPLE: (*Laughing*) By Timothy, you really are the limit, Steve!

STEVE: Anyway, I saw Reggie and I asked him if he could find out whether a Mrs Fletcher had deposited a deed box at their branch in Tenterhurst.

TEMPLE: (*Interested*) Go on …

STEVE: He telephoned Northampton and said an enquiry had come through about the garage in Westerton, and he wondered if the bank held the deeds. Northampton said that they didn't but that Mrs Fletcher had certainly deposited a deed box with them some little time ago.

TEMPLE: I see … And it's your deduction that the deed box contains a great more than just the deeds of the garage?

STEVE: Well – what do you think?

TEMPLE: I think you're right, Steve; I think you're a hundred per cent right – but in future, young woman, please let me do the investigating around here!

STEVE: (*Laughing*) All right, but thank you for the "young" anyway. (*A moment*) Well, how did you get on – did you see Midge Harris?

TEMPLE opens a drawer in the writing bureau.

TEMPLE: Yes, I did, and I want you to do something for me, Steve. Where are the postcards, darling?

STEVE: On the left of the writing paper.

TEMPLE: Oh, yes.

TEMPLE takes out a postcard.

TEMPLE: Steve, you were always a pretty good hand at drawing … I want you to sketch a girl's head on the back of this postcard … Here you are, dear – use my pen.

STEVE: (*Puzzled*) A girl's head?

TEMPLE: Yes; just a rough drawing, Steve, showing a girl's head under a dryer at the hairdresser's.

STEVE: You don't want much!

TEMPLE: It doesn't matter how rough it is.

There is a pause during which STEVE does the sketch.

TEMPLE: (*Calling*) Charlie! (*To STEVE*) How's it going?

STEVE: (*After a moment*) Will that do?

TEMPLE: (*Amused*) Oh, that's very good, Steve. Now write underneath: "So much for your friends. Still sweating my guts out. Sal."

STEVE: (*Laughing*) That's a bit crude, isn't it?

TEMPLE: Midge isn't exactly the sophisticated type.

CHARLIE enters.

CHARLIE: You called, sir?

TEMPLE: Yes – wait a minute, Charlie, I want you to post something for me. It's all right, Steve, I'll address it.

The telephone rings.

STEVE: I'll take it, Paul.

STEVE lifts the receiver.

STEVE: (*On the phone*) Hello?

KELBURN: (*On the other end of the line*) Mrs Temple?

STEVE: Speaking …

KELBURN: (*Very affable*) This is George Kelburn, Mrs Temple. Could I possibly have a word with your husband?

STEVE: Yes, just hold on a minute, will you, Mr Kelburn? (*To TEMPLE*) It's Kelburn, Paul.

TEMPLE: Right. (*To CHARLIE*) Go down to Camden Town, Charlie.

CHARLIE: Camden Town?

TEMPLE: Yes, Camden Town – and post this in the first letter box you see.

CHARLIE: Okay, Mr Temple.

TEMPLE: (*To STEVE*) Kelburn?

STEVE: Yes – and he sounds particularly cheerful.

TEMPLE: (*On the phone*) Hello, Temple speaking …

KELBURN: (*Pleasantly*) Temple, I'm sorry to disturb you, but I wondered if you and Mrs Temple would care to drop in for a drink this evening? It's very short notice, but I'd particularly like to have a chat with you.

TEMPLE: (*After a momentary hesitation*) Yes, I think that would be very pleasant, Kelburn. About what time?

KELBURN: Seven o'clock?

TEMPLE: Splendid.

KELBURN: Look forward to seeing you both, then. Goodbye.

TEMPLE: Goodbye.

TEMPLE replaces the receiver.

A pause.

STEVE: (*Quietly*) What is it, Paul? Is anything wrong?

TEMPLE: I don't know. Kelburn's asked us round for a drink this evening.

STEVE: He sounded different, didn't he? Much more affable.

TEMPLE: Yes – why? Why, I wonder?

FADE IN of music.

FADE DOWN of music.
FADE IN a doorbell ringing.
A front door opens.

MAID: Good evening. Mr and Mrs Temple?

TEMPLE: Yes.

MAID: Please come in. Mr and Mrs Kelburn are expecting you.

TEMPLE: Thank you.

The door closes.

MAID: May I take your coat, madam?

STEVE: Oh, thank you.

LANGDON: (*Approaching*) That's all right, Mary – I'll look after Mr and Mrs Temple.

MAID: Thank you, sir.

LANGDON: Hello, Mrs Temple!

STEVE: Hello, Mr Langdon …

LANGDON: Nice to see you, Temple. Glad you could both make it.

TEMPLE: I thought you'd be on your way back to New York by now.

LANGDON: No, no, not yet. I'm keeping my fingers crossed; any moment now, with a bit of luck.

TEMPLE: There's been a change in the situation?

LANGDON: (*With a little laugh*) There certainly has!

STEVE: What's happened, exactly?

LANGDON: Well, Kelburn's had a change of heart. He's decided he's still very much in love with his wife and he's made it up with her.

TEMPLE: When did this happen?

LANGDON: Within the last twenty-four hours.

TEMPLE: Really?

LANGDON: Don't ask me to explain it, it's a mystery to me. Right now you wouldn't think they'd ever seriously considered leaving each other for a weekend, let alone parting for good. Still, I'm all for it! It's a wonderful idea – especially if it gets me back to New York!

LINDA: (*Brightly*) Hello, Steve! How lovely to see you, my dear!

STEVE: Good evening, Linda!

LINDA: Hello, Mr Temple – how sweet of you to come. (*To LANGDON*) Is George in the drawing room?

LANGDON: I think so, Linda.

START FADE.

LINDA: Come along, then – let's go in …

COMPLETE FADE.

FADE IN to the opening of the drawing room door.

LINDA: George, our guests have arrived!

KELBURN: (*Pleasantly; friendly*) Ah, good evening, Mrs Temple! How very nice to see you. (*Shaking hands*) Temple, my dear fellow, how are you?

TEMPLE: I'm very well, thank you.

KELBURN: So glad you could make it at such short notice. Mike, will you see to the drinks?

LANGDON: Delighted! What can I get you, Mrs Temple?

STEVE: May I have a dry Martini?

LANGDON: Linda?

LINDA: Oh – a gin and tonic, please.

KELBURN: Temple, what would you like?

TEMPLE: Whisky and soda?

KELBURN: Of course. Scotch and soda, Mike – and I'll have the same.

LANGDON: (*Busy at the drinks table*) D'you like it very dry, Mrs Temple?

STEVE: (*Hesitantly*) Well …

LANGDON: (*Laughing*) That's okay, don't worry – leave it to me …

KELBURN: Temple, I owe you an apology.

TEMPLE: An apology?

KELBURN: Yes. I'm afraid I've wasted a lot of your valuable time – getting you involved in family affairs which don't concern you. Naturally, I shall see that you're not the loser financially, but that's not the point.

TEMPLE: (*Pleasantly*) What is the point, Kelburn?

KELBURN: Linda and I have decided to forget the past and make a fresh start.

TEMPLE: I'm delighted to hear it.

KELBURN: I ought never to have doubted her in the first place, I know, but …

LINDA: (*Softly*) Oh, George …

KELBURN: Well, things haven't been too easy for me just lately … what with Julia and …

LINDA: … Darling, we understand …

KELBURN: Yes, I know <u>you</u> do, my dear – but I wanted Mr and Mrs Temple to realise that I – well – that I'm sorry I ever doubted you, Linda.

LINDA: That's very sweet of you, darling. Now you've said your little piece we'll all drink to it.

LANGDON: Here we are, Mrs Temple – one dry Martini.

STEVE: Thank you.

LANGDON: Scotch, Temple.

TEMPLE: Thank you very much.

LANGDON: Linda …

LINDA: Thank you, Mike.

KELBURN: It's all right, Mike, I can help myself to soda.

LANGDON: Well, Linda – George – here's to both of you. I can't tell you how glad I am that everything's straightened out.

LINDA: (*Laughing*) You're just a line-shooter, Mike – you just want to get back to little old New York, that's all you want!

LANGDON: (*Amused*) Whatever gave you that idea?

KELBURN: (*Pulling LANGDON's leg*) Why don't you come along with us, Mike?

LINDA: I thought you said this was going to be a second honeymoon, darling?

KELBURN: I'm only joking, Linda.

STEVE: Are you going away, Mr Kelburn?

KELBURN: Yes, we're going on a cruise. We fixed it up last night, didn't we, Linda? We sail from Southampton at the end of the month.

TEMPLE: What's the ship?

KELBURN: It's an American ship – the Wisconsin. It goes down to Jamaica. We'll be away about six months.

STEVE: How wonderful! I've always wanted to go to Jamaica.

TEMPLE: Does Sir Graham know about this trip?

KELBURN: (*Faintly surprised by the question*) No; I haven't told him. We only knew ourselves last night.

TEMPLE: I think I'd have a word with him, Kelburn. The file on your daughter's case is by no means closed. They may want to get in touch with you.

LINDA: But that's the whole point of taking this cruise! George wants to forget about the whole thing – he wants to get away from Sir

Graham Forbes and Superintendent Raine and people like that.

TEMPLE: Yes, I know, Mrs Kelburn. Unfortunately, that isn't quite as easy as it sounds.

There is an awkward pause.

LANGDON: How's the dry Martini, Mrs Temple?

STEVE: Excell … hic … Excellent, Mr Langdon.

They all laugh.

FADE SCENE on the laughter.

FADE IN background noises of a London Square.

A car door opens.

TEMPLE: Will you drive, Steve?

STEVE: Yes, all right, dear.

TEMPLE and STEVE get into the car.

TEMPLE: Go through the park, will you; I want to stop in Wimpole Street.

STEVE: Why Wimpole Street?

TEMPLE: I'm calling on Dr Benkaray.

STEVE: She's probably in Westerton …

TEMPLE: Well, if she is, we'll go down to Westerton.

STEVE: (*Surprised*) What – tonight?

TEMPLE: Yes, tonight. But don't worry, it's my bet she's right here – in Town.

STEVE: But why do you want to see Dr Benkaray?

TEMPLE: I'll tell you later, dear. (*Looking behind*) All right – you can pull out now …

The car drives away.

FADE SCENE.

FADE BACK to the car.

STEVE: Is anything wrong, darling?

TEMPLE: Wrong? No – why do you ask?

STEVE: You're very quiet.

TEMPLE: I was just thinking, that's all.

STEVE: Well – you've certainly got plenty to think about. Have you ever seen such a change in people? Even Mike Langdon seemed different. And Linda – well, she was positively human, for once. Maybe it's the thought of going to Jamaica.

TEMPLE: (*Quietly*) Yes – maybe … (*A moment*) You know, I find this sudden departure of everybody a little worrying, Steve.

STEVE: What do you mean?

TEMPLE: The Kelburns going to Jamaica, Langdon returning to New York, and Mrs Fletcher off to Australia.

STEVE: Well?

TEMPLE: (*Softly*) Well – I don't like it. I hope The Fence isn't going to slip through our fingers, Steve.

FADE UP the noise of the car.

FADE DOWN the noise of the car completely.

FADE IN the sound of the car drawing to a standstill.

A car door opens.

TEMPLE: I shan't be five minutes, Steve. If Benkaray's out I'll come straight back.

STEVE: Yes, all right, Paul.

We hear the sound of footsteps.

The footsteps stop.

Sound of a door knocker.

A pause.

The front door of a house opens.

LARRY: (*Surprised*) Hello, Mr Temple! I didn't expect to see you …

TEMPLE: No, I don't expect you did, Mr Cross. I'd like a word with Dr Benkaray.

LARRY: I'm sorry, but Dr Benkaray's got several appointments this evening and can't be disturbed.

TEMPLE: I see. Well – do you think I could speak to her on the telephone sometime – possibly late tonight?

LARRY: (*Hesitantly*) Yes – I should imagine so. I should ring about half past eleven.

TEMPLE: Thank you. (*Casually; turning away*) Tell Dr Benkaray we now know who murdered Julia Kelburn, but there's just one small point I'd like to check with the doctor. It won't take a minute, I can do it on the telephone.

LARRY: (*Suddenly*) No … no, wait a minute! Er – come in, Mr Temple. I'll see if the doctor can spare you a minute.

TEMPLE: Oh – thank you very much, that's very kind of you.

TEMPLE enters the house.

The front door closes.

LARRY: (*Opening the waiting room door*) If you'll just wait in here – I shan't keep you a moment.

TEMPLE: Thank you.

A door opens and closes.

A pause.

A clock chimes the hour.

The door opens again.

BENKARAY: (*Approaching*) Good evening, Mr Temple. I understand you wish to speak to me?

TEMPLE: Oh, good evening, Dr Benkaray. How very kind of you to see me. Yes, I wanted to have a word with you, Doctor, before you left because I thought …

BENKARAY: (*Surprised*) Before I left?

TEMPLE: Yes. (*Politely*) You are going away, aren't you, Doctor?

BENKARAY: (*Puzzled*) Yes, as a matter of fact, I am – but how did you know?

TEMPLE: (*Glibly*) Oh, I thought it was common knowledge. My wife overheard someone say something about it at a party – one of your patients, I imagine.

BENKARAY: I see.

TEMPLE: Where are you going to, Doctor?

BENKARAY: I'm going to Canada, on a lecture tour.

TEMPLE: (*Laughing*) Well, take it easy – those lecture tours can be terribly tiring. I know what I'm talking about, I've just returned from one.

BENKARAY: My secretary tells me that you know who murdered Julia Kelburn.

TEMPLE: Yes – we know; but I'm afraid I can't tell you who it is. The police are being rather cagey about it.

BENKARAY: (*Annoyed*) What do you mean – cagey? I'm not used to these Americanisms.

TEMPLE: You'll have to get used to them, Doctor, if you're going to Canada. Incidentally, is Mr Cross going with you?

BENKARAY: Yes, he is.

TEMPLE: Ah, well – he'll put you right, I'm sure.

BENKARAY: What is it you wanted to ask me, Mr Temple?

TEMPLE: During your consultations with Julia Kelburn, did she ever mention a friend of hers called Fiona Scott?

BENKARAY: No, she didn't.

TEMPLE: You've never heard the name before?

BENKARAY: No, I haven't. (*A note of sarcasm*) Sorry to disappoint you.

TEMPLE: Oh, I'm not disappointed; on the contrary – I should have been disappointed if she had mentioned it, Dr Benkaray. Good night …

FADE IN of music.

FADE DOWN of music.

A door opens.

CHARLIE: Would you like some more toast, Mr Temple?

TEMPLE: No, thank you, Charlie. Is Mrs Temple up?

CHARLIE: Yes – she's just coming down, sir.

TEMPLE: Were there any messages last night?

CHARLIE: No – no messages. Ah, good morning, Mrs Temple.

STEVE: Good morning, Charlie. You're very early, darling.

TEMPLE: Yes, I'm expecting Sir Graham. I telephoned him last night.

The doorbell rings.

CHARLIE: That's probably Sir Graham now, sir.

TEMPLE: If the Superintendent's with him show them into the drawing room.

CHARLIE: Yes, sir. I'll fetch you some more coffee, Mrs Temple.

STEVE: Thank you, Charlie. Paul …

TEMPLE: Yes?

STEVE: You didn't tell me what you found out last night – from Dr Benkaray?

TEMPLE: I found out that Mike Langdon, the Kelburns, and Mrs Fletcher aren't the only people who are leaving the country. Dr Benkaray and Larry Cross are going to Canada.

STEVE: I see. Now I know why you're worried, darling. Time's running out.

TEMPLE: Yes. I'll see you later, Steve.

FADE SCENE.

FADE IN of SIR GRAHAM's voice.

FORBES: … Ah, good morning, Temple.

TEMPLE: Good morning, Sir Graham … Superintendent …

RAINE: Good morning.

TEMPLE: Do sit down.

RAINE: Thank you.

FORBES: I hope we're not too early for you; but you sounded quite anxious when you telephoned last night.

TEMPLE: I was more than anxious – I was very worried. I still am. Sir Graham, as you know, we've suspected for some time that the murder of Julia Kelburn was linked up with the activities of The Fence.

FORBES: Yes.

TEMPLE: Well, I've good reason to believe that The Fence has made plans to leave the country. He suspects that we're on to him and he's getting out while the going's good. Now, the point is this, Sir Graham: I know this man, but I haven't sufficient evidence – not real evidence – for you to get a warrant out for him. On the other hand, once he leaves the country …

RAINE: He mustn't leave the country! That would be an impossible situation …

TEMPLE: Well – how do we stop him, Superintendent?

RAINE: (*Worried*) I don't know, but …

FORBES: Have you a suggestion, Temple – a possible plan?

TEMPLE: Yes; but I'm afraid it's a very unorthodox one, Sir Graham. I doubt whether you'll approve of it.

RAINE: It doesn't matter how unorthodox it is. If it's going to help us to …

FORBES: Just a moment, Raine! What is this plan of yours, Temple?

TEMPLE: Well, first of all I've got to have a quiet little chat …

The telephone rings.

TEMPLE: Excuse me …

TEMPLE lifts the receiver.

TEMPLE: (*On the phone*) Hello? Paul Temple speaking …

MILTON: (*On the other end of the line*) Mr Temple, this is Inspector Milton – Scotland Yard.

TEMPLE: Oh, hold on – I'll get the Superintendent for you …

MILTON: (*Stopping TEMPLE*) No, it's you I wanted, sir. There's been a phone message through from Brixton … Midge Harris has asked the Governor if he can have another interview with you. They've arranged an appointment for three o'clock this afternoon. Will that be convenient, Mr Temple?

TEMPLE: (*Delighted*) Yes, quite convenient. Thank you, Inspector.

TEMPLE replaces the receiver.

FORBES: What's all that about?

TEMPLE: (*Pleased*) Midge Harris wants to see me.

RAINE: But you've seen him!

TEMPLE: Yes, I know. He wants to see me again.

RAINE: (*Puzzled*) But why? I'm damned if I could get a word out of the fellow!

TEMPLE: (*Smiling*) Ah, but you didn't send him a postcard, did you, Inspector?

START FADE.

TEMPLE: Now let me tell you about this plan of mine. First of all, it depends on whether Midge Harris …

COMPLETE FADE.

FADE UP the opening of a door.

GOVERNOR: Good afternoon, Mr Temple. Do come in. How nice to see you again.

TEMPLE: I'm afraid I'm giving you rather a lot of trouble, Governor.

GOVERNOR: Not at all, my dear fellow.

TEMPLE: I presume Harris got the postcard all right?

GOVERNOR: Yes, indeed. About half an hour after receiving it he asked for an interview and said he wanted to speak to you again. I got the impression that he was angry about something.

TEMPLE: That doesn't surprise me.

GOVERNOR: I'll take you to him now. He's waiting in the chaplain's room. This way, Mr Temple.

FADE SCENE.

FADE UP on a door opening.

GOVERNOR: Ah, there you are, Harris. Here's Mr Temple.

HARRIS: (*Quietly; subdued*) Thank you, sir.

GOVERNOR: I'll be in my office, Mr Temple, if you want me.

TEMPLE: Thank you.

The door closes.

TEMPLE: Well, Midge – I came as soon as I got your message.

HARRIS: Thanks. I had to see you, Mr Temple. For one thing, I wanted to say I'm sorry I didn't believe you last time you were here. You know – when you came out with all that stuff about my girl Sal.

TEMPLE: You've heard from her?

HARRIS: Yes. I had a postcard. She 'aint in the South of France like I told you; she's still in her old job, sweating her guts out. I've been led up the flippin' garden, and that's a fact.

TEMPLE: I take it your friends have let you down, then?

HARRIS: Let me down! You can say that again! Yes, well, he ain't flippin' well goin' to get away with it – not this time, he ain't!

TEMPLE: I'm glad to hear you say that; after all, apart from the predicament you're in, it's not fair on Sally.

HARRIS: You're dead right it ain't fair on Sally! (*Puzzled*) I don't know what's gone wrong. He's always looked after the other boys, always taken care of them …

TEMPLE: Yes, well, he hasn't looked after you, Midge – has he?

HARRIS: No, he 'asn't!

TEMPLE: (*Quietly*) Now, Midge, listen: I want you to tell me about The Fence. I give you my word that whatever you tell me about yourself will be treated in strictest confidence. I'm only interested in The Fence and the Kelburn murder.

HARRIS: (*Quickly*) I didn't have nothing to with any murder! You got to believe that or you don't get another word out of me!

TEMPLE: All right, Midge, I believe you. Now tell me how you first got in touch with The Fence.

HARRIS: I'd never heard of him until a few years back when I knocked off a jeweller's and tried to get rid of the stuff through the usual channels. The boys wouldn't hear of it – wouldn't touch the stuff. The Yard had got the heat on just about then – sending scores of Dicks round the pawn shops and places. I tried one or two of the provincial boys but it was the same story – they all said the stuff was too hot.

TEMPLE: Go on …

HARRIS: Well, one day I was in a little caff off the Tottenham Court Road when the geezer who runs the place said I was wanted on the blower. It was a woman – she didn't give her name but she 'ad a bit of a funny accent; foreigner, I suppose. Anyway, she said she'd heard I was interested in doing a deal and she told me to go to a pet shop in South Dock Road, Shoreditch. I was to ask for Oscar. Well, I went round to this place – it's next door to a pub called The Greyhound – and spoke to the bloke behind the counter. He was a big, tough looking chap with a Brummy accent.

TEMPLE: What happened?

HARRIS: I showed him a diamond ring I wanted to flog and told him there was plenty more where that came from.

TEMPLE: Did he buy it?

HARRIS: No, 'course he didn't; not right away. They weren't takin' no chances. This Oscar bloke asked me to leave it with him for a couple of days while he had it valued. Well, what'd I got to lose? I couldn't flog it anywhere else. Two days later I got another phone call, telling me to take all the stuff to a place called Breakwater House, not far from Brighton.

TEMPLE: And what happened there?

HARRIS: A youngish chap let me in – tough looking, slick operator type. He collected the stuff off me and took it into the next room. After a minute or two I heard several voices – there seemed to be a bit of an argument going on. I began to wonder what was happening … I mean to say, I was all on my own, and there were three or four of them, as far as I could tell. Still, in the end this young bloke comes back with a real good offer – and what's more it was cash down and no messing about.

TEMPLE: You didn't see any of the other people?

HARRIS: No, I didn't. But the young bloke asked me if I'd be interested in another little job they'd cased out at Ealing – dead easy it was, too. After that, one thing led to another. They kept me pretty busy … Sometimes with one or two other chaps, sometimes on my own …

TEMPLE: And you never actually saw The Fence?

HARRIS: No, never set eyes on 'im. But he always played fair, Mr Temple – paid a good price and looked after the wife and kids if any of the boys got nabbed. (*Puzzled*) That's what I don't understand about this lark. Why didn't he take care of Sal?

TEMPLE: Yes, well – it's just one of those things.

TEMPLE rises and shakes hands with HARRIS.

TEMPLE: Thank you, Midge, you've been a great help. Take care of yourself.

HARRIS: Well, I won't over-eat, if that's what you're worried about!

TEMPLE laughs.

FADE SCENE.

FADE IN of CHARLIE's voice.

CHARLIE: (*Approaching*) … Some fresh coffee, Mr Temple, and the morning papers.

TEMPLE: Oh, thank you, Charlie.

CHARLIE: Shall I pour the coffee?

TEMPLE: No, Mrs Temple will be down in a moment.

CHARLIE: Big robbery last night in Pont Street, sir; jewellers – nearly eighty thousand pounds' worth of stuff …

TEMPLE: (*Looking at the newspaper*) Yes, I'm just reading the headline …

CHARLIE: It was on the eight o'clock news. And they say crime doesn't pay!

STEVE: (*Approaching*) Good morning, Charlie.

CHARLIE: Good morning, Mrs Temple.

STEVE: You were very late last night, Paul. What were you up to?

TEMPLE: I went down to Fleet Street and had a couple of drinks with the crime reporter friend of yours – Ken Sinclair.

STEVE: That's the second time you've seen Ken within the past fortnight.

The doorbell rings.

TEMPLE: Yes; I've asked him to look up an old friend of ours – Wally Stone.

STEVE: Who's Wally Stone?

TEMPLE: Don't you remember? He used to be one of the best cats in the business.

STEVE: Cats? Pantomine cat?

TEMPLE: (*Laughing*) No, darling. (*Changing the subject*) Steve, you know the bracelet I bought you last Christmas – the diamond and ruby one.

STEVE: Yes.

TEMPLE: I'd like to borrow it for a couple of days. I think the clasp needs attention.

STEVE: (*Puzzled*) It doesn't – the clasp's perfectly all right.

TEMPLE: (*Casually*) I don't think so, Steve. I noticed it the other evening when we went to the Kelburns. It needs looking at. It'll only take a day or two.

The door opens.

CHARLIE: Sir Graham Forbes is here, sir.

STEVE: (*Surprised*) Hello, Sir Graham!

TEMPLE: Come in, Sir Graham! Let me see what you look like at this time of the morning.

FORBES: I – I just happened to be passing so I thought I'd – I'd pop in.

TEMPLE: (*Amused*) Jolly good idea. We don't get many people for breakfast, do we, Steve?

STEVE: (*Puzzled*) Would you like some coffee, Sir Graham?

FORBES: Yes; yes – thank you, Steve, thank you very much. I – I see you've seen the newspapers, Temple.

TEMPLE: Yes, I've seen them.

FORBES: Well, we've done what you wanted – we've included the ruby and diamond bracelet in the list of stolen property. A description has been sent out to all stations – jewellers – pawnbrokers – and the press.

STEVE: Did you say a ruby and diamond bracelet?

FORBES: Yes.

STEVE: But Paul's just asked me to …

TEMPLE: (*Quickly*) Pour the coffee, darling – don't keep Sir Graham waiting …

STEVE: Look, what is this? What's this all about? Sir Graham, what's going on?

FORBES: (*With a little laugh*) Don't ask me, lady, I'm a stranger in these parts!

TEMPLE: (*Excessively polite*) The coffee, darling.

FADE IN of music.

Slow FADE DOWN of music.

A shop door opens: the sound of a spring bell.

A background of pet shop noises.

OSCAR: (*An unfriendly man; Birmingham accent*) Good morning. What can I do for you?

TEMPLE: You've got a dog collar in the window – it's marked twenty-eight and six …

OSCAR: That's right.

TEMPLE: Is it leather?

OSCAR: Yes, 'course it's leather – genuine leather.

TEMPLE: Do you think I could have a look at it?

OSCAR: Yes – I've got one here. It's a different colour, but it's just the same.

OSCAR opens a drawer and produces a dog collar.

OSCAR: Very good value for twenty-eight and six.

TEMPLE examines the collar.

TEMPLE: Yes, it is ... but it's not quite the same as the one in the window, is it?

OSCAR: It's exactly the same – that's leather, that is – genuine leather.

TEMPLE: (*Ignoring the remark; pleasantly*) I'll take it.

OSCAR: (*Resentfully*) Okay ...

TEMPLE: Are you Oscar?

OSCAR: Yes.

TEMPLE: I think you know a friend of mine – Midge Harris.

OSCAR: Don't know anyone called Harris.

TEMPLE: A small, rather scruffy little man with a red ...

OSCAR: (*Interrupting TEMPLE*) Don't know anyone called Harris.

TEMPLE: No?

OSCAR: No ...

TEMPLE: Oh, I'm sorry about that. I thought you might be able to tell me what this was worth.

OSCAR: (*Taken aback*) Strewth! (*Nervously*) Where did you get that bracelet from?

TEMPLE: I'll give you three guesses.

OSCAR: That's from the Pont Street job!

TEMPLE: That's right.

OSCAR: (*Rather frightened*) Have you got the rest of the stuff, then?

TEMPLE: Yes.

OSCAR: Where?

TEMPLE: (*With a laugh*) Don't be silly, do you think I'm going to tell you that?

OSCAR: Why did you come here? You didn't want a dog collar …

TEMPLE: Of course I didn't! I'm in a spot; I've got to get rid of this stuff, it's red hot. Look, if you're prepared to help me I'll cut you in …

OSCAR: Listen, pal – don't get me wrong. I'm not The Fence, I'm just the go-between. (*A moment*) How do I know this bracelet is genuine, anyway?

TEMPLE: Does it look genuine?

OSCAR: Oh, yes, it looks genuine – but so does the dog collar!

TEMPLE: (*Apparently irritated*) Well, what do I do – ditch the stuff? I've got eight thousand quid's worth tucked away in … Okay, if you're not interested …

OSCAR: (*Quickly*) No, wait a minute! He'll have to see this bracelet, you know – he'll have to take a butcher's at it …

TEMPLE: All right. That's all right by me. I'll leave the bracelet with you. How long will it take him to make up his mind?

OSCAR: (*Examining the bracelet*) About forty-eight hours. Come back on Thursday morning.

TEMPLE: Thursday morning …

The shop door opens: the spring bell rings.

FADE SCENE.

FADE IN the sound of a key being fitted into a front door lock.

The door opens and closes.

STEVE: (*Approaching*) Oh, hello, Paul!

TEMPLE takes off his coat.

TEMPLE: Any messages, darling?

STEVE: Yes, that friend of yours is here. He's in the drawing room.

TEMPLE: What 'friend'?

STEVE: The man you saw Ken Sinclair about.

TEMPLE: Oh, Wally Stone! Yes, of course. How long has he been here?

STEVE: About ten minutes.

The drawing room door opens.

TEMPLE: Good afternoon, Mr Stone. I'm sorry to have kept you waiting.

WALLY: (*A quiet, faintly parsonic voice*) Good afternoon, Mr Temple. I just happened to be in Town for the day and Mr Sinclair said you were anxious to see me.

TEMPLE: Yes, that's right. Would you care for a glass of sherry?

WALLY: (*Flattered*) Thank you, Mr Temple, that would be very agreeable.

TEMPLE starts to pour out the sherry.

WALLY: What a delightful room. I've been admiring your fireplace.

TEMPLE: Yes; it is rather pleasant, isn't it?

WALLY takes his glass from TEMPLE.

WALLY: Thank you.

TEMPLE: Mr Stone, I'm sure you'd prefer that I didn't beat about the bush and came straight to the point. I'm working with the police on an important case – unfortunately our investigations are held up because we've failed to secure a vital piece of evidence.

WALLY: Yes?

TEMPLE: Well, it seems that the only way for us to secure this evidence is for someone to break into a certain house and – search for it.

WALLY: I see. And I take it, that's why I'm here? That's what you'd like me to do, Mr Temple?

TEMPLE: Yes.

WALLY: And what is this piece of evidence, exactly?

TEMPLE: It's a diamond and ruby bracelet. It belongs to my wife.

END OF EPISODE SEVEN

EPISODE EIGHT

THE VISITOR

OPEN TO: *FADE IN TEMPLE's voice.*

TEMPLE: Mr Stone, I'm sure you'd prefer that I didn't beat about the bush and came straight to the point. I'm working with the police on an important case – unfortunately our investigations are held up because we've failed to secure a vital piece of evidence. I've tried to think of all sorts of alternatives, but it seems that the only way for us to secure this evidence is for someone to break into a certain house and – search for it.

WALLY: I see. And I take it, that's why I'm here? That's what you'd like <u>me</u> to do, Mr Temple?

TEMPLE: Yes.

WALLY: And what is this piece of evidence, exactly?

TEMPLE: It's a diamond and ruby bracelet. It belongs to my wife.

WALLY: (*Surprised*) Your wife? Then the bracelet was stolen from you?

TEMPLE: (*Smiling*) Don't worry too much about the finer details of the assignment, Wally. Here's the address. If you don't find the bracelet, give me a ring. If you do – come straight back here.

WALLY: And what if anything goes wrong?

TEMPLE: Nothing must go wrong – that's important.

TEMPLE pats WALLY's arm.

TEMPLE: However, if you do get into trouble, don't worry; I'll get you out of it.

WALLY: All right, Mr Temple.

TEMPLE: (*Smiling*) You haven't asked me what the job's worth?

WALLY: Well – what is it worth? Ten per cent of the value of the bracelet?

TEMPLE: (*Laughing*) We'll talk about that later.

WALLY: Anyway, it isn't so much the money, Mr Temple, it's the nostalgia that appeals to me … it'll be just like old times …

TEMPLE: Yes, well, don't forget – we're only interested in the bracelet …

WALLY: No, of course not. I won't forget.

WALLY sips his sherry.

WALLY: Delicious sherry, Mr Temple …

START FADE.

TEMPLE: Drink up, Wally – and I'll pour you another glass …

FADE SCENE.

FADE IN the sound of a typewriter.

A door opens and the typewriter stops.

STEVE: Oh, here you are, Paul! Has your visitor gone?

TEMPLE: Yes, about ten minutes ago.

STEVE: Paul, what are you up to?

TEMPLE: I'm just typing the third chapter of …

STEVE: You know what I mean! This man Wally Stone … Why did you want to see him?

TEMPLE: I've asked him to do something for me.

STEVE: What?

TEMPLE: I'll – I'll tell you later, Steve. I can't tell you now.

STEVE: Paul, what is it? You look worried … You've looked like this for the last two days.

TEMPLE: I am worried, Steve. I've a terrible feeling that this case might well turn out to be one of our failures.

STEVE: But why should you think that?

TEMPLE: I think The Fence realises that the game is up, and there's a very good chance that he might slip through our fingers.

The door opens.

STEVE: But surely … Yes, Charlie?

CHARLIE: Sir Graham Forbes is here, sir.

TEMPLE: Come in, Sir Graham!

FORBES: Hello, Steve!

STEVE: Hello, Sir Graham.

TEMPLE: I've been trying to get you on the phone all day but they told me …

FORBES: Yes, I know, I'm sorry. I've had quite a day, Temple!

STEVE: Sit down, Sir Graham.

FORBES: Thank you, Steve.

TEMPLE: Has something happened?

FORBES: Yes. We've had a message through from Westerton. You know that woman that worked for Dr Benkaray?

TEMPLE: Mrs Fletcher – yes.

FORBES: She has a son …

TEMPLE: … That's right – Bill. He runs the garage.

FORBES: He was knocked down by a car early this morning. He's in Westerton hospital.

STEVE: Is he badly hurt?

FORBES: Yes, I'm afraid he is.

TEMPLE: What happened?

FORBES: We don't know exactly. The car didn't stop. But the point is, Temple, the boy's asking for his mother and we just don't know where she is. She's not at the garage …

STEVE: No, I don't expect she is, Sir Graham.

FORBES: What do you mean?

STEVE: I saw her this morning. She told me she was leaving for Australia.

FORBES: Australia!

TEMPLE: That's what I wanted to tell you, Sir Graham. Mrs Fletcher told Steve that not only did she work for Dr Benkaray but that she …

The telephone rings.

TEMPLE: Excuse me …

TEMPLE picks up the receiver.

TEMPLE: (*On the phone*) Hello?

RAINE: (*On the other end of the line*) Mr Temple?

TEMPLE: Yes …

RAINE: Raine here. Is Sir Graham with you?

TEMPLE: Yes. Hold on, Superintendent. It's for you, Sir Graham.

FORBES: Thank you.

TEMPLE hands the receiver to FORBES.

FORBES: (*On the phone*) Hello? What is it, Raine?

RAINE: We haven't located Mrs Fletcher yet, sir, but we've discovered that she's got a B.O.A.C. booking for tonight. Flight B.107 to Melbourne …

FORBES: What time does it leave?

RAINE: The take-off is scheduled for 9.15 …

FORBES: Right, thank you, Raine.

FORBES replaces the receiver.

FORB ES: Did you hear that, Temple?

TEMPLE: Yes, I did. And I've got a suggestion to make, Sir Graham.

FORBES: What is it?

TEMPLE: Let Steve deal with Mrs Fletcher …

FADE IN music.

FADE music.

FADE IN background noises at London Airport.

VOICE: Will B.O.A.C. passengers on Flight 109 to New York please proceed to Channel 2 … Passengers for New York – Channel 2 … (*A moment*) There is a delay of half an hour for passengers on Majestic Flight 188 to Malta. Passengers will be informed when the aircraft is ready …

STEVE: Good evening, Mrs Fletcher!

MRS FLETCHER: (*Astonished*) Why … it's Mrs Temple …

STEVE: That's right. I've been looking for you everywhere, Mrs Fletcher. I made a mistake and went over to the main building.

MRS F: What is it you want?

VOICE: Passengers on Flight 107 to Melbourne please report immediately to Channel 9. Flight 107 to Melbourne … Channel 9 …

MRS F: That's my plane … I must go …

STEVE: Wait a minute, Mrs Fletcher! I'm afraid I've got some bad news for you.

MRS F: This is a trick! I know what you're up to! It's a trick to try and stop me from …

STEVE: Bill's had a serious accident. He's in Westerton Hospital.

MRS F: I don't believe you!

STEVE: It's true, I assure you.

MRS F: (*Hesitantly*) What – what happened?

STEVE: He was knocked down by a car early this morning. The car didn't stop. Whether it was an accident or not we don't know.

MRS F: How – how bad is he?

STEVE: Well – he's on the danger list. He wants to see you, Mrs Fletcher. He keeps asking for you.

MRS F: If this isn't true – if this is some kind of a plot to keep me from leaving …

STEVE: Look, Mrs Fletcher – if you want to catch that plane, catch it! I'm not stopping you! I promised my husband I'd see you and tell you what had happened. It's up to you whether you believe me or not!

MRS F: (*Still hesitant*) You say he's in Westerton hospital.

STEVE: Yes – in the Casualty Ward. You can ring the hospital if you like. Westerton 824.

MRS F: (*Distressed*) No … no, I believe you … This accident, Mrs Temple … You say the car didn't stop? …

STEVE: That's right …

MRS F: The swine … I ought to have realised something like this would happen …

STEVE: I've got my car outside. I'll run you straight down to Westerton.

MRS F: *(Trying to control her tears)* Thank you, Mrs Temple, but – but what about my ticket and …

START FADE.

STEVE: Don't worry, I'll see to that … I'll see to everything … Come along, Mrs Fletcher.

FADE SCENE.

FADE IN the noise of a typewriter.
A clock chimes the hour.
It is two o 'clock.
The door opens and the typing stops.

CHARLIE: Oh! Sorry, Mr Temple …

TEMPLE: Anything wrong, Charlie?

CHARLIE: No, sir, but I heard a noise. I didn't know you were down here.

TEMPLE: Sorry if I disturbed you.

CHARLIE: No, that's all right, Mr Temple. It's two o'clock in the morning, you know …

TEMPLE: (*Smiling*) Yes, I know.

CHARLIE: Is Mrs Temple still out?

TEMPLE: Yes, she's still out. It's all right, Charlie, she's not on the tiles, if that's what you're thinking! I know where she is. She had to go down to Westerton.

CHARLIE: Oh. Oh, I see. Well, would you like me to get some coffee, Mr Temple, while you're waiting for her?

TEMPLE: No; I'm all right. Just leave me, Charlie, I want to get on with …

We hear the sound of the front door opening and closing.

TEMPLE: Is that the front door?

CHARLIE: Yes, it must be Mrs Temple!

STEVE: (*From the hall*) Paul!

TEMPLE: (*Calling*) I'm in the study, darling!

The door opens.

STEVE: Paul, you shouldn't have waited up. (*Surprised*) Or you, Charlie!

CHARLIE: Good evening – morning, Mrs Temple …

TEMPLE: Charlie, I think we'll take you up on that offer of some coffee.

STEVE: Yes; that's a wonderful idea!

CHARLIE: Okey … Right away, Mrs Temple!

TEMPLE: Well – how did you get on, Steve?

STEVE: It all went according to plan. Mrs Fletcher was a bit suspicious at first, but eventually she realised I was telling the truth.

TEMPLE: And what about Bill?

STEVE: He's had the operation and he's still very ill but they think he'll pull through. Mrs Fletcher was so relieved when she heard he'd got over the operation that she agreed to do everything you wanted. She's staying the night at the hospital. I said we'd drive down there tomorrow.

TEMPLE: Good.

STEVE: She's very bitter about Dr Benkaray, Paul. You know, I'm sure Mrs Fletcher isn't really a crook – at least, not a professional one.

TEMPLE: I never thought she was; and that's the danger, Steve. The other people realise that, too; they know she's the weakest link in the chain. But tell me: what else did she say?

STEVE: She explained about the coat – with the name Margo in it – that was found in my car.

TEMPLE: Yes?

STEVE: It appears that just about that time Mrs Fletcher discovered that the gang had extended its activities – and were going in for drug smuggling.

TEMPLE: And she disapproved?

STEVE: She certainly did; particularly when she discovered that she'd been distributing drugs without realising it. You see, from time to time they asked her to take certain coats down to Brighton; the coats were handed over to Margo, the fortune-teller, who distributed the drugs.

TEMPLE: The drugs were concealed in the coats, then?

STEVE: Yes, in the buttons. Apparently when an addict contacted Margo they were handed one of the coats. Then, in order to get another supply of heroin, they had to return the "empty" coat. This also established identification.

TEMPLE: I see.

STEVE: Anyway, when they gave Mrs Fletcher another coat to deliver she decided she wouldn't and that she'd tell them so. Larry Cross was just leaving for the airport when she tackled him about it. The argument continued all the way to the airport . Finally, Cross lost his temper, pushed her to one side, and concentrated on the matter in hand …

TEMPLE: Which was the kidnapping of you?

STEVE: Yes. Mrs Fletcher was furious, and she tossed the coat into my car and caught the next bus back to Town. She thought Cross would return to the car and pick up the coat.

TEMPLE: I see. Did she let you into any more of her secrets?

STEVE: She admitted that she tipped us off about the fortune-teller – then blackmailed the woman into telling us about Breakwater House. You know, Paul, I can't help but think that we owe a great deal to …

The doorbell rings.

STEVE: (*Surprised*) That's the front door!

TEMPLE: Yes.

STEVE: Are you expecting anyone?

TEMPLE: Yes; Wally Stone.

The door opens.

CHARLIE: (*Surprised*) There's a gent to see you, Mr Temple. He says you're expecting him …

TEMPLE: Yes. Ask him in, Charlie.

CHARLIE: In here, sir.

WALLY: (*Entering brightly*) Good morning, Mr Temple!

TEMPLE: Hello, Wally! You know my wife?

STEVE: Yes – good morning, Mr Stone.

WALLY: Good morning, Mrs Temple.

TEMPLE: Charlie, bring in the coffee as soon as it's ready. You'll join us in some coffee, Wally?

WALLY: Delighted, Mr Temple. Can't think of anything I'd like better – except perhaps a whisky and soda.

TEMPLE: Yes, of course. Bring in the decanter, Charlie.

CHARLIE: Yes, sir.

TEMPLE: (*To Wally*) Well – what happened?

WALLY: I had to open the safe, Mr Temple. Very neat little job it was too, concealed in an alcove just behind the fireplace. Took a bit of finding.

TEMPLE: Was it much trouble to open?

WALLY: Tiresome, you know – a little tiresome …

TEMPLE: And what was inside?

WALLY: Loads of stuff. My goodness, yes … Had a bit of a job sorting out what I'd come for. Lucky you gave me a good description … There we are – that's the bracelet, isn't it, Mr Temple?

TEMPLE: Yes! That's the one!

STEVE: (*Surprised*) But that's my bracelet, Paul!

TEMPLE: Yes, I know, darling.

STEVE: But how on earth …

TEMPLE: I left your bracelet with a man called Oscar. He thought it was stolen property. He's a go-between; works for The Fence.

STEVE: Then how did Mr Stone get hold of it?

TEMPLE: He's just told you. He stole it – from a house in London. From The Fence …

FADE IN of music.

FADE DOWN of music.

NURSE: Can I help you?

TEMPLE: My name is Temple – this is my wife. We have an appointment with a Mrs Fletcher.

NURSE: Oh yes, Mr Temple, she's expecting you. This way, please …

STEVE: How is Mr Fletcher this morning?

NURSE: He had a fairly good night. I think the doctor's quite pleased with him.

STEVE: Oh, good.

NURSE: In here, please.

The NURSE opens the door.

NURSE: Some visitors for you, Mrs Fletcher …

The door closes.

TEMPLE: Good morning, Mrs Fletcher.

STEVE: Hello, Mrs Fletcher. How are you this morning?

MRS F: I'm all right, thanks. Bill hasn't had a bad night – they seem quite pleased with him, in fact.

STEVE: Yes, I know, the nurse has just been telling us.

MRS F: Mrs Temple, I do apologise for my behaviour last night. Believe me, I'm most grateful … When I think that – if it wasn't for you – I'd be on the other side of the world this morning, I just don't …

STEVE: That's all right, don't worry about last night.

MRS F: Mr Temple, what d'you think will happen to me?

TEMPLE: You mean – with the police?

MRS F: Yes. You see, although I worked for Dr Benkaray I didn't really know what was going on. I thought that … Well, the point is, Mr Temple, will the police believe me or will they say ignorance is no excuse for what's happened?

TEMPLE: I don't know, Mrs Fletcher, but I'll certainly have a word with Sir Graham and make a point of telling him what you've done to help us. But first of all tell me: have you seen Dr Benkaray or spoken to her since last night?

MRS F: Yes, I have. I did exactly what Mrs Temple asked me.

TEMPLE: And what happened? Tell me exactly what happened.

START FADE.

MRS F: … Well, soon after breakfast I asked the Matron if I could use the telephone in her office …

COMPLETE FADE.

FADE IN of MRS FLETCHER dialling a number on the telephone.

She finishes dialling the number.

The number rings out at the other end and after a moment the phone is answered.

LARRY: (*On the other end of the line*) Dr Benkaray's house.

MRS F: (*On the phone*) Is that Mr Cross?

LARRY: Yes, speaking. Who is that?

MRS F: This is Mrs Fletcher.

LARRY: (*Surprised*) Fletcher? I thought you'd gone abroad!

MRS F: I – I changed my mind.

LARRY: Well, if you take my tip you'll change it again and get the blazes out of here!

MRS F: I want to see Dr Benkaray …

LARRY: What do you want to see her for?

MRS F: I'll tell that to the doctor!

LARRY: She's extremely busy this morning, she can't see anybody …

MRS F: (*Tensely*) I've got to see her, I tell you! It's important!

LARRY: (*With sarcasm*) Important to you – or the doctor?

MRS F: (*With equal sarcasm*) The doctor!

LARRY: (*After a moment*) What's this all about, Fletcher?

MRS F: It's about some letters I have, and some tape recordings. Dr Benkaray knows all about them. They're in a deed box at the bank. Tell the doctor if she'll meet me I'm now prepared to do a deal …

LARRY: (*A pause, then:*) All right. Come to the house this morning – about eleven o'clock. I'll tell the doctor to expect you.

MRS F: (*Now in command of the situation*) No; I can't do that!

LARRY: Why not? It's broad daylight …

MRS F: It was broad daylight when Ted Angus turned up, wasn't it? I'm at the hospital at Westerton; I think you know why. I'll meet you both outside the hospital in about an hour. We can talk in your car.

LARRY: (*After a momentary hesitation*) Yes, all right, Mrs Fletcher.

MRS FLETCHER replaces the receiver.

FADE SCENE.

FADE UP the noise of traffic.

FADE traffic noises to the background.

MRS FLETCHER is sitting in a car with DR BENKARAY and LARRY CROSS.

BENKARAY: … Now pull yourself together, Mrs Fletcher, and let's try to be sensible.

MRS F: If I'd really known what was going on, Dr Benkaray, I'd never have let you talk me into it. For weeks and weeks I've been trying to get away …

LARRY: You're too involved, Mrs Fletcher. You've got to take your chance with the rest of us. You didn't object to the money!

MRS F: I would have if I'd known what it was all about!

LARRY: Don't be a hypocrite – you knew, all right!

BENKARAY: Larry, please!

MRS F: I kept telling you that Bill knew nothing about all this – yet you ran him down like that, in cold blood!

BENKARAY: I assure you we know nothing about that accident, nothing whatever.

MRS F: The trouble is, I can't believe you any more! That's why I've been trying to get away!

BENKARAY: I can only repeat that the accident had nothing to do with me. Now what's all this about letters and tape recordings? You mentioned this to me once before. What are they, exactly?

MRS F: You know what they are! They're photostat copies of letters you received and tape recordings of telephone conversations. I took them while I was working for you.

LARRY: (*Angrily*) Why, you interfering …

BENKARAY: Shut up, Larry!

MRS F: When I found out what was going on I had to protect myself. Especially after Ted Angus was murdered. I – I always had a soft spot for Ted.

BENKARAY: And what exactly did you plan to do with these letters?

MRS F: I was going to hand them over to the police, if there was ever any attempt on my life – or Bill's.

BENKARAY: I assure you no one is going to make any attempt on your life.

MRS F: How can I be sure of that? Look what happened to my son …

BENKARAY: (*Interrupting MRS FLETCHER*) Mrs Fletcher, will you please listen to me! You must realise that you can't leave that box at the bank without taking some precautions. What's to prevent your son opening it at any time? Don't you see, it would get a lot of people into serious trouble – yourself included.

MRS F: It's a safeguard …

BENKARAY: It's not, and you must be made to realise that! If your son took that box to the police and they found out who murdered Ted Angus and Julia Kelburn …

MRS F: (*Quickly*) I had nothing to do with those murders!

BENKARAY: I know you didn't – but someone did! And if you value your son's life you'd better hand that deed box over straight away.

MRS F: (*Quietly*) I'm prepared to hand it over – but not to you.

BENKARAY: Well, who are you prepared to hand it over to?

MRS F: (*After a momentary hesitation*) The Fence …

BENKARAY: But you don't know The Fence; you've never met him – so why should …

MRS F: I know that, but I'm not prepared to hand it over to anyone else – and I'm only prepared to hand it over to him on one condition. He's got to give an assurance – a definite assurance – that he'll leave Bill alone in the future.

BENKARAY: I think he'll agree to that, Mrs Fletcher. Get the box from the bank and take it to your garage. You'll have a visitor this evening – about eleven o'clock.

MRS F: (*Quietly*) All right, Doctor …

MRS FLETCHER opens the car door and gets out of the car.

FADE UP of traffic noises.

FADE DOWN of traffic.

FADE SCENE.

FADE IN the voice of MRS FLETCHER.

MRS F: … After that I left Dr Benkaray and came back into the hospital. Bill was asking for me so I was allowed to go up to the ward for two or three minutes. I hope I did the right thing, Mr Temple – about Dr Benkaray, I mean?

TEMPLE: You certainly did, Mrs Fletcher, and I'm very grateful to you.

MRS F: Well, I felt it was the least I could do.

TEMPLE: You've been very frank about the whole affair, but now, I'm afraid I've got to ask you to do something else.

MRS F: I'll do anything – anything you ask, Mr Temple …

TEMPLE: I'd like you to go through with this, Mrs Fletcher. I'd like you to get the deed box from the bank and take it to the garage. I'd like you to be there tonight – when The Fence arrives.

MRS F: It's – it's quite a risk, Mr Temple. He's a desperate man and he's in a tight spot!

TEMPLE: Yes, I know that, Mrs Fletcher.

MRS F: (*After a moment*) All right. If that's what you want – I'll be there.

START FADE.

TEMPLE: Thank you, Mrs Fletcher. Now this is what I want you to do … Listen carefully …

FADE IN of music.

Slow FADE OUT of music.

FADE IN a distant background of a church clock striking the half hour.

An owl hoots.

FORBES: How many cars have we got, Raine?

RAINE: Four, apart from us, Sir Graham. There are two near the wood, one in the corner by the gate over there, and another one on the main road.

TEMPLE: Well, when our visitor arrives, I think one of the cars had better block the entrance to the garage, Superintendent.

RAINE: (*Dryly*) Yes, I had that in mind, sir. Mr Temple, who exactly are you expecting to see this evening – Dr Benkaray?

TEMPLE: No. I think Dr Benkaray is the prime mover so far as the drug smuggling is concerned, but I don't think she's The Fence.

FORBES: No, neither do I. I believe she persuaded The Fence to handle drugs and he's regretted it ever since.

TEMPLE: I agree, Sir Graham; but I'll go further than that. I think Dr Benkaray and Larry Cross have had definite designs to take over the organisation and just recently … (*He stops*)

FORBES: What is it, Temple?

TEMPLE: There's a car coming …

In the background the sound of a car can be heard approaching.

FORBES: It's probably one of the locals on the way home from the pub.

RAINE: If it is – that pub wants investigating. It's half past eleven …

TEMPLE: This isn't one of the locals – he's put his lights out …

FORBES: Yes, he's turning into the garage …

The car draws to a standstill.

TEMPLE: (*After a moment*) He's stopped …

A pause.

The car door opens and closes.

RAINE: (*Tensely*) There he is.

FORBES: I can't see who it is! He's got his coat collar turned up …

RAINE: … He's going down the passage at the side of the garage … This is our man all right!

FORBES: Is Mrs Fletcher armed?

TEMPLE: Yes, I gave her an automatic – but she won't use it except in an emergency.

RAINE: How long are we going to give him, sir?

FORBES: Four minutes – five at the outside. Check your watch, Raine …

A long pause.

We hear the sound of another car approaching.

RAINE: There's the sergeant … He's pulling up in front of the entrance …

TEMPLE: Good.

A pause.

FORBES: We'll give him another four minutes and then move in …

RAINE: Right …

Another long pause.

The sound of the owl is heard in the background and the noise of a distant train.

TEMPLE: (*Worried*) I hope she's all right, Sir Graham. I feel responsible for her. If anything happens to Mrs Fletcher I'll never …

RAINE: (*Suddenly*) There he is! He's coming out of the house …

TEMPLE: Where?

RAINE: Over there, near the petrol pumps!

TEMPLE: Yes, you're right!

FORBES: He's got the deed box …

TEMPLE: (*Quickly*) I think he's spotted us!

FORBES: Give the signal, Raine!!

RAINE: (*Shouting through the car window*) Lights!!!!

There is the sudden noise of a car horn.

TEMPLE: He's running for it!!!

RAINE: He's coming this way …

FORBES: Temple, look out – he's got a revolver!

RAINE: Get down!!!

There is the sound of revolver shots and the sudden smashing of the car windscreen.

FADE IN noises of police whistles and excited voices.

The car door opens.

RAINE: He's dropped the gun!

FORBES: Careful, Temple!

FADE UP of excited voices, etc.

RAINE: Temple's got him! Quickly, Sir Graham!

FADE UP of TEMPLE struggling with MIKE LANGDON.

LANGDON: (*Panting*) Let go … Let go! I warn you, if you don't let go I'll …

TEMPLE: (*Struggling with LANGDON*) It's no good, Langdon! It's all over … The police are here!

LANGDON: (*Desperately*) Temple, I warn you, if you don't let go …

TEMPLE: (*Angrily*) All right – you've asked for it!

There is a sudden sound of a blow followed by a groan from LANGDON as he falls.

FORBES and RAINE arrive on the scene.

FORBES: (*Breathlessly*) Temple, are you all right?

TEMPLE: (*Gasping for breath*) Yes, but you know, I'm getting a little too old for this sort of thing!

RAINE: I don't know about that, Mr Temple – you've made a nice mess of Mr Langdon!

TEMPLE: (*Staring at Langdon; surprised*) Yes, by Timothy, I have – haven't I?

FADE IN of music.

FADE DOWN of music.

Slow FADE IN of a ship's siren.
There is a background of a busy ocean liner.
FADE noises to the background.

KELBURN: ... We should be sailing in about fifteen minutes.

LINDA: Yes. Don't you want to go on deck?

KELBURN: Not particularly.

LINDA: This is a change for you, isn't it, George? No last-minute instructions to anyone, no attempt to ... (*Suddenly*) What are you staring at?

KELBURN: (*Quietly; still staring*) I was just looking out of the porthole, that's all. (*Turning*) Linda, this is supposed to be a pleasure cruise. Let's try not to get on each other's nerves.

LINDA: (*Petulantly*) There aren't enough hangers for my dresses.

KELBURN: All right – ring for the steward. Or better still, go and have a word with the Purser. You'd better get to know him anyway. Let the poor devil know what he's in for!

LINDA: Well, if I see the Purser I shall complain about the accommodation. This bathroom is absurd!

KELBURN: (*Wearily*) All right – do that. See where it gets you.

LINDA: Don't leave the cabin.

KELBURN: That, you can depend on, Linda. Oh – perhaps you'd be kind enough to pass me that carafe of water ... Thank you.

The door opens and closes.
A slight pause.
KELBURN drinks the water.
The cabin door opens.

TEMPLE: (*Quietly*) Good afternoon, Kelburn. I thought you weren't taking your trip until the end of the month?

KELBURN: I changed my mind.

TEMPLE: A sudden decision?

KELBURN: Yes – a sudden decision. (*Resigned*) Where are the police? I saw them through the porthole …

TEMPLE: They're talking to your wife.

KELBURN: You picked up Langdon, I suppose?

TEMPLE: We did. Also Dr Benkaray – and Larry Cross.

KELBURN: Langdon talked?

TEMPLE: He had to, otherwise the police might have believed he was The Fence – instead of you. He was most anxious that they shouldn't think that, Mr Kelburn. Still, we've got enough evidence against you – without Langdon.

KELBURN: You mean Mrs Fletcher and the deed box?

TEMPLE: Yes – and the fact that my wife's bracelet turned up at your house in Eaton Square.

KELBURN: (*Surprised*) Your wife's … So that was it? You were the burglar?

TEMPLE: By proxy. You know, you've worried me, Kelburn. I should have been on to you earlier – I should have realised what Tony Wyman meant when he said "Kelburn – The Fence." He wasn't warning you against the electrified fence – he was warning me against you, Kelburn.

KELBURN: (*Irritated*) That young fool overreached himself!

TEMPLE: I don't think you can criticise him on that account.

KELBURN: He thought he knew all the answers, Temple – just like you do. (*Hesitating; suddenly in pain*) But … you … don't … know …

TEMPLE: (*Suddenly*) What is it, Kelburn?

KELBURN: (*Gasping*) I – I took something just before … you … came … in … I didn't intend the police to …

TEMPLE: Kelburn, you fool! You fool! …

There is a sudden gasp and KELBURN falls forward across the table, knocking over the carafe of water.

TEMPLE: Kelburn …

The door opens.

RAINE: Mr Temple, we've taken Mrs … (*He stops*) What is it? What's happened to Kelburn?

TEMPLE: (*After a moment*) He's dead …

FADE UP of the ship's siren.

CROSS FADE to music.

Slow FADE DOWN of the music.

FADE music completely.

STEVE: … Would you like another brandy, Sir Graham?

FORBES: No, thank you, Steve.

TEMPLE: What about you, Superintendent?

RAINE: (*Hesitantly*) Well, I think I …

TEMPLE: Just a drop more …

TEMPLE pours brandy into RAINE's glass.

RAINE: Thank you.

FORBES: (*Smiling*) Well, Temple, I noticed you studiously refrained from talking shop all through dinner, in spite of the fact that Raine and I have been patiently waiting for the full background to the Margo case.

RAINE: Yes, there are quite a few aspects of the case to be explained.

TEMPLE: Well, as we now know, The Fence was George Kelburn …

RAINE: Yes, but what puzzles me is why a man in his position should turn to crime? I mean to say, he was a director of over fifteen companies … How did he find time, apart from anything else?

TEMPLE: It's a fallacy that big business men have no time for any other activities, Superintendent. You've only to read the gossip columns to appreciate that.

FORBES: Yes, but why crime?

TEMPLE: I don't suppose we'll ever know the full answer to that. There may even be more than one. But you have to admit the idea of a big time fence operating on an international scale is a tempting one. Carried to its furthermost limits a man like that could become extremely powerful. And there's no doubt that Kelburn was obsessed with power.

RAINE: I agree that's a fair estimate of the general picture. Now, let's get down to details. Who exactly was in this organisation?

TEMPLE: We may never know the full extent of the organisation. Mike Langdon, Dr Benkaray, and Larry Cross were certainly his chief lieutenants, and there were several smaller fry like Ted Angus, Oscar at the pet shop, Mrs Fletcher, and Julia Kelburn.

STEVE: His own daughter!

TEMPLE: Yes, that's why he resented her friendship with Tony Wyman. He thought that Wyman might find out that she was working for The Fence – which is exactly what happened, of course. Wyman tried to get in on the easy money and found himself out of his depth.

STEVE: But surely Kelburn's troubles started when he allowed Benkaray to persuade him that the biggest money lay in smuggling drugs?

TEMPLE: Yes, that's true, Steve. His own daughter became an addict. Langdon had been against the drug activities right from the start, and Kelburn turned to him to try and get Julia out of the habit. But by this time Benkaray had realised that Julia was Kelburn's weak spot.

RAINE: You think Benkaray wanted to gain control of the organisation, then?

TEMPLE: Everything points that way. Naturally, Kelburn fought like a tiger. He had built up the organisation and he resented anybody taking it over. At first, it wasn't open opposition; in fact he gave them a bigger cut in the profits to keep them quiet.

FORBES: I take it Larry Cross was on Benkaray's side.

TEMPLE: Naturally. However, one condition of the extra cut was that the doctor should stop supplying Julia with drugs. This drove Julia frantic; she made a special visit to Westerton to see the doctor, and on her father's instructions Mike Langdon went to fetch her back. He had a lot of trouble with the girl and she threatened to tell all she knew about her father's activities. This frightened Langdon, especially when he discovered she had already told quite a lot to Tony Wyman. When he found this out he challenged her, and she was so defiant that he lost his temper and strangled the girl.

RAINE: And Wyman, of course, was the suspect?

TEMPLE: Yes, Kelburn saw to that. You remember what Tony Wyman said, Sir Graham, just before he died? He tried to tip me off about Kelburn being The Fence but unfortunately I misinterpreted him.

FORBES: Yes, but what was he doing at Breakwater House?

TEMPLE: He'd been tricked into going there, just as Steve and I were lured there by that message from the girl, Fiona Scott. Wyman had been told to meet Kelburn at Breakwater House at the same time that Steve and I were due there. He was captured by the gang and tied up – he overheard them talking about the steel rope and the electrified fence. The accident with the rope was to have got rid of us – the fire was to have put paid to Wyman.

RAINE: Then what about the murder of Ted Angus?

TEMPLE: Angus was ordered to murder Tony Wyman; when he failed he was told to report to Dr Benkaray. He was murdered by the doctor and the body dumped in the wood.

STEVE: What a dreadful night that was! I don't think I shall ever forget it!

TEMPLE: No …

FORBES: And what did Angus mean when he told you to ask Mrs Fletcher about the coat?

TEMPLE: He was referring to the coat worn by Julia Kelburn. This coat had the name Margo in it. Julia stole this coat and made arrangements to go to Brighton to see the fortune-teller …

STEVE: … To try and get another coat with a supply of heroin in it?

TEMPLE: Exactly. Well – we know what happened. Langdon stopped the visit and murdered her.

FORBES: Temple, do you think Langdon wanted to be top dog – d'you think he had any design on Kelburn's position?

TEMPLE: No, I don't think so – although Benkaray, of course, obviously had. Langdon was a typical executive; not a leader. Kelburn depended on him for the unpleasant jobs.

STEVE: Then that nonsense about having to watch Linda Kelburn was a sort of diversion – a deliberate attempt to take you away from the main issue?

TEMPLE: No, not entirely, Steve. Langdon knew that Linda had been seeing Larry Cross and Kelburn was afraid she would tell Cross about his contacts and methods of working. It was Kelburn's practice to keep all this to himself as much as possible. That was one of the things, of course, that Benkaray resented.

FORBES: Yes, well, it seems to me it'll take a couple of years to straighten out Kelburn's affairs, legitimate and otherwise.

TEMPLE: Yes, well, just at the moment I'm more concerned with some of the smaller fry. Mrs Fletcher, for instance. You know she saved our lives, Superintendent, and she's been more co-operative this past week or two.

RAINE: Yes, I know.

TEMPLE: I'm relying on you and Sir Graham to see that she's let down lightly.

FORBES: (*Smiling*) All right, Temple; I was wondering when you were going to mention Mrs Fletcher. I'll have a talk with the Public Prosecutor.

RAINE: Incidentally, I hear her son is off the danger list.

TEMPLE: Yes, I think he'll be all right now. Larry Cross denied running him down …

RAINE: He's denied quite a lot of things that will be brought home to him in the next week or so.

FORBES: Well, this has been quite a case, Temple – quite a case! I should imagine you and Steve are ready for a pretty good holiday.

TEMPLE: Yes – and we're going to take one, Sir Graham. We're flying out to Jamaica on Thursday.

STEVE: (*Surprised; delighted*) Darling, I didn't know that!

TEMPLE: (*Laughing*) No, I know you didn't!

STEVE: But this is wonderful! How long are we going to be away?

TEMPLE: Oh, five weeks – six weeks – ten weeks, perhaps …

RAINE: Well, don't stay away too long. London isn't the same without the Temples …

FORBES: Well said, Raine!

TEMPLE: Thank you, Superintendent – Sir Graham.

STEVE: (*Laughing*) Don't worry, we'll be back! We'll be back, Sir Graham!

FORBES: (*Almost to himself*) By Timothy, I hope so …

THE END

ALTERNATE ITALIAN ENDING

Why and how did an alternate ending to *Paul Temple and the Margo Mystery* come about? Here, Italian superfan Antonio Scaglioni gives a possible explanation.

In Italy fiction on the radio has always played a subordinate role to other genres, such as music programs, variety or news. Then from the second half of the 1960s it underwent a further downsizing, remaining relegated in practice to only a quarter-hour more or less in the morning, with an audience almost exclusively composed of housewives and retirees, and for Francis Durbridge there was no exception. Despite the great success that Durbridge was experiencing in Italy through his TV serials in the same period, only four radio serials featuring Paul Temple were produced in about a decade, from 1967 through 1977 before his name disappeared permanently from Italian radio schedules, each divided into ten episodes of about fifteen minutes and broadcast Monday through Friday invariably around ten o'clock in the morning. The four stories were *Margò* (*Paul Temple and the Margo Mystery*) in 1967; *Chi è Jonathan?* (*Paul Temple and the Jonathan Mystery*) in 1971; *La ragazza scomparsa* (*Paul Temple and the Conrad Case*) in 1975; and finally *Cabaret* (*Paul Temple and the Spencer Affair*) in 1977. This is just to explain how little impact radio dramas had in the ratings both in terms of air times and the length of the broadcasts themselves. Then knowing that the original British serials had for each episode double the length one can easily guess that the stories had to go under careful editing to adequately summarize the events. Real adaptations that, however, did not sacrifice any major plot elements, starting with the cliffhangers that closed each episode. Anyway, some changes and actualizations (some of the original stories were even twenty years old) were physiological, such as replacing the disk in *The Spencer*

Affair, transformed from an unknown, at least in Italy, "My Heart and Harry" into "Cabaret," the famous musical soundtrack. But these were always or mostly small changes that did not affect the development of the events. Except in two cases: in both *The Margo Mystery* and *The Conrad Case*, the guilty party who was unmasked by Paul Temple in the finale turned out to be different from the one in the original serial. How was this possible?

There were only two possibilities: either it had been an initiative taken arbitrarily by those who had adapted the stories (in this case the Italian translator Franca Cancogni with the directors of the two serials, Guglielmo Morandi for *Margo* and Umberto Benedetto for *Conrad*), or the changes had been made by Durbridge himself, which by the way he had done already in the past especially in his adaptations for Germany. But why should the Italian adapters have taken the burden and risk of changing without permission the endings of these two stories alone? (Let's recall here that Franca Cancogni was the translator of almost all the Italian radio versions of Durbridge's scripts, and never on any other occasion do the endings turn out to be changed from the originals.) Besides, unlike television serials, where millions of viewers and constant media attention justified any expedient to protect the secrecy of the ending, the interest aroused in the public and the press by radio serials was not so great as to require such major interventions.

So, it doesn't seem very likely that the translator or the director took the trouble to change the ending on their own. Moreover, as I mentioned above, Durbridge was no stranger to even heavily tweaking his earlier scripts that did not convince him, and it would not be the first case for Italy either. It had already happened at least once, in 1960 for an hour-long radio drama, *Preludio al delitto*, which had been rewritten from scratch with several changes and new names for the characters, when the plot had clearly come from an earlier work of his, *The Caspary Affair*, broadcast in the UK in 1946 and now published in *Three Plays for Radio - volume 1* (Williams & Whiting, 2022).

The alternative ending of *La ragazza scomparsa* (and the doubts it inspires) have already been discussed in the appendix to the volume *Paul Temple and the Conrad Case* (Williams & Whiting, 2023). Let's deal here instead with *Margò*. In this case, the change of ending made by Durbridge himself is the most likely scenario, because in the original serial the ending seemed to have many similarities, perhaps too many, with *Paul Temple and the Jonathan Mystery*, already published in this series (which, I want to remind you, would arrive in Italy only four years later, but actually written and broadcast by the BBC ten years earlier than the original *Margo Mystery*).

Without revealing anything important, let's say that in both serials' final scenes, the mastermind behind all the crimes in the affair suddenly decides to leave, (by ship in *Margo*, by air in *Jonathan*) evidently feeling closely hunted by Paul Temple; in both he is joined by the detective at the last moment before leaving; and in both a dialogue takes place between the two, in which, before surrendering, he cautiously inquires what his already arrested accomplices have confessed to. Not to mention another, much more important detail, I prefer not to reveal here, that sharply accentuates this similarity (however if you have read both serials you will not have any difficulty in recognizing). In short, we are dealing with two almost interchangeable scenes, names and locations aside.

Probably the truth is that in many cases Durbridge, in order to meet the deadlines for his radio scripts, was forced to work quickly by recycling situations from previous plots, but being also a perfectionist, he sometimes went back over his own stories to remedy those things that did not satisfy him, particularly when it came to important points such as unmasking the guilty party. So it is not impossible that realizing these similarities, he had rectified it with a new solution to the riddle even before selling the script to Italian radio, a solution more surprising and unpredictable, more congenial to his typical startling ending than the original was.

But now you can judge for yourselves.

MARGÒ (from *Paul Temple and the Margo Mystery*)
translated by Franca Cancogni
10 episodes aired daily from June 19th to June 30th 1967,
length: about 15 minutes each episode,

Cast:

Paul Temple . . . . Aroldo Tieri
Steve Temple . . . . .Lia Zoppelli
Sir Graham Forbes . . . . . . Francesco Sormano
George Kelburn . . . . .Adolfo Geri
Linda Kelburn . . . . .Giuliana Lojodice
Mike Langdon . . . . .Cesare Polacco
Tony Wyman . . . . Alfredo Senarica
Ted Angus . . . . Carlo Ratti
Larry Cross . . . . Corrado Gaipa
Doctor Benkarai . . . . .Renata Negri
Mrs. Fletcher . . . . .Wanda Pasquini
Bill Fletcher . . . . Saverio Moriones
Inspector Raine . . . . Lucio Rama
Charlie . . . . Franco Scandurra
Edgar Northampton . . Corrado De Cristofaro
Fiona . . . . .Anna Maria Sanetti
Margò .Cecilia Polizzi
Mrs. Perkins . . . . .Grazia Radicchi
Midge Harris . . . . .Guido Marchi
Oscar . . . . .Giampiero Becherelli
Wally Stone . . . . .Dante Biagioni

Directed by Guglielmo Morandi

The following scenes start right after Langdon's arrest and close the story.

FADE IN the sound of the ship's siren.
A cabin door closes.

KELBURN: Here you are, Linda.

LINDA: Yes, George.

KELBURN: I was looking for you on deck. We sail in ten minutes.

LINDA: Come here! Come and look through the porthole.

A pause.

LINDA: There over on the dock. Do you see them?

KELBURN: Yes, I see them.

LINDA: They're both there. Sir Graham Forbes and Inspector Raine. Along with who knows how many other policemen in plain clothes.

KELBURN: Let them come. At least it will be over.

LINDA: (*Angrily*) Over for you! Not for me!

A gun magazine is engaged.

KELBURN: What are you doing, Linda? Put that gun away! Are you crazy?

LINDA: Not quite. (*A pause*) Go to meet them, George. Spare them the trouble of coming here. As far as they are concerned you are The Fence.

KELBURN: What are you suggesting? No! I won't!

LINDA: They have no suspicions about me. Why should they suspect a mere woman of being The Fence? Anyway, I've taken precautions.

KELBURN: What are you talking about? What have you done, Linda?

LINDA: I went to my friend Steve and made a full confession to her. I told her that I knew you were The Fence, that I have always known but kept quiet out of fear – that I was your victim, under your total control – and that no matter how hard I tried I couldn't get away from you.

KELBURN: That's not true and you know it! It's quite the opposite, in fact! Since I found out the kind of monster you are I've not had a minute's peace. I tried to get rid of you and in revenge you had Julia murdered!

LINDA: You fool! It wasn't out of revenge – it was because she would have talked!

KELBURN: You used her to ferry drugs. You tied me with the fear of scandal!

LINDA: Prove it! It's my word against yours and no one is going to believe anything you say. Even to your faithful lackey Langdon, you are The Fence. Didn't you order him to go and get those papers in Westerton tonight? No one knows that it was me who told you to send him. I've nothing to worry about - there was nothing against me in those papers. I wasn't worried about getting them back. He was arrested just as I'd hoped, and now Langdon is going to put the blame on all of us. It was you who gave him the order, as always. And it's facts that matter, dear George, not words. Come on, now! Do what I tell you! Go and meet them!

KELBURN: No, Linda, I won't!

LINDA: I don't want to have to use this gun, George …

Suddenly the cabin door bursts open.

RAINE: Stop!

LINDA: (*Shouting*) No! Cowar …

RAINE slams into Linda knocking the gun out of her hand.

LINDA: Ah!

TEMPLE: Here, Inspector! In some cases handcuffs are a necessity …

We hear the snap of handcuffs being put on LINDA.

KELBURN: Oh, Linda! Linda!

TEMPLE: I'm sorry I had to intervene this way, Kelburn. The lady herself said so. Facts matter, not words. (*A pause*) Even if sometimes words …

FADE IN music.

FADE music.

FADE IN voices coming from a tape recorder.

LINDA: They have no suspicions about me. Why should they suspect a mere woman of being The Fence? Anyway, I've taken precautions.

KELBURN: What are you talking about? What have you done, Linda?

LINDA: I went to my friend Steve …

The tape recorder is switched off.

It is fast forwarded distorting the tape and making the voices incomprehensible.

KELBURN: That's not true and you know it! It's quite the opposite, in fact! Since I found out the kind of monster you are I've not had a minute's peace. I tried to get rid of you and in revenge you had Julia murdered!

LINDA: You fool! It wasn't out of revenge – it was because she would have talked!

KELBURN: You …

The tape recorder is switched off.

FORBES: We couldn't have got more damning proof, not counting the bracelet in Kelburn's safe.

TEMPLE: But the bracelet would have still left us in some doubt: Linda or George?

FORBES: But you say you suspected her from the start …

TEMPLE: Well, I got my first suspicion when she phoned me saying they wanted to kill her stepdaughter.

RAINE: Yes, but why come and tell you, Temple?

TEMPLE: She knew I'd investigate The Fence anyway … as the papers said … and she's been trying to double-cross me ever since. Linda was a succubus – she used her sexual powers over George to control him – she knew how to keep him under pressure, she was sure of it until the end.

FORBES: Well, this tangled web has been unravelled! Thanks to you, Temple. And to you too, Steve.

STEVE: Ah! I'm glad you remembered me.

TEMPLE: Of course we remembered you, darling! Do you know what I've got here?

STEVE: What is it? Oh, Paul! Is it a gift?

TEMPLE: Yes. Two plane tickets to Haiti.

STEVE: Oh, Paul, darling! (*She laughs*) I've always wanted to go to Haiti!

TEMPLE: Yes, and it took Margo to remind me!

They all laugh.

THE END

Printed in Great Britain
by Amazon

27717520R00169